SHATTERED DREAMS

Charlie
It was supposed to be a regular day out.
Three couples celebrating the last days of summer.
When tragedy struck.
I thought I was going to marry her.
Instead, I was burying her.
I blamed the world for my pain.
I buried it all.
I became a man I didn't even recognize.

Autumn
In a blink of an eye, everything changed.
My best friend was gone, and I was responsible for it.
I may not have been driving the truck, but I didn't stop it.
Escaping the town was the only thing I could do to survive the guilt.
I thought I was strong enough to go back.
I was wrong.
One look from him and I knew I wasn't welcome.
But this is my home, and I wanted to come back.
One night turned into more. But at the end of the day, I know he'll never love me.
Besides, we all have shattered dreams.

BOOKS BY NATASHA MADISON

Dream Series
shattered dreams
forbidden dreams
buried dreams
stolen dreams

Meant For Series
Meant For Stone
Meant For Her
Meant For Love
Meant For Gabriel

Made For Series
Made For Me
Made For You
Made For Us
Made for Romeo

Southern Wedding Series
Mine To Kiss
Mine To Have
Mine To Hold
Mine To Cherish
Mine To Love
Mine To Take
Mine To Promise
Mine to Honor
Mine to Keep

The Only One Series
Only One Kiss
Only One Chance
Only One Night
Only One Touch
Only One Regret
Only One Mistake
Only One Love
Only One Forever

This Is
This Is Crazy
This Is Wild
This Is Love
This Is Forever

Southern Series
Southern Chance
Southern Comfort
Southern Storm
Southern Sunrise
Southern Heart
Southern Heat
Southern Secrets
Southern Sunshine

Hollywood Royalty
Hollywood Playboy
Hollywood Princess
Hollywood Prince

Something Series
Something So Right
Something So Perfect
Something So Irresistible
Something So Unscripted
Something So BOX SET

Tempt Series
Tempt The Boss
Tempt The Playboy
Tempt The Hookup
Tempt The Ex

Heaven & Hell Series
Hell and Back
Pieces of Heaven
Heaven & Hell Box Set

Love Series
Perfect Love Story
Unexpected Love Story
Broken Love Story

Mixed Up Love
Faux Pas

Cover Design: Jay Aheer
Editing done by Karen Hrdicka Barren Acres Editing
Editing done by Jenny Sims Editing4Indies
Proofing Julie Deaton by Deaton Author Services
Proofing by Judy's Proofreading
Formatting by Christina Parker Smith

Shattered
DREAMS

DREAM SERIES

NATASHA
MADISON

One

CHARLIE

"YOU READY?" JENNIFER asks when she walks into the walk-in closet as I pull on my white T-shirt. I smile at her standing there in jeans and a white T-shirt, matching me.

"I'm ready," I reply, grabbing my baseball hat and putting it on my head. "I was waiting for you." The small smile I had on my face widens as she closes the distance to me and puts one hand on my stomach, while the other hand grabs the hat off my head.

"I like it when you don't wear this ratty thing." She waves the hat in her hand, looking up at me, her golden-brown eyes warm like whiskey. "I like to run my fingers through your hair." She drops the hat from her hand and proceeds to do exactly that through the top of my wettish hair.

"You win." I lower to kiss her, wrapping an arm around her waist, then bending her back to kiss her lips.

"You always win." I pull her closer, burying my face in her neck and smelling her.

"Not always." She smirks at me and she's about to give me another kiss when we both hear the honking from outside. "Shall we finish this when we get home?" she asks with a twinkle in her eye as she leans forward to kiss my neck before I let her go. She turns in my arms, my hand reaching for hers as we walk out of the closet and head to the front door, going through the house. Picture frames of us are scattered throughout every single part of the house, something she did when she moved in a month ago. Even though I've been begging her to move in with me as soon as I moved here. Even though she would be here five days out of seven, she never gave in until she was ready.

She's almost to the front door and about to unlock it when the doorbell rings twice, and she pulls it open. "Hey, can I use the bathroom?" Autumn practically barges in, hopping from one foot to the next.

"Go ahead," Jennifer says, and Autumn comes down the hallway. When she spots me, her blue eyes light up.

"Hey." She quickly comes over to kiss me on my cheek. "Got to use the bathroom," she mumbles, then turns and rushes toward the bathroom.

"I'm going to go wait in the truck!" Jennifer yells, grabbing her green jacket and slipping it on. "You'll close up?"

"Will do." I nod at her, going to the back door and making sure it's locked before walking over and checking the window above the kitchen sink that she likes to keep open so she can hear the birds.

I'm walking to the front door when I hear honking again. "He's in a great mood today," Autumn mumbles sarcastically behind me, making me laugh because Waylon is almost always in a great mood. "Tonight is going to be fun," she says over her shoulder as she walks out of the house. I follow her, closing the door behind me.

"Took you long enough," Waylon snaps when Autumn opens the passenger door and then looks over at me. I look around her to see he's got his baseball hat on backward, his blondish hair sticking out from the back of the hat.

"You sit up front." She tries to hide that she's pissed off at him and his words, but she fails miserably as she walks over to the back door and opens it, sliding in and slamming the door, not giving me an option.

"Hey," I greet, getting into the truck and looking over to see the four of them are squished in the back. "How's everyone doing?" I ask Brock, who is sitting with his girlfriend Everleigh's ass practically in his lap, his arms wrapped around her to keep her safe. I barely have my seat belt on before Waylon drives off, making Brock shake his head. "Good times," I say, looking at Jennifer and winking at her. She scrunches up her nose at me and then smiles before turning to Everleigh and saying hello, and the two of them start chatting. Autumn is looking out of the window and not talking to them.

We head over to Waylon's family hunting cabin, some fifteen minutes away, on the outskirts of town. The log cabin is painted red, with a wraparound porch and four rocking chairs on it. Waylon and I became friends two years ago when I came into town and went to the town hall to apply for permits to start building my barn here. My family and I bought property with a barn on it, but I wanted to expand it. Waylon's family has been around this town, dating back to the 1920s, when his great-grandfather started a construction company and went into lumber trading or something like that. Now, they just do construction. If a building goes up in town, it's always with the Cartwright family building it. They were the ones who did all the renovations to the barn.

We walk to the side of the house where eight big logs lie in an octagon shape around a firepit. We are here almost every single weekend just to sit and shoot the shit, or even during the week, we go out and eat and then just come here and chill. Sometimes we even bring the food with us.

The sun is slowly going down when Waylon comes back with some wood and starts the fire while I sit on a log. "Here," Brock offers, handing me a beer he took out from the cooler that he just carried over from the back of Waylon's pickup.

"Thanks." Holding my beer, I clink it with his. The heat from the fire comes to me as I look over and see Jennifer, Autumn, and Everleigh sitting on a log across from me, laughing at something one of them said. The three of them have been best friends since kindergarten. I met Jennifer through Waylon, who brought her to the barn one day. The next day, I called her up, and we'd been together for the past year. I watch Brock walk over to the girls with the cooler in his hand, and the three of them open up their own beers as Everleigh tells them a story.

"I'm wiped," Brock states when he comes back and sits next to me, stretching out his legs in front of him. He just graduated with a Bachelor of Architecture and is starting his three-year internship with the Cartwright Company. Plus, he works on the weekend and sometimes at night at his family mechanic shop. I take a pull of my beer as Waylon comes over to sit next to me, holding a water bottle. "No beer?" Brock asks him, and he shakes his head.

"Nah," he says, "I'm driving." He takes a big gulp of his water. "Plus, I have to help my father tomorrow at the house." He shakes his head. "Like he couldn't get someone else to help him or my brother. He's been on my ass these past couple of weeks." We both chuckle at him as he goes on to talk about how his father has been on his case. Something that I can understand since he dropped out of college to help work at the construction company, but then bailed the first week of working. He opted to work in the office except he practically never shows up, and when you talk to him, he's usually on the golf course. He finishes the bottle of water, then crushes it before going to his truck to get another one.

The crackling from the fire fills the night air as we all talk about little things here and there, the girls on their side of the fire laughing away and giggling. I catch Jennifer watching me a couple of times and I wink at her

each time, giving her a little grin. I want to leave and go back to our place and just be together when Waylon gets up and goes to his truck. I watch him walking there, wondering what he's doing. He opens the driver's side door and turns the pickup on, blasting the radio loudly. The sound of a country song now replaces the sound of the fire branches snapping. He holds one hand up in the air as he sways his hips. "Autumn, get your ass over here and dance with me." He grabs another bottle of water from the truck. I shake my head and laugh as Jennifer gets up and comes over to me, sitting on the ground between my legs. I put my beer bottle down next to the three other empty bottles I've drunk since we got here, before wrapping my arms around her chest. "Having fun, baby?" I ask her when she looks up at me, smiling.

"More fun than them." She motions with her chin toward the truck where Waylon and Autumn are having what looks like a heated argument. He's trying to get her to dance, but she's whipping off his arm and fighting his advances. "I don't know what she's doing with him. She deserves so much better than him." Waylon pffts in Autumn's face before she shakes her head. He grabs her wrist when she's about to walk away from him, yanking her to him, jerking her shoulder, and then hugging her. "I mean, it's not a night out unless they are fighting," Jennifer says when she stands up and holds out her hand for me. "Dance with me?"

"Anytime." I grab her hand, getting up. "Anywhere." I wrap an arm around her waist as I sway her to the song playing on the radio. I bury my face in her neck, smelling the berry scent from her shampoo. "Forever." I rub my nose against hers. "Have I told you lately that I love you?" I ask her softly as she grips the back of my neck in both hands.

"You might have mentioned it a time or two," she replies, and she's about to kiss me when Waylon starts.

"We should get the fuck out of here," he urges, his voice almost in a scream as he tries to be louder than the music, "hit up the bar in town and see what's going on there."

"We shouldn't do that," Autumn quickly says to him, and he looks at her, and it's a look of a glare and a sneer.

"No one asked you, Autumn," he retorts, shaking his head, turning toward the four of us. "Who is with me?" He looks at the four of us. "Should we take off or what?"

I put my arm around Jennifer's shoulders when she wraps her arms loosely around my waist. "We can't leave until the fire is out." I motion with my head toward the fire that is still going strong.

"No problem." Waylon storms to the side of the porch where they keep the hose, bringing it to the firepit and putting out the fire in no time. "There, now let's get the fuck out of here."

"I think we're going to go home," Everleigh says, "I have an early morning."

"Fuck that," Waylon spits out, going back over to the pickup, "get your ass in the truck."

"Watch the tone, man," Brock warns him, and he just laughs it off, as he does with everything.

"It's all good, man," Waylon says. "Let's just get

out of here and get to the bar. Then if you guys want to leave, I'll drive you home." He looks back at Everleigh. "There, happy?"

Brock and Everleigh share a look and then glance over at us, and for the first time I do not have a good feeling about this. "Let's go, people." Waylon swings his arm around and around to get us moving toward the truck.

The four of us start walking to the pickup. "I'll drive," Autumn offers. "I can drive." She walks over to Waylon, who just glares at her. She ignores his glare and smiles at him. "I can drive you around for once." Her voice goes soft as she holds on to his hips and he shakes off her hands.

"No way." He shakes his head. "My truck, I drive."

"Waylon," she murmurs his name softly, in a plea.

"Get in the truck," he orders her, his tone tight like he's losing his patience with her, his teeth clenched together, "or fucking walk home."

"Relax," I finally say, trying to break up the drama with the two of them, "we're supposed to be having fun."

"I'd be having more fun if we could get the fuck out of here," Waylon almost snarls, stomping over to the truck. "Now get the fuck inside or else I'll leave you all here."

"I don't know if that would be a bad thing," Everleigh mumbles as Brock chuckles beside her, putting his arm around her neck and pulling her to him, kissing her temple.

"I'm not sitting in the front, that is for sure," Everleigh says.

"I'll sit in the front," Jennifer offers, "that way the

two of them will be happy at least."

"No way." I shake my head. "You sit in the back; I'll sit with him up front."

"Fine," Jennifer relents, watching Autumn get into the back seat. She gets on her tippy-toes, kissing my jaw, before she climbs into the back seat in the middle. Followed by Everleigh, who moves as much as she can before Brock gets in with her.

The driver's window is open and I see Waylon finish his fifth water bottle since we've been here. He tosses it out the window. "Let's go, bro." He smirks at me and I just shake my head, walking around the front of the truck, opening the door, and getting in.

Jennifer reaches out and squeezes my arm as Waylon turns his pickup around and then speeds up at the same time. He puts the music on a bit louder. "Love this song!" he shouts, turning down the long stretch of road lined with trees on each side.

I'm watching the road, seeing him swerving a little all over the place, but since it's a backroad, he isn't paying that much attention.

"Can you focus on the road, please?" Autumn says from the back; she's literally saying what we are all thinking.

"Can *you* focus on the road?" Waylon mimics her as he picks up speed even faster. "Pain in my ass," he says and then turns his head around to talk to Autumn. "You're a pain in my ass. You focus on the fucking road!" he yells at the same time Everleigh shouts something, but I'm looking at Waylon—who is looking in the back—and by the time I look forward again, the bright headlights are shining straight into the truck.

He jerks the vehicle right, going off onto the gravel, and then quickly turns the wheel to the other side. The sound of him hitting something fills the truck, along with the screams from the back. I hold on to the dashboard, looking out the windshield as he's swerving back onto the road, hitting something else. All of sudden, it feels like someone hit the back of the pickup because we are spinning. The next thing I know, I hear the sound of metal crunching and scraping as I close my eyes, and the blackness hits me.

I taste metal in my mouth as I try to open my eyes. I hear people talking all around me, and I have the biggest headache of my life. I open my eyes, looking around at the pitch-black darkness. My arm is stuck, and I can't move it as I look around and see I'm upside down in the cab. The seat has me pushed against the dashboard; the white airbag popped under me. "Jennifer!" I call for her and hear moaning coming from the back seat, but with me pushed against the dash, I can't see behind me. "Jennifer." I try pushing the seat back, but my arm feels like it's out of place. "Jennifer!" I call her name more frantically now.

I hear sirens approaching. "Help!" I shout. "Somebody!" I try again, but the darkness takes me again right after I whisper her name, "Jennifer."

I hear the sound of rustling coming from the side of the truck. "We have help coming," a woman says.

"What about the other car?" a man asks, the voice

foreign to me. The sound of people bustles around beside us, but no one is doing anything to help us.

"It's in the ditch, and we just pulled the driver out," a man answers as I try to pry open my eyes. "The ambulance just got here."

I fight the darkness, but it's too strong. "Holy fuck," a man says right before I'm sucked back in. "We're going to need the Jaws of Life."

Two

Autumn

I HEAR THE sounds of crunching metal as I try to pry open my eyes, "How the fuck did this end up upside down?" someone asks once the crunching metal stops, and then I hear a buzzing sound coming from my ears. My left side feels like it is being crushed as I try to take a deep breath, but the pain rips through me. I groan softly, trying to push away the pain, and open my eyes, though they feel like they are sealed shut. I lick my lips, but my mouth is dry, and I notice the metallic taste right away as I fight to open my eyes.

"We got this door open!" someone shouts. I'm not sure if it's right beside me or far away.

"Fuck," another voice yells, "let's get him out!" The pain in my side is making it so hard to breathe that everything comes out in what feels like pants. I try to remember where the fuck I am.

Waylon's voice cuts into my thoughts. "You shut the

fuck up and don't say a fucking word," he hissed at me, *"you're a waste of my time."* I flinched at the words, but *I'm not sure why since he always goes down this road when he's had too much to drink.*

I knew I should have said something to someone, but I also knew he would kill me if I did. I was so dumb. "Jennifer!" Charlie calls her name. "Jennifer." The last time I saw her, she was beside me as we swerved in the road. Waylon was looking back at me instead of looking forward. The bright lights of the car filled the cab, and I think I screamed, or maybe someone else screamed, but we were jerked from one side to the other. I think he hit the car, or the car hit us, but all of a sudden, we were going through the air. My eyes closed, and the darkness took me, and now I am fighting against it to open them back up.

"Everleigh?" Brock mumbles from beside me, or at least I think it's beside me. "Everleigh, are you okay?"

"Hmm," someone mumbles, "my head." I feel movement and try with all of my strength to push myself away from the seat that I'm against. "It hurts."

"Guys, how is Jennifer?" Charlie asks from the front seat.

"I think she's on top of me," I can barely get out. "I can't move." I lick my lips again.

"Brock, are you okay?" Charlie asks.

"Foot is stuck. Feels like something is in my leg." His voice is pained.

"Help!" Charlie screams from the front seat as we hear sirens and then people rushing all around the truck.

"Do we know how many people are inside?" The question is asked, and I want to answer it, but I'm so tired. I just want to close my eyes, if only for a minute.

It sounds like a saw is working near us and then the sounds of crunching metal. "We got a door off!" someone shouts. "Fuck, I think he's DOA." What the hell does that mean? DOA? My mind spins as to what they are saying. "We need more hands."

"We got the second door opened!" another man shouts. "We're going to get you out."

"Everleigh," Brock says to the man.

"We have to get you out first and then get her," the man states, and then I hear the sound of roaring in pain from Brock, and I flinch at the sound of it. I want to move my hand, but I can't move it. Everything feels like it's a thousand pounds. "Fuck," someone else says, "we need a paramedic here."

"His foot is jammed," someone announces, "if we pull him out, it'll rip through his whole thigh."

"We need to get the driver out." I hear more footsteps from the other side of the car.

"What a fucking mess," another voice adds, "three-car accident. One man struck on the side of the road."

"How many are in this car?" a woman asks as I hear shouting from far away, and then more sirens fill the night. Red lights flash into the truck's darkness for a couple of seconds, but I don't have time to look around before it's dark again.

"We have three in the back and two in the front." I want to tell him we have four in the back, but my mouth is dry, and I suddenly taste metal.

The sound of metal clunking fills right outside my door, and I wince as my head throbs. "We got you," someone says right after the clunking sound stops. "We got him out."

"Jennifer," Charlie says. "My girlfriend," he says frantically, "she's in the back."

"We're trying to get them out," the man assures him, and I finally am able to open my eyes and look around. We are upside down, my head tilted to the side. My hair is in front of my face as I try to lift my hand to push it away, but it's being crushed by a body.

"Jennifer," I call her name since she was the one sitting next to me. "Jennifer is here," I try to say, "she's here."

"We're coming to get you out." The voice sounds like it's right next to me. "We'll get you out."

It sounds like a hundred people are working around me. "Jennifer," Charlie screams, "she was in the back!"

"How many people were in the back?" a man calmly asks him.

"We were six people," Charlie snaps. "Four in the back."

"There are only three people in the back." I hear the words, but nothing makes sense.

"There are four people in the back," Charlie tells him, frustration in his voice. "Three girls and one guy."

"Okay," the man again says calmly. "We'll go check again."

"She's in there," Charlie declares, and then I hear him

roar out in pain.

"Sir, you need to sit down and let us work on your leg," a woman urges. "Your leg is broken; you won't be able to stand."

"I need to go to her!" Charlie screams. "Why aren't you guys trying to get her out?"

I blink as a white light fills the back seat, so I close my eyes. "There are only three people back here," a man says softly, "unless she's under…"

"Fucking front of the cab is on the floor; we can't even see." I try to make sense of the bits and pieces of the conversation going on around us. I want to keep my eyes open, but they are so heavy. *I just need to close them for a minute*, I think to myself, and then I feel like I'm being moved.

"Had to pry her out," someone relays, and I try to open my eyes but not before I hear Charlie's shrieking.

The agony in his voice runs through my bones. "Where is she?" he yells. "I'm not leaving without her."

I feel like I'm floating. "Her arm seems to be broken, I think. Her blood pressure is high."

"She has to be fucking here somewhere!" Charlie screams. "Get me a phone. Someone, please, I need a phone!"

I open my eyes and turn my head for a minute, seeing Charlie sitting beside the upside-down truck. The front of the pickup looks like it's been crushed. A tree branch lies on top of the bottom of the truck. The four doors are pried open, and one of the tires is not too far from the wreckage. I turn my head to the other side, noticing two other vehicles. A pickup looks like it's been crashed into on the side, and the other car is missing the front tire and smashed up on one side.

I try to lift my arm, but it feels like it's stuck to the gurney. My body bumps up and down, and I groan, but it's swallowed by the sound of two doors being slammed shut, then the banging on the back, and I feel like I'm moving.

My eyes open, and I look around to see I'm in an ambulance, or at least I think I'm in the ambulance. "Hurts." That's the only thing that comes out.

"I bet it does," the woman tells me. "We're on the way to the hospital."

"Is everyone okay?" I ask, blinking open my eyes and focusing on the top of the ambulance.

"Um," the girl says, avoiding my eyes, "I'm not too sure."

"Waylon," I say his name, "the driver. Is he on his way to the ambulance?"

"I'm not sure," she repeats. "All I know is I have you, and we are going to get you to the hospital." "It hurts," I whisper.

"I bet it does," she comforts. "You probably have a couple of broken ribs." That's the last thing I hear before I shut my eyes and take a little nap.

I wake only when my eyelid is lifted, and light is flashed into my eyeball, going from one to the other. I groan and want to push the hand away from my face, but I literally can't lift my hand. "Stop." That's the only thing I say. "My friends?" I ask, looking at them and then wincing at the pain in my side.

"We need to get an MRI and an X-ray," the doctor orders as he presses my side, and I have no choice but to cry out in pain. "We'll get you all better," he assures me, turning and rushing out of the room.

"Where is she?" Brock shouts from somewhere. "Where the fuck is Everleigh?"

I'm about to ask something when my head falls forward, the sounds of rushing all around me. "We have a code…" That is the last thing I hear before I feel like I'm sinking into the blackness.

I feel someone touch my hand as my eyes try to open, but they can't. The sound of beeping fills the room. "She has five broken ribs. One of them punctured her lung, so we had to go in and stop the bleeding." I hear hissing. "She has a severe concussion, a broken leg, and her shoulder was dislocated." *That doesn't sound good.* It's the only thing I can think of as I try to open my eyes. I take a deep inhale, which makes me moan.

"It's okay, princess," my dad says as my hand is squeezed. "Rest. You'll be okay." I feel his lips on my forehead.

I want to tell him I don't want to rest. I want to tell him that I'm up, and I'm fine. I want to ask him where I am. I just want to open my eyes, but I'm pulled back into the darkness instead.

Three

CHARLIE

"SIR," THE PARAMEDIC says, "you have to come with us." He is crouched down beside me. "You can't stay here; we have to get you to the hospital." My back is against a tree from when they pulled me out of the wreckage. The pickup is flipped over, and the front of the truck looks like it's missing, probably from hitting a tree and being spun around. The bottom of the vehicle is facing up, with a tree branch lying on it. The front right tire lies five feet from the truck, not too far from another pickup involved in the accident. The front of the hood rests on the grass. You can't even see inside.

"I'm not leaving without her," I tell them through clenched teeth. "I don't care if I'm here for the rest of the fucking night. I'm not leaving." My whole body feels like it's about to snap in half. I'm not even thinking about the pain shooting through me or the fact that something stabbed my side. The only thing I'm thinking about is finding Jennifer.

"Sir," he starts again, and if my leg wasn't busted, I would get up and punch him right in the fucking throat.

"I need a cell phone," I tell him, "like now." I put out my hand to him, expecting him to place his phone in my hand so I can call my father.

"Sir," he tries again. This time, I move my face toward him, going almost face-to-face with him.

"Here." The cop who has been walking around comes over and hands me his cell phone. "You get one call, then I need some questions answered."

"Yeah, whatever," I respond, as I look over and see they are taking Brock out of the truck. "Is he okay?"

"So far," the cop says as I put the phone to my ear and listen to it ring twice before my father answers it with a groggy voice.

"'Lo," he answers.

"Dad," I start, my voice in a whisper, "there was an accident." All the fear I have is now coming back in full force when I have to say the words out loud.

"What?" he snaps, and I hear him moving around on his side. "Talk to me."

"I need you to come," I tell him. "I don't know where Jennifer is." The tears fall down my cheeks, and all the pain I've felt in my body is now straight in the middle of my chest. Like someone has shoved a knife in the middle of my chest and is twisting it left and right, ready to crack it open. "They don't know where she is, Dad." I try to take a breath, but the pain is too much to bear. "Dad, she was in the truck with us, but now she's not there."

"I'm coming," he says. "I'm calling your grandfather, and we're coming." I hear a door slam in the background.

"I'm not leaving this place until they find her…" My voice trails off. "I won't leave here without her."

"We'll be there as fast as we can. Are you okay?"

"I have a busted leg," I admit to him. "Not sure what else. I don't care. Dad, I'm not fucking leaving here without her." My teeth clench as I tell him and hope everyone around me is listening.

"We'll be there as soon as we can," he assures me. "Charlie." His voice is almost broken. "I'll be there in less than an hour." I don't answer him. I can't, my voice would break, and then it would be the longest hour of his life. Instead, I hang up the phone and hand it to the officer waiting there.

"Thank you," he says, taking the phone from me. "We have a couple of questions, and you are the only one who seems to be awake." I look up at him. "How many people were in the vehicle?"

"Six," I reply. "I was in the front with Waylon," I say, my voice trailing off, "four of them in the back. Brock, Everleigh, Jennifer, and Autumn."

"Waylon," he repeats as if he didn't hear properly. "Cartwright?" He says his name right away and then hisses when I nod. "Fuck," he swears, shaking his head.

"That's his truck." I point at his pickup. He takes his radio out and says something, but my eyes are watching the firefighters use the Jaws of Life to cut off the back door. They remove the door, and I don't know why I hold my breath. It all feels like it's happening in slow motion.

Blond hair is revealed instead of Jennifer's brown hair. Autumn falls to the ground, and I see she has blood in her hair. She groans as the firefighters get out of the way so the paramedics can take over. The sound of wailing is coming from across the street, and I look over to see a woman sitting by one of the wrecked vehicles with a man lying on the road. His limp hand is in hers as the paramedics move away from him, and her head falls on him. I see the paramedics shake their heads at the firefighters, and I know the man is gone. My eyes go back to the truck, and I see a firefighter getting into the cab and pulling a woman in his arms. I'm about to get up, even with a busted leg, to rush to see if they found Jennifer when I see him slowly moving Everleigh out.

"Do you know what happened?" he asks me, and I look over at the wreckage of the other two vehicles.

"It happened so fast," I admit. "I looked forward, and Waylon, I think, lost control. He swerved, and then I felt like we were going in the air."

"Do you know how fast he was going?" the officer asks, and I shake my head.

"Please," I plead with him, "if you can go and see if my girlfriend is in there."

He nods and walks back to another officer, taking someone else's statement, who stands up and is quietly sobbing in her hands. He looks at him, then at me, and then at the ground before he comes to me.

"There were only five people in the vehicle," he says softly, not sure what else to say.

"That's impossible." I shake my head. "We were all

in there." I point at the truck, the frustration in my voice.

"Was Mr. Cartwright drinking tonight?" he asks, and I shake my head.

"No, he was drinking water all night," I tell him, "because he was driving."

"How is he?" I ask, and he avoids looking at me. "Is he bad?" I ask, and someone calls his name.

The officer just looks at me and then the paramedic. "I'll be back." He walks away from me, and I look at the EMT.

"You need to go and help someone else because I'm not leaving," I inform him. He nods and gets up to walk away from me.

I don't know how long I sit here with my eyes on the pickup, willing Jennifer to pop up from the truck. I see the firefighters on the other side of the truck at the driver's door. They stand around waiting for something, who or what I don't know. I hear a car door slam and look up to see my father walking over to the yellow tape that has the area closed off. The police try to stop him. "I got a call from my son," he says, looking over, and I sit up.

"Dad," I call to him, and he runs over my way, followed by my grandfather, who is right behind him.

"Holy shit," my father swears once he gets close enough to see the truck. "Charlie." He gets on his knees. "You're hurt." He grabs my neck, squeezing it.

"Dad," I start, putting my hands on his arms. "Dad, I need you to find Jennifer."

"What are you talking about?" my grandfather asks,

getting on the other side of me.

"No one knows where she is," I tell them. "People are all around, I don't know what they are doing, but no one is looking for her."

I'm about to say something else when I look to the side and see a van get here. The two doors open, and they walk over to the police officers who are there. Another van follows the first. One of them approaches us, and my grandfather stands by my side.

"Good evening, I'm Lieutenant McCaffrey," he introduces himself. He looks at my grandfather, then down at me.

"Please," I plead, "my girlfriend is missing."

He nods. "We have the K-9 unit coming in, and we're also assembling a search party," he informs us, looking at my father next. "It's just we'll see more when daylight hits."

"Fuck that," I say, trying to get up but wincing, "she could be hurt and need help."

"Charlie," my father assures me softly, "we'll find her."

"In the meantime," Lieutenant McCaffrey says, "it's best we get you to the hospital and get you taken care of."

"I'm not going anywhere until they find her," I grind between clenched teeth.

"Charlie." My grandfather now gets down beside me. "I think you should go and get taken care of, and as soon as they fix you, you can come back here."

"No," I snap at him, "I'm not leaving."

"You can't do anything for her sitting here with your back against the tree," he reasons. I hate that he's right, but there's no way I'm leaving her.

"I'll stay," he tells me. "I'll stay here and search with them, and I promise you I won't stop until we find her."

"No one else I would trust more," my father declares. "It won't take us long," he tries to persuade me, "to get your leg set and in a cast, and then you can come and help search."

I look over at my grandfather. "Promise me."

"I've never once let you down," he speaks the truth, "and I won't do it now. I promise I will not stop searching, and when you return, we can search together."

I look at the two of them and then at the lieutenant. "Okay, I'll go and get sorted." The lump in my throat feels like a baseball. "But I'm coming back here."

He nods. "Sounds good." He waves over to the waiting EMT, who rushes over with a gurney.

They load me up into the ambulance, and my father gets in with me. They put the blood pressure machine on me. "What the fuck happened?" my father asks.

"We were driving, and he looked away for a second. The next thing I know, we were flying through the air." I swallow. "I woke up and was upside down. I was stuck to the fucking dashboard." My father puts his elbows on his knees and hangs his head. "Dad," I call his name, and he looks up at me with tears in his eyes.

"I could have lost you," he finally croaks out. "Did you see that fucking truck?"

"Jennifer, she's out there somewhere."

27

He puts his hand on mine. "We're going to find her." His hand squeezes mine. "We are going to fucking find her."

"When we find her, I'm going to marry her," I tell him, and he looks at me. "I'm going to fucking marry her tonight if I can." He doesn't say anything to me. He just nods because the ambulance stops and the doors swing open.

The paramedic starts talking to the doctor about my blood pressure and all that. "I just need my leg checked," I tell him, "and then I'm leaving."

"Let's get you checked out." He looks at my father. "We need an X-ray." They are wheeling me down the hallway, and I spot Waylon's father going in and out of the rooms looking for his son, I'm assuming.

They take me down to X-ray, and it's no surprise my leg is broken in two places. The doctor says something about surgery. I look up and see that over an hour has passed, and by the time they get someone in to stitch up the cut on my side and put the cast on, it feels like it's been five days.

I'm sitting on the side of the bed, waiting for the nurse to cover the wound, when I look up and see my grandfather standing in the doorway. I sit up, and my father stands, coming over to my side of the bed. "What are you doing here?" I ask, but the look on his face should have been my first clue.

"Charlie," he says my name, and his voice is hoarse.

"Did you find her?" I'm ready to jump off the bed. I grab my father and stand, ignoring the shooting pain from my foot. "Where is she?" I look over his shoulder to see if maybe they're wheeling her in.

"We found her." He comes in and stands in front of me. The relief that they found her is so overwhelming I feel like my chest is going to explode.

"Oh my God," I say, smiling. "Where is she?" I'm ready to go to her.

"Charlie," he says again, and his tone is flat. "I'm so sorry." It's then I know my life will never be the same. It's then I know the pain I feel will stay with me forever. It's then I know all of my dreams are being shattered. He says two words, and then the blackness gets me. "She's gone."

Four

AUTUMN

Eight years later.

I LOOK AT the computer screen in front of me, adding the numbers on the paper while grabbing my cup of steaming hot coffee beside the computer. When my phone rings next to the papers, I look down and see it's my brother, Brady. A smile fills my face as I answer, "Good afternoon to you." I look at the top of the computer screen to see it's just a little past one in the afternoon.

"Hey," Brady sighs. His tone is low, and I instantly know something is wrong. "What's up?"

"What's up with you?" I quickly answer him. "You sound like someone stole the lunch money you were saving up to buy naked magazines." He chuckles at that, making me relax just a touch.

"I wish this was that kind of problem," he says, and I gingerly put the coffee cup down.

"You're scaring me," I say softly, leaning back in the wooden desk chair that is as old as me, if not older. "What's going on?"

"I'm at the hospital," he replies, and my stomach immediately surges to my throat, "and it's not good."

The back of my neck tingles. "What do you mean?"

"It's Dad," he says, and every single cell in my body feels like it's being drained, only to be refilled with ice-cold water.

"What happened?" I try not to get ahead of myself, but the tears come anyway.

"He didn't want me to tell you." Just that sentence alone should make me stop in my tracks. My father has been my rock for my whole life, or at least for as long as I could form memories. My mother passed away when I was a baby. She got sick one day and then found out she was terminal at the ripe age of twenty-nine. I have pictures of her holding me, forever frozen at that stage. He never moved on, never remarried. His life was my brother and me and, of course, the distillery my great-grandfather created. "We just met with the oncologist."

"What?" I snap, and my hand hits the desk in front of me. "Oncologist," I whisper as my head is spinning. It's a good thing I'm sitting down because I would have fallen to the ground, but this time, I didn't have my father to help me stand.

"It's stage four, and they don't give him much longer." Brady's voice cracks as the tears stream down my face. "You need to come home."

"Of course," I agree without a second thought. Forget

the fact I haven't been home in the past six years. Forget the fact I said I would never step foot in that town again. Forget the fact my life ended the day my best friend and boyfriend died because of me.

"He's going to be pissed I told you," Brady shares, and I can hear the anguish in his voice mixed with the sadness.

"Well, too bad," I reply, trying to be strong for him. When I took off six years ago, everything dropped on Brady and my father. We were scheduled to help take over the whiskey production as well as the bar, but now it's all Brady's. "I'll get there as soon as I can."

"Sounds good." I can hear the tiredness in his voice, and the guilt of not helping him just adds to the guilt that lingers in my soul. "Call me with the details."

"Will do." I look up when I see Mildred walking into the room with a smile on her face that fades as soon as she takes one look at me. "I love you." It's something I've done in the last eight years, after that fateful night. I never, ever get off the phone without telling him I love him.

"Love you too," he replies and disconnects as my hand slowly lowers from my ear to place the phone on the desk. My eyes are on the phone in a trance.

"Hey." Mildred comes to the side of my chair and squats down beside it. Her white hair is perfectly styled and pulled back at the nape of her neck in a ponytail, which is probably tied with a ribbon. It's the same style she's had for the past forty years. Her warm hazel eyes watch me. "What happened?"

"It's my dad." The words come out of my mouth in a low tone. She puts her hand on top of mine. "He's not doing good."

"Oh, sweetheart." Her voice is filled with kindness. She was the first friend I made when I moved here six years ago. I drove through the town and stayed a couple of nights at the local motel, which had the sweetest man running it. I didn't know where I fit in, but I knew here in the middle of nowhere, no one knew me. No one knew my story. No one looked at me with hatred or anger or pity. I was just Autumn, the new girl in town. One day turned into three, and on the fourth day, while having a piece of pie at the local diner, Mildred walked in. She oozed confidence in skintight jeans and a tight top, and her silver hair made me do a double take. Truth be told, if I had her body at her age, I would probably have been dressed the same. She got on the stool next to me, and we started talking. She ran the local bar in town and was down a server, so I figured, why not? Now, six years later, I help her run it by doing her books and working side by side here on the busy days. She's the closest thing I've ever had to a mother figure.

"I have to go home." The thought alone makes me want to throw up. In the past six years, I have never had the pull to go home. Do I think of home every single night right before I go to bed? Yes. Is it a good memory? No. It's what nightmares are made of. It's the reason I'm breathing through life and not actually living. In reality, I died eight years ago. My heart is the only thing that didn't stop that night. Everything else did.

"Time to face those demons." My eyes fly back to hers. Even though we are close, she has no idea about the accident, and I wasn't going to tell her. To her, I was just Autumn, the lost girl who wandered into this small town and stayed. She loved me for who I was, the Autumn who smiles because she has to. The Autumn who laughs and then feels the immense guilt that I'm laughing. The Autumn who wakes every single morning with a burning hole in her stomach and wondering when her heart is going to put her out of her misery. "I knew you were running from something. You are a shell of a person." She squeezes my hand. "Stop running." She gives me a sad smile. "Trust me, I ran and wish I hadn't." I knew she held secrets; she knew I held secrets. I think that's why we bonded. We both hold those secrets so close to our hearts that no one is ever going to be let in.

"I'm coming back," I tell her, "so don't think you're replacing me." This is my home now, the only home I want.

"I could never replace you." She gets up and kisses the side of my head that eight years ago was laced with twenty-seven stitches. It was the least of my injuries.

I inhale deeply, looking down at the papers in front of me. "I'll finish this and then make my arrangements," I inform her, and she shakes her head.

"No, you won't." She grabs the papers from the desk. "You will go upstairs, pack your shit, and go to your father." I tilt my head to the side.

"Being mean isn't you." I try not to laugh at her, but I can't help it as she glares.

"Do you want me to get the bat?" She mentions the baseball bat she keeps behind the bar in case someone acts up, and she has to stand up for herself. It's hard being a bar owner who is also a woman. She makes sure that everyone knows not to fuck with her.

"Fine, I'm going." I get up out of the chair. "When I come back, I'm bringing a cushion for that chair."

"Hmm." She shakes her head. "If I take you back."

I can't help but throw my head back and laugh, clapping my hands. "You love me."

"Love is a strong word, my girl." She softens when she says my girl. "Now get out of here and go to your father." Her eyes fill with tears. "You call me if you need me, and I'll come."

"He'll be pissed as hell if you show up," I tell her. "He wants you to think he's macho."

Now it's Mildred's turn to laugh. "He's about as macho as it comes." She shakes her head. Over the years, he's come to visit me, and he and Mildred would always be trying to best each other. Even down to drinking, which he would win because he had a hundred pounds on her.

I walk out of the office, opening the side door to head to the wooden staircase that leads to my studio apartment above the bar. I let myself in, going to the bed and sitting on it. "You can do this," I tell myself. "You have no choice." My legs move up and down as I have a one-sided conversation. "Get up and go." I put my hands on the side of the bed and stand. "I have to do this."

Twelve hours later, I'm driving past the town sign, the dread rearing up so hard and fast my hands grip the steering wheel. My heart speeds up to an abnormal pace, and I feel like I've just completed a marathon. My chest rises and falls as I try to swallow down the bile that is rising. I take a deep inhale and puff out, then breathe through my mouth, the radio playing so softly that my breathing drowns it out.

The darkness is almost too much to bear as I drive down the road where the trees look like they hide the monsters inside them. I should have stopped five hours ago and continued my journey tomorrow, but I thought it would be okay. It's not. I never, ever drive at night anymore. It's why I live upstairs from the bar where I work. The memories are just too vivid, the panic attack that rails from it too strong to take. The last time this happened, I pulled over and slept on the side of the road. From that day on, I drove when it was daylight and only daylight. Sometimes when it started to get dark, it was okay, but as soon as nighttime would hit, I was not driving.

I'm so in my thoughts that I don't even notice I'm driving down the road I never wanted to be on again. I'm so in my thoughts I don't notice the tears running down my face. I'm so in my thoughts that I don't even notice I'm at the accident site.

I stop the car on the side of the road where my life changed. Putting the car in park, I look across the road at the tree that stopped the truck from going even farther into the forest. My hand shakes as I open the door and put one foot out and then the other. I take three steps onto the road and look around. The memories of that night come rushing back, and I see where the other vehicles were. I feel like the road is spinning under my feet, or maybe I'm moving my feet in a circle, as if I'm watching it replay again in my head.

My feet move toward the tree, the night silent, without even a cricket making noise. It's like the world stands still as I step from the road to the grass, getting close enough to see the white wooden cross planted right next to the tree. A green wreath hangs around it. I put my hand to my mouth, thinking that I'm going to be sick. I close my eyes at the same time I hear the sound of twigs breaking. My head flies to the side, and I see him come out of the darkness. "What the fuck are you doing here?" The venom in his voice cuts my breath off again. I take a second to look at him. Eight years changed us all, but Charlie looks almost the same, except for his haunted eyes. His frame is bigger, as if he's been working out, and the scruff on his face makes him look more rugged.

There is no mistake; Charlie Barnes holds me accountable for what happened that night. Little does he know, he's not the only one. "Hello, Charlie."

Five

CHARLIE

I THOUGHT MY eyes were playing tricks on me. It wouldn't be the first time that happened, especially when I'm here. Sitting with my back against the tree, with my hand on the cold, wet ground as if I could touch her. The same spot where they found her, the spot where she lost her life. The same spot I come and sit at a couple of times a week. It used to be every day, but now I alternate from being here or being at her grave site. I watched from the darkness as she got out of her car and onto the road where our lives changed, her feet moving her around in a circle, probably reliving the horror that was that night. I slid up the bark of the tree in the darkness as she walked toward me. Toward the scene where my life turned into the hellhole it is now.

My eyes narrowed to slits as I saw her take steps toward where the white wooden cross I planted sits, along with the wreath that I replace monthly. I stand here in the darkness, my body tense and burning like it's on fire with rage as I look at the woman who could have stopped all of this. The woman who with one word could have changed the lives of five other people. Selfish, that is what she is, and I hate every single bone in her body.

The silence of the night is almost deafening. I watch her short blond hair move side to side as she stands in front. I can't help myself, nor do I fucking care. "What the fuck are you doing here?" The harshness of my voice is tamer than what I feel inside me. The hatred I have for this woman feeds my soul. I hate the world. I hate the whole fucking world for the pain I walk with every single day. But I don't hate anyone as much as I hate Autumn.

Her body looks like it's shaking, like she's outside in a snowstorm without a jacket. "Hello, Charlie," she says softly.

"I asked you a question," I growl out, ignoring she was trying to be polite at the same time watching the tears run down her face, tears she has no right having. "What the fuck are you doing here?"

"My father is sick." Her voice comes out broken. "I won't be here long." I watch her body shake even more, her arms wrapping around her stomach. She's changed in the last six years since I've last seen her; she looks like she's skin and bones.

Her face is ghostly. "You come home, and the first fucking place you come to is here?" I say in disgust.

"I shouldn't have." She shakes her head, her hand coming up to wipe away the tears streaming down her face.

"Yeah, you're right. You shouldn't have," I snap at her. "Let's hope this is the last fucking time I see you." I don't stand here long enough to see her reaction. Instead, I turn and walk back into the darkness, past the tree where she died, and toward the path that after eight years I could find with my eyes closed.

I hear a car door close in the distance and know it's her. It has to be since it's the middle of the night. The sound of a car driving by makes me turn to the side as I see her. It takes me forty-five minutes to walk back to my house. Coming out of the dense forest into the clearing, I walk past the barn and straight to the house I moved into four years ago. When we bought the property, it came with a main house, but it was falling apart. So my parents had it renovated slowly, and when it was done, they came down and helped me move in here.

My parents were beside themselves watching me drown in the house I shared with Jennifer. I hadn't touched anything that was Jennifer's. Her clothes still hung in the closet with mine. Her clothes still folded in the drawers. Every single thing she left was still out, untouched. I never wanted to move from the house Jennifer and I shared, but I gave in. It was easier than fighting with them day in and day out. I was a shell of myself. I'm still a shell of myself. I've just learned how to hide it from everyone now.

I walk up the back steps, going to the sliding door. Grabbing the handle and pulling it open, I feel the cold air from the air conditioner hit me right away. I kick off my boots on the little mat before I make my way to the kitchen. Going straight to the cabinet over the fridge, I grab the half-full bottle of whiskey before going to the couch. I sit down and place the bottle on the coffee table. Twisting the cap off, I toss it across the room and watch it land somewhere in the corner before I bring the bottle to my mouth and take a big pull of the amber liquid. The burning is almost nonexistent anymore since I drank some before I took my walk after dinner.

"Fucking hell." I shake my head, seeing Autumn in my mind before I take another pull and sit back into the cushions of the couch. She was standing there alive, breathing, while Jennifer rots under six feet of dirt. I ignore the way her eyes looked, just as haunted as mine, if not more. I ignore that Jennifer would not want me to blame her. I ignore it all while I take another pull of the amber liquid. My eyes go to the frame sitting in the middle of the coffee table of Jennifer and me from the first night we met, standing beside her with my arm around her shoulder. The regret of not marrying her is something I carry with me daily. Not making her mine forever will always be my biggest mistake.

My heart feels the usual pressure when I look at the picture, as the sorrow comes slowly after. I take another long pull before putting my head back and closing my eyes, bringing me back to the day my life ended.

In that hospital room, staring at my grandfather. His stoic expression, his face saying what I think I already knew in my heart but not in my head yet. "She's gone." The words cut me off at the knees, and I swear I blacked out for a minute. All I saw was darkness until I felt two strong arms lift me and place me on the bed.

I snapped out of the darkness. "No!" I shook my head in disbelief. "No, no, no, no, no," I chanted over and over again. "You're lying," I hissed at him. "You're lying. She's not gone." I looked at my father, wanting him to tell me it wasn't true. But I could tell from his eyes, from the way he was looking at me, he wasn't lying to me.

"I'm so, so sorry." His voice sounded as broken as my soul was at that moment. It felt like half of me, fuck that, the whole of me was gone with her. Like a piece of me was going to be forever lost.

"I have to go to her." I turned to get out of the bed. "I have to go and be with her."

"You can't." My grandfather came to stand beside the bed next to my father.

"It's cordoned off; no one can go in." He said the words, and I thought at that moment I hated him. I hated him for telling me this.

"Where was she?" I asked, my voice as dead as my heart.

My grandfather looked at my father, not sure if he should tell me. "He's not going to stop until you tell him," my father communicated to my grandfather.

"She flew out of the window. She died on impact." He said the words, and all I knew was I had to turn to the side, and I threw up everywhere.

"Fuck," my grandfather said as he rushed out of the room to get someone. The nurse came back in and called

someone to come and clean it up.

My father went to get me something to drink, and all I could do was stare at the cream-colored wall. "Where is she?"

"She's going to be sent to the coroner," he murmured softly. "There is going to be an autopsy performed."

"What about everyone else?" I asked, even though, to be honest, I didn't care. At that moment, I wished everyone had died, including me.

"Waylon didn't make it either," my grandfather said, and I laid my head back on the bed and closed my eyes, never wanting to wake up again. But sadly, I did.

Every day, the alarm rings, and I have to ask whoever is listening why. Why keep me here? My eyes open again, taking in the darkness as I take another gulp of the whiskey, getting up right after and heading to the bedroom. I place the bottle on my bedside table, falling onto the covers of the bed.

I look up at the ceiling. "I miss you," I tell the empty room, "every fucking day." My eyes close. "I wish you were here," I mumble as my eyes get heavier. "I wish I was there." Those are the last words I say before the darkness takes me.

It feels like it's been five minutes when the alarm blares from the side. I reach out my hand and move it around, knocking the bottle of whiskey to the floor. It shatters all over the place. I get up on my elbow, looking down at the amber liquid with glass shattered around it. "Well, this is a wake-up," I say, rolling to the other side of the bed and grabbing a pair of shoes before going to get a broom. I sweep up the glass. "What a waste of good alcohol," I mumble as I finish cleaning it. I look over to the bedside table at the picture of Jennifer. "Morning, baby," I greet her before turning and heading to the shower.

Thirty minutes later, I'm grabbing my mug of steaming, hot black coffee and heading out the back door. My hair is still wet from my shower when I slide my boots on as I walk down the steps, headed to the backyard. I look at the side, at the sun slowly coming up.

I walk past the two black pickup trucks parked right next to the shed where we keep the tools, going to the far corner of the yard where the red barn is located. I'm making my way to the office building that is halfway to the barn. I open the glass door and turn on the lights before I make my way past the reception desk toward my office. "Time to start the day." I pull out my chair. "Another day I'm closer to death."

Six

Autumn

THE SOFT SOUND of bells ringing makes me reach out from the quilt and turn it off. It wasn't like I was sleeping anyway. I turn to the side, grabbing my phone and shutting it off before my arm goes back under the cover where it was. I look around the room I moved back in with my father a couple days after the accident. I haven't been in for over eight years, eight years and nothing in this room has changed. A house where my mother grew up and we inherited when her parents died. Brady wanted nothing to do with it, mostly because he knew how much I loved this house, so he didn't care that I moved in as soon as I turned eighteen. A house Waylon hated because it was beneath him to be in something that didn't have fifteen bedrooms. Another reason I should have hated him, but instead I just ignored it.

Turning to my other side, I look at the window. The shade's open as the daylight streams into the room. My body feels like it's been run over with a Mack truck, front and back. I blink a couple of times, not looking anywhere else but the window, until I take a deep inhale and throw the covers off me and get out of bed. The cool air makes me shiver as I reach for the long sweater lying across the bottom of the bed. Wrapping it around myself, I move to the kitchen to make myself a cup of coffee.

Walking over to the pantry cupboard, I see my brother at least went out to get things to make coffee. Setting it up to brew myself a pot of coffee, before pouring myself a cup, I pick it up and walk over to the back door, pulling it open and then pushing through the storm door before standing on the back deck. The swing chair my father put up for me when I inherited this place ten years ago sways softly with the warm breeze. Instead of walking over and sitting in the swing, I walk to the steps and sit on the top one and look out into the field. The sounds of birds chirping fill the morning air as I take a sip of my hot black coffee. My mind goes back to last night and coming face-to-face with the one person I never wanted to see again. Was it irony or maybe it was karma? Whatever it was, I saw that Charlie had not changed in six years.

I mean, his appearance changed for sure. He was always handsome and the hate definitely didn't dimmish that. The words from the last conversation we had, some all those years ago, fill my head. It was also the last night I stayed in this house, after that, I moved in with my father, right before I left town.

"You fucking knew he was drunk!" he roared in my

face; his face filled with anguish and hatred. His eyes were filled with rage. It was also one o'clock in the morning when he knocked on my door, scaring the ever-loving fuck out of me. "You did this." His face advanced to mine. "You could have stopped him."

"I tried," I finally said, "I tried to get him to give me the keys."

"You didn't try hard enough." His words sliced through me like little shards of glass getting under your skin. "It should be you in that grave, rotting in hell with him." That was the last thing he said to me before he turned and stumbled into the forest like a thief in the night. My legs gave out from under me, and I sat there rocking side to side until daylight.

I take a sip of the coffee, closing my eyes and blinking the last tear away. I knew coming back home would bring back all of this. I was just hoping I would be strong enough for it.

I finish the cup of coffee before getting up and moving back inside where my phone is ringing. I place the cup in the sink, not rushing to the phone. The phone stops ringing as I walk back to the bedroom. Picking it up, I see it's my brother.

I'm about to call him back when he sends me a text:

Brady: *Just checking in. Call me when you're up.*

I put the phone on speaker, calling him back. "Hey," he says when he answers the phone, "did I wake you?"

"Nope," I reply, picking up the pillows and tossing them to the foot of the bed as I make it. "I was up and at 'em."

"You got in so late last night," he reminds me, "you should have slept in."

"I'm fine," I assure him, avoiding telling him I ran into Charlie. He has enough on his mind with Dad. He doesn't need to worry about me and how I'm doing. "I was planning on getting in the shower and picking up some donuts and surprising Dad."

"What time do you think that is going to happen?" he asks me. "Because he's going to want to kick my ass, and I'd rather be far away from him when you do this."

I laugh at him. "In about an hour. Is he still at the hospital?"

It's Brady's turn to laugh. "You think that stubborn man would stay in the hospital if he didn't need to be there? His words to the nurse were, 'I can do all this lying around in my own damn house.'" I grab the pillows, putting them back up to the headboard.

"Sounds about right," I say, "he'll probably kick my ass for being here."

"Well, there is more stuff we need to talk about," he says, and I sit down. "How about you swing by the bar when you're done?"

"Sounds good." I close my eyes. "I will also note I don't like your tone."

"Duly noted, little sister," he responds softly. "See you later."

"Love you," I say before pressing the end button, then getting up and going into the shower. I comb out my shoulder-length hair before fluffing it with my hands. I've always had long hair, but now I don't let it get longer than my shoulders.

The dread that fills me is something I can't explain or put into words. I slip my light-blue jeans with holes in the knees on before grabbing the gray tank top that sits right above the waist of the jeans, showing you just a touch of my stomach. I grab my gray sweater and put it on before snatching up my black bag and putting on my white sneakers.

I walk out the front door to my car, my hands shaking when I pull open the door and get behind the wheel. "It'll be fine," I tell myself. "The worst that can happen already happened."

I make my way down the familiar roads, turning on Main Street and heading straight to the little coffee shop that makes the best sugar donuts I've ever tasted in my life. I park on the street, getting out of the car and closing the door. I look around to see that people are already looking at me. One woman turns her head and then does a double take, her mouth hanging open in shock at me being here.

I try not to let it bother me; I should be used to it by now. I had to endure it for a full two years before I left. The finger-pointing, the whispers as soon as I walked into the room, the snide comments and remarks until everyone else won, and I packed up and left.

Pulling open the door to the bakery, I'm assaulted with the smell of sugary goodness right away, and my mouth waters. The woman, Maddie, behind the counter looks up from placing a tray in the window stand. "Well, I'll be." She wipes her hands on her apron. "If it isn't

Autumn Thatcher." She smiles at me. "You're a sight for sore eyes."

"Hello, Ms. Maddie." I walk to the counter, trying to hide the fact that my hands are shaking and so is my voice.

"You are skin and bones." She looks me up and down. "They don't feed you where you are." The worry is in her voice and also in her eyes.

I laugh. "Nothing like home cooking, I guess," I tell her. "Can I have a box of donuts?" I look at the case. "Half sugar, half powdered."

"Sure thing, missy." She grabs a box to fill it, and the sound of bells ringing behind me means someone opened the door. My hands instantly start to shake, wondering if it will be someone I know. I mean, it's a small town. The question is, who is it going to be?

My neck gets heated, but I don't turn my head to look behind me as I wait for Maddie to hand me the blue-and-white box. She rings up the amount, and I pay her. I turn my head down and walk past the two people waiting in line. Lucky for me, it's not someone who recognizes me. My chest gets tight, making breathing harder and harder. It comes in little breaths now as I rush toward my car. Getting in, I set the donuts on the seat next to me before putting my hands on the steering wheel. My head falls forward as I try to focus on my breathing, knowing I'm in the middle of having a panic attack. I haven't had one in six years since I left town.

I close my eyes, counting to ten and then to twenty. Only when I'm at a hundred do I feel even remotely better. I start the car, making my way to my family home. The street is lined with willow trees, and I have this sense of peace when I'm driving down it. Like nothing can hurt me and it's okay that I'm here.

I pull into the driveway, parking behind my dad's pickup, before grabbing the box of donuts. I have one foot out the door when I hear the storm door slam shut. "What in God's name are you doing here?" His voice feels like a big hug, and I have to close my eyes to stop myself from breaking down. Instead, I turn to him and put a big smile on my face, though it's mixed with tears.

"Is that any way to welcome your only daughter home?" I ask him as I walk up the four steps to the house I grew up in, ignoring the fact he looks pale and he's lost about thirty pounds since the last time I saw him. "Especially when I come with donuts."

He takes the box from my hand, placing it on the floor before he pulls me into a big bear hug. A hug that I feel right down to my bones. A hug that you know, no matter what, everything will be okay. A hug I didn't know I missed and needed until this very moment. "What are you doing here?" he asks me in my ear, but his arms never move from around me. "Did your brother call you?" I laugh and cry at the same time in his arms. "I'm going to kick his ass."

"I'm going to kick your ass"—I move out of his embrace and then bend to pick up the donut box—"from here to Timbuktu." I look up into his gray eyes. "Why didn't you tell me?" I ask softly, and he takes a deep inhale.

"What was it going to change?"

"Well, for one, I would be here for you," I snap.

"Baby girl, you ran away from here because it was killing you." He puts his big strong hand on my face. "You think I was going to try to get you back here?" He shakes his head. "Ain't no way in hell I would do that."

"Well, ain't no way in hell I was not going to be here for you," I tell him, just as stubborn as he is, "and I'm not going to be mad at you for not telling me either." I raise my eyebrows. "But I am pissed you put this box on the ground." I hold up the donut box. "What if it got ruined?"

He chuckles. "Let's get you inside and get you a glass of milk to go with your donut."

"Dad, I'm not ten anymore." I turn to walk into the house with him. The smell is like home, and I admit I buried the fact I missed it. I buried the fact I wanted to be here, but I didn't deserve it. I buried it all, and now that the door is open, it's coming back in full force. No matter how quick or how fast I try to close the door, the pressure is stronger than me. The memories coming so fast and so quick, I can't stop it.

"How long are you staying?" he asks, grabbing two glasses and going to pour them both with milk while I pull out a chair and sit down.

"For as long as I need to be." The words come out of my mouth, surprising both of us. In reality, I was thinking of this week and then coming back when the time was needed, but being here, seeing my dad, I need to be here. I'm going to be here.

He's about to say something when the storm door opens, and then slams shut. I look over to see Brady walking into the house. "I figured you would hunt me down"—he puts his hands on his hips, looking at my father, who is glaring at him—"so I saved us both the time and energy." I bite my lower lip. "Plus, I heard she got donuts." He bends to give me a side hug and kisses the top of my head.

He pulls out the chair beside me while my father pulls out another glass. "So what are we talking about?"

"How long I'm going to be in town," I fill him in, and he looks at me and then at Dad.

"Well then," he says, opening the box, "now is a good time to talk about Thatcher's and Sweet Southern Country Whiskey." I look at him and then my father, who comes back to the table with two glasses of milk, putting them down in front of us before going back to get his own.

"What about them?" I ask of the distillery that has been in our family since the twenties. My great-grandfather made his own whiskey and sold it out of the trunk of his car. Once Prohibition ended, he opened up the Sweet Southern Country Whiskey distillery with its own bar attached to it called Thatcher's. He figured he would make it and sell it at the same time, cutting out the middleman. It's been passed down from one son to the other. My father taking it over from his father, and when Dad's ready, he'll hand it over to both of us, not just my brother.

"Things aren't looking so good," my father says, and

I turn back to him, confused.

"That's putting it lightly," Brady states, taking a bite of the powdered donut. "That is putting it very mildly." He looks over at me. "I don't know if we'll last the rest of the year."

My mouth opens in shock. "What the hell are you talking about?" I look at both of them, my eyes going back and forth.

"Things haven't been…" My father pulls out a chair. "As productive as we had hoped."

"Dad," Brady grumbles, "stop with the bullshit. She is going to find out."

"Find out what?" I ask him, then look at my father. "What are you guys not telling me?"

"We lost a couple of big contracts," my father admits.

"A couple," Brady mumbles. "More like all of them. Let's just say the Cartwrights are still holding a grudge," Brady declares, and I gasp. "Not one restaurant in town will hold our whiskey," he continues, "and it seeps to all the surrounding areas." I blink, and I think my heart is going to come out of my chest. "We have the stock; we just have nothing to do with it. We haven't had a run in five months." Just that thought alone is unfathomable. We used to sell out and have people on waiting lists to get our product.

I look at them. "What about shooting it out globally?" I ask them. "Selling it from a website?"

"There is only so much we can do," my brother says. "We were going to ask you if you could help." He looks at my father. "But Dad said no."

"Did he?" I glare at my father. "You don't think I should have known that my inheritance is being flushed down the tubes?" He shakes his head.

"You had enough on your plate," my father says calmly. "We could have handled it."

"Really?" I ask. "How is that going for you two?" I don't wait for him to answer before I get up and push away from the table. "Let's go." I look at my brother.

His mouth is full of donut. "Go where?"

"I want to look at the books," I tell him, "see what we have to work with."

"I'm not even finished with my donut," he groans out but gets out of his chair. "I forgot how bossy you are."

I grab my own donut. "I guess I did too." I take a bite of the donut. "Now, let's get to work."

Seven

CHARLIE

I SLAM THE truck door closed, walking over to the door with Earl's Diner across it. Pulling it open, I hear the sound of plates and utensils meeting at the same time. I walk straight to the long counter with round leather stools and sit on one, looking around to see the place jam-packed since it's lunchtime. "Hey, Charlie." I look over to see Isabel holding two plates in her hands. "I'll be right with you." She smiles shyly at me, and I just smirk at her.

"Take your time, Isabel," I say, my fingers nervously beating against the counter while I wait for her to come back.

"What can I get you?" she asks me softly, taking out her server pad.

"I'll have a bacon burger to go," I say, "and a side of fries and rings."

"Is that all?" she asks, her blue eyes lighting up. I nod

and wink at her. She smirks at me before she turns and walks away. My eyes go to her ass as she sways her hips from side to side.

"What's up, Charlie?" I look over to see Fred sitting down beside me.

"Not much," I reply. "Was out and decided to stop in for lunch."

"Good choice," he says and I look over at the old man, wearing gray pants with a flannel shirt and his suspenders. "Heard you got some new horses in."

"You heard right," I tell him of the five new horses we got in last week. "You have time, you can come over and help break them in."

He nods. "You betcha," he says, "it's been too long."

When Isabel returns and places a cup of coffee in front of Fred, she places a brown bag in front of me. "That'll be twelve seventy-four," she announces. I reach into my back pocket, pulling out my wallet before tossing a twenty on the counter for her.

"Keep the change, Isabel." I get up.

"Hope to see you soon," she says before grabbing the twenty from the counter and smirking.

"You just might." I grin before walking out of the diner. I hold the door open for a couple, who thank me, before I walk toward my truck.

I pull up to my house and go straight to the office instead of into my house. My eyes go to the red barn as I see a couple of trainers leading some horses out of it.

I pull open the front door that has Mustang Creek Ranch in the middle of it. I named it this as soon as I got the papers for the barn, putting my own stamp on it. I walk around the reception desk in front of five chairs in the waiting room.

Ten years ago, I moved to Montgavin to expand the Barnes therapy farm. Something my father started when he was twenty with two horses. Initially, it started with soldiers who would come home with PTSD symptoms. They would come by every day and do a couple of hours with the horses. Then he expanded it to women who came from abusive homes to kids who suffered anxiety and also special needs. It's a different approach to healing. He now has barns all over the South. I came to town to do the startup and then met Jennifer and decided I would take over this branch. Now we have twenty-five horses that are working with people. Fifty people work the farm, along with twenty therapists working one-on-one with all our clients.

I had the best of both worlds: the woman I was in love with and the new branch that was starting to grow at a fast pace. Then in a matter of seconds, it was over, and I was a changed man. I think I spent every day for six months drunk. From the time I opened my eyes until I closed them, I was drunk and in a fog. I would attempt to come to work, but I would end up passing out in my office with the bottle of whiskey in the middle of my desk. I hated every single second that I wasn't drunk because it was the only time I didn't see her. I didn't feel her beside me. I didn't hear her tell me she loved me or call my name.

The more drunk I got, the closer I felt to her until my

parents intervened. Not just my parents, but my father, my great-grandfather, grandfather, all of my uncles, and most of my cousins. They picked me up off my floor while I was passed out, and I woke up in my childhood home, pissed at the world. I said things I could never take back. Hurt the people who loved me most in the world. Ravaged my father to the core and kept kicking him while he was down. It was my grandfather and my cousins, Ethan and Gabriel, who literally took me by the scruff of the neck and pulled me out of my house. They tossed me into a cold fucking shower and watched me go cold turkey.

They sat there while I raged on. While I blamed the whole fucking world for my grief. I would see the sorrow and pity in all their eyes, and watching my parents cry tears for their son, who was still alive, bothered me. I didn't want them to shed a tear for me. Especially since they watched me cry more tears than I thought a body could create before I accepted the help. I listened to the doctors and more therapists than I can count on one hand. It was a waste of everyone's time because the anger and rage I held inside me fed my blood. I would pretend I was fine, and then when I was alone, I would hate the whole fucking world. I would drink after hours when no one would see. I became the man I am today. A man I'm not proud of. A man I think I hated. A man who was lost and never was going to be found.

I walk down the hallway to my office and toss the bag on the desk before walking to the kitchen and grabbing a bottle of water and going back to my office.

Pulling out the black chair to sit, I open the bag and pull out the burger with a folded note on top of it. I put the wrapped burger on top of the desk while I open the note.

It's been a while. Why don't you stop by tonight?
Isabel

I fold the note back up and toss it in the garbage can beside my desk before unwrapping the burger and taking a bite. Another thing I started doing was having a revolving door of women. The first time I slept with someone else, I came home and threw up, then I went to Jennifer's grave and lay with her. My head on her cold tombstone, I asked her to forgive me. A string of one-night stands. A string of nameless women. A string of faceless women. Without fail, as soon as I would sink my cock into them, all I saw was her. It might have been the booze. Whatever it was, I didn't care. Thursday, Friday, Saturday, and Sunday I would go and sit with her and then go out, get drunk, and fuck some random. Over the years, there were a couple who I would go back to, but other than fucking them, I wanted not one thing from them. And it wasn't a surprise to anyone. Everyone who knew me knew my story, knew my heart belonged to one woman and one woman only. I would never give my heart away to someone else, it wasn't even mine to give anymore.

I take another bite of the burger before taking the fries and rings out of the bag and tap the mouse to start the computer. I'm opening the emails I have to go through when I hear the sound of boots coming into the office.

I look up and see Emmett walking down the hall toward my office. He's wearing jeans and a long-sleeved shirt pushed up to the elbows. A hat that has seen better days sits on his head backward. The dust and sand from the barn is on his face. "Hey," he greets, watching me as he walks into the office, "I was looking for you."

"Not too hard," I say, "since you found me."

"Funny," he fires back, not laughing. Emmett started with me at the beginning of this. I hired him to be in charge of everything, not thinking that I would make this place my home, but then I ended up staying so the two of us could work side by side. He's been my right-hand man for the last ten years and one of the closest friends I've ever had. He tells me when I'm being a dick, which is more often than I care to admit. He's seen me at my best, and he's definitely seen me at my worst.

"What's up?" I ask, taking a bite of my burger.

"I heard." He just looks at me, and my eyebrows pinch together.

"I'm sorry, you are going to have to give me a bit more than that." I laugh. "Is this like a code word or something?"

"I was in town this morning," he states, and again, I just stare at him. "Jesus, you're going to make me say it, aren't you?"

"I'm going to have no choice but to have you say it since, for the life of me, I have no idea what the fuck you are trying to say." I pick the burger back up.

"Autumn," he says her name, and I drop the burger onto the wrapper. My blood goes ice cold. "Someone saw her in town this morning, grabbing donuts." I chew the food in my mouth, the taste is suddenly sour as I grab the bottle of water to wash it down before I throw it up. "I see you haven't heard."

"Didn't need to hear," I finally say, leaning back in my chair. "Saw her last night."

His eyes about come out of his sockets. "Excuse me?"

"Ran into her last night at the crash site," I explain, and he hisses. "Welcomed her back with open arms."

"I bet you did," he sneers. "I heard about the last time you met, so I could just imagine." I shrug, and all he does is shake his head.

I watch him walk out of the room, and I think about the last time we met. I was walking through the forest, stumbling mostly. My goal was to go to the crash site, but instead, I ended up at her house. The darkness of the house loomed as I walked up the steps and pounded on her door.

The minute she opened her door and stepped outside, I roared in her face, "You fucking knew he was drunk!" The shock and horror on her face should have stopped me, but nothing could stop me. I saw red. "You did this." My face went into hers so she could see the damage she caused. "You could have stopped him!"

"I tried," she finally said, her voice cracking. "I tried to get him to give me the keys."

"You didn't try hard enough." She winced when I said that as if I hit her. "It should be you in that grave, rotting in hell with him." I turned and stumbled back into the forest. Looking over my shoulder for a second, I watched

her fall to her knees.

She left town after that, and now she was back. For what? I have no idea, but I know one thing. I never want to fucking see her face again.

Walking out of the house after dinner, just as the sun is going down, I look around, seeing that no one is left working in the barn. My horse is outside waiting for me as I get on him for my after-dinner ride. Pushing him to go faster and faster as we go down the trail, which I can probably do with my eyes closed. I'm a sweaty mess when I finally get him back into the barn and get him water before walking out into the black night.

I debate whether to shower before I make my way over to Jennifer. Instead, I head towards the forest, Deciding that I would shower when I got back. My feet make their way down the beaten path as I think about where I will go today. It's one of two places: the crash site or the cemetery. My thoughts going back to last night and the confrontation with Autumn, I opt for the cemetery.

Walking through the forest, listening to the sounds of birds chirping and twigs snapping as I mindlessly make my way over. Pulling open the black cast-iron gate, I hear the squeaking as I step up the two steps and follow the pebbled path.

My head down as I walk towards her, and when I look up, I see a figure on their knees in front of the tombstone. My body going tight, my blood turning to ice. "You've got some fucking nerve." The words are out of my mouth, echoing in the night. Autumn looks up and over at me, and I can see the tears in her eyes, making me even angrier. "What the fuck are you doing here."

"Charlie," she says my name in a whisper as she gets to her feet, "I didn't know."

"I don't want to fucking hear it," I hiss at her, this woman who I hate more than anything in the world. More than myself, more than Waylon, more than the one who decided to take Jennifer from me instead of taking me with her, "I don't want to see you; not here, not at the crash site, not fucking anywhere."

"I'm sorry." The words barely a whisper before she turns her head to the side and starts to walk away from me.

"I need to know that you understand what I'm saying"—she stops at my words—"I don't even want to fucking breathe the same air you breathe."

I see her chest inhale as she turns her head to the side, her eyes looking past me towards the tombstone. "You aren't the only one who loves her," she says before she runs off and away from me, leaving me to watch her as she runs through the trees and disappears into the night.

Eight

AUTUMN

I SHUT THE car door and make the stupid mistake of turning and looking around. It's been a week since I've been in town, and it's been a week since I've been seen. Which means the whispers are back, the finger-pointing, the leers from some of the old people who have been around for a long time. Also, who have an allegiance to the Cartwright family. A week of feeling like I'm about to crawl out of my skin, also a week since I've come to realize how much I missed having my brother and father around me daily. Even though we used to FaceTime each other often enough, it's never the same thing as seeing the person in real life. Being able to hug them or glare at them is so much better face-to-face.

I try to pretend that it doesn't bother me, but every single time it eats at me. If it wasn't for my father being sick and them needing help at the distillery and the bar, I would be gone so fast. Fuck, I wouldn't even be here.

I pull open the back door to the office, my flannel shirt I tied around my waist flows side to side. I have on a pair of black jeans, which have been in my closet here for the last eight years, with a white sleeveless bodysuit. The sound of the heels of my boots echoes in the big room. I stop in my tracks and listen to hear if someone else is in, but the sound of emptiness greets me. Looking at my watch, I see it's a little past nine in the morning. I walk past the column stills to the office, dumping my bag on the chair in front of the desk. The office is enclosed, but it has windows all around showing you the distillery room.

I pick up my phone and text my brother.

Me: Early bird catches the worm.

I put my phone on the desk before I walk out and make my way to the front of the building where the bar area is. Down the long wooden hallway, the walls are stacked with pictures of when the company started. A picture of my great-grandfather standing with two of his friends is fading as the years go by. I always laugh when I see the picture because they look like three mob bosses. Then the pictures go from black and white to color. One picture is one that we all have displayed in our homes. The picture of Mom and Dad when I was born. She had just left the hospital, and my father had to quickly come here. They took the picture as soon as they walked into the distillery. My mother smiles with me in her arms while Dad held Brady. I smile at the picture as I walk through the swinging door that leads to the bar area.

The wood floor has been worn over the years but is still shiny. I walk past the area in the back where I thought it would be great to host private parties and maybe even tasting events. Something I was going to work on before everything happened. Walking into the bar area, the ceiling opens up and I take a look around at how pretty this bar is. The exposed red brick around the bar pops out against the dark metal cladding surrounding it. It's a rustic feel but almost modern at the same time. The big brown square bar area is in the middle of the space, with the square metal piece suspended over it with different glasses all hanging in their place ready to be used.

Old wooden barrels that have been used over time also help with the decor. Dark brown leather stools are all around the bar area, while little round tables scatter against the outer wall area. I walk over to the side where the kitchen is, which is never used, and start to make a pot of coffee. I look around the kitchen, wondering why we've never offered food in here. I know it was something else I wanted to do. I had all these plans, excited to put them on paper, and then the accident happened. Nothing else mattered after that. I was frozen in time, sometimes I think I'm still frozen there.

"There you are," I hear from behind me and look over to see my brother walking in wearing jeans and a blue T-shirt. "I'll take a coffee."

"Is that your way of saying, 'Autumn, can you make me a cup of coffee, please?'" I ask him and he just smirks.

"Almost," he says, "just missing a couple of words."

"Yes," I reply, grabbing two white mugs. I put them down and fill them with the piping hot black coffee. "Especially the word please." I put the pot down, handing him his mug before taking mine and smelling it before taking a sip. "Is there anything better than coffee in the morning?"

"Yes." He grins. "There is something better in the morning."

"Can you be more gross?" I ask, leaning my hip against the counter and putting one foot on the other, my eyes wandering around the room. "Why don't we use this kitchen?" I ask, and he looks at me. "We could offer some pub food. You know, drinks and food so they stay later?"

"They have to come in the door first. We had three customers last night. I closed up at seven thirty." He takes another sip of his coffee. "And I'm sure that they came in looking to see if you were here." I close my eyes, trying to tell myself that eventually, it'll go away, but knowing it will probably be like this for the rest of my life. I'm a pariah. I knew it would come to that when I spoke up. I just didn't think it would last so long. I still would never go back and change my decision to do what I did.

"It's a good thing we hit up that little B and B outside of town and left them the two-for-one specials," I remind him of the little flyer I created. Luckily, the owner had no idea who the hell I was, so she was glad to put them at the front desk.

"We are going to need a lot more than that." He turns and walks out of the kitchen.

"Well, we have to start somewhere," I tell him, stopping in front of the bar. "Maybe we offer happy hour from five to seven," I suggest to him things he probably did over the years, but they didn't work, "but with a food special. Like two-for-one, but you have to order a burger."

"Why would they come here to order a burger when they can go to the diner?"

"Can you get a pitcher of beer or try the new whiskey flavors at the diner?" I counter.

"I guess," he concedes, "but that's just throwing money away we don't have."

"I have money saved up," I inform him. "Six years of living in a studio apartment and paying nothing for rent will make a good cushion."

"I'm not taking your money." He shakes his head. "And Dad sure as fuck is not going to take your money."

"What choice do you have?" My voice goes higher than I want it to be. "You are literally drowning right now." I shake my head. "And that is putting it mildly."

"Autumn," he says my name softly, "if you put everything you have into this, then what? You could end up with nothing, and then what?"

"And then I deal," I tell him. "I go back to work and start over again. It won't be the first time. And we can always sell my house."

"Absolutely not." He slaps the bar with his hand. "No fucking way. That's nonnegotiable."

"We can take a mortgage on it."

"And what if you can't pay it?" he asks me. "Then what, you lose Mom's family home?"

"Well then, I guess we are going to have to go with plan A." I try to cover my smile with the mug.

"Which is?" His eyebrows pinch together when he knows he just agreed to something without knowing he agreed to something.

"I'll write you a check. A loan, and when we make it back." He rolls his eyes and shakes his head. "I want it back."

"Fine." His words are laced with annoyance. "But"—he then smiles—"you get to tell Dad."

"Or we don't tell Dad." I start to walk away from him. "Then he is none the wiser."

"I'm pretty sure he's going to ask questions when we start serving food." He follows me to the back.

"Well, until then, we keep it to ourselves." I push open the swinging door and look over my shoulder at him. "Now, I have some other ideas I want to run by you." He immediately groans. "Aren't you happy I'm back?" I fake smile at him, walking into the office and sitting behind the desk.

"So happy," he says, sitting down. "Now, what else did you have in mind?" he asks, and I lean back in my chair, giving him a grin. "Ugh, I hate that face."

"Get ready to work." I wink at him and proceed to tell him about my ideas.

Ten hours later, I'm behind the bar while he's on the floor. It's Friday night, so a couple more people are in. I try to ignore the whispers coming from tables, which is why I'm behind the bar and not out on the floor. "Table four wants another round of Midsummer Night," he orders. "Good idea, offering samples." I walk over to grab the bottle, plucking the cork out, and pouring two fingers into the small glasses.

"See, my ideas are already working," I gloat to him as I place the glasses on his tray and look at a man come in the door. A man I've never seen before, wearing jeans and a button-down shirt with a sweater over it. His black hair is combed back as he walks straight to the bar and pulls out a stool. "Hi there." I smile at him. "Welcome, what can I get you?"

"What do you recommend?" He folds both hands on top of the bar, tapping his finger.

"I can give you a little sampler you can choose from there," I tell him, and he nods.

"Sounds good," he says with a smile.

I turn away, walking to the side, taking five little shot glasses out and filling each with a little bit of whiskey before going over and placing them in front of him. "Let me know which one you would like."

I walk back over to grab a rag and wipe down the bar for the millionth time. "I'll take the second one." He holds up the glass and finishes it.

"Neat or on the rocks?" I grab the glass in my hand.

"Neat," he replies, so I pour two fingers into the glass before walking over to him and placing a square white napkin down, then putting the glass on top of it.

"Let me know if you need anything else," I tell him, and I'm about to walk away.

"There is something you could help me with, actually." He picks up the glass, brings it to his mouth, and sips.

My back goes up, and my neck tingles at his voice, and I feel Brady at my back. "My name is Darren Trowel," he starts, and my body goes on high alert. I just don't know why yet. "I'm a reporter for a New York magazine called *The Future and the Past*." I swallow down, but something is lodged in my throat. "We are doing a follow-up segment on the Cartwright accident." I put my hand on the bar. "I'd love to ask you some questions about it."

"Not interested." I try to remain calm on the exterior, but inside, my whole body is shaking.

"It's just a couple of questions." He takes another sip. "About the accident and what you have been doing since. How your life has changed." He places it back down in front of him.

"I said I'm not interested." I grab his glass from in front of him. "That one is on the house."

"I don't want to—" he says.

"You heard her," Brady declares from behind me. "You can show yourself out." The man looks over my shoulder and nods before reaching into his back pocket and pulling out a fifty-dollar bill, placing it on the bar. "Here is my number." He leaves a card on top of the money. "Call me if you change your mind. I'll be in town for a few days." He turns and walks out of the door, and only when he's out and I don't see him do I let go of the breath I was holding on to.

"You okay?" Brady asks. I shake my head and make the mistake of glancing around the bar at a couple of people looking over at us. Knowing that this little scene will be all over town by the time I walk into my house.

"I just need a minute," I tell him, turning and walking away from the bar and toward the back. My knees shake as I walk through the swinging door. Taking a couple of steps into the room and leaning against the wall, I let it take my weight. I let my eyes close and tip my head back, and I take a deep breath through my nose and out through my mouth. Putting my hands on my knees, I try to steady my breathing.

The door swings open and then closed, and I know Brady has followed me in. "Why don't you go?" he suggests, coming to squat in front of me. "It's not like it's crazy busy."

"I'll be okay in a minute," I tell him, and he gets up and rubs my back.

"It's been a long day, go home." His voice is soft. "You are doing too much too soon. You literally came back and didn't even test the waters. You just jumped in with both feet."

"So dramatic and bossy." I try to make light of the situation, but the last thing I want is to go back out there. "I'll close up tomorrow," I tell him, and he just laughs.

"You're on." He shakes his head, about to turn around. "I know this week has been rough, but"—he runs his hand through his dark hair—"it's good to have you back."

I listen to the settling of my heart, as the thumping in my ears eases. "I can't believe I'm going to say this." I laugh nervously. "It's good to be home." The tears well up in my eyes as I lift my hand and pinch my fingers together. "But only this much." We both have our laugh before I turn and walk to the office to grab my stuff, picking up a bottle of whiskey and tossing it in my black bag before walking out the back door.

I drive home with the windows down, the hot night feeling like the world is on hold. I don't bother with the lights when I get home. I kick off my shoes before placing my bag on the floor next to them and grabbing the bottle of whiskey. Going straight to the counter, I put the whiskey on it before walking over to the cabinet on the side and grabbing a shot glass. I pour the whiskey to the rim before taking a shot, which leads to two, then slowly leads into three before I open my eyes. My breathing becomes easier, and the burning down my throat goes numb. My head hangs forward, and I hear the voice of the reporter fill my head, "follow-up segment." I shake my head, grab the bottle as my hand shakes, and take another shot. I untie the shirt from around my waist and toss it on the table before walking to my bedroom and grabbing a pair of shorts and a tank top.

The moonlight comes in from all the open shades as I grab the bottle and head out to the back to sit in the swing. Sitting in it, I listen to the deadness of the night. Some chirps are going on here and there as I stretch my feet on the bench and put my arm on the back of it, laying my head down on it. Taking a pull of the whiskey, I try to forget the day.

My eyes watch the fireflies in the distance as I put one foot on the wooden deck to push myself back and forth gently. Minutes turn into hours, and I take a pull from time to time. I look at the clearing as I see a figure there, but I'm not sure if my eyes are playing tricks on me. I watch him move closer and closer to me, his white

T-shirt sort of shining in the darkness, his jeans dark as the night. He looks down as he makes his way to me, and I take another shot of the whiskey to brace for whatever it is Charlie wants to throw my way. The last time I saw him at the cemetery I made sure that I avoided him like the plague. It wasn't hard since I went to work and then home. I never ventured out anywhere, especially at the two places he told me never to go.

He must feel me looking at him because he glances up and his eyes see me, and I know because his body goes tight. I take a deep inhale as I turn on the swing and put the bottle of whiskey on the floor before getting up on my feet and walking over to where the three stairs are. My head spins just a bit. "Seriously?" My mouth is talking before my brain can even realize it is. "You have got to be kidding me."

"Seriously," he replies when he's standing at the bottom step, looking up at me. His hair is longer than I remember it ever being. "What the fuck are you still doing here?"

I swallow down the lump in my throat. "Fuck you, Charlie." Everything is building up inside me.

"No, fuck you!" he roars, and I can smell the alcohol rolling off him. "You ruined my life."

I shake my head. "Your life is ruined?" I ask him and laugh bitterly. "Your life is fucking ruined? I lost everything that night. Everything," I hiss at him.

He takes a step up. "I lost my whole life that night."

"Really?" I ask, baiting him. In the past eight years, I've never, ever challenged Charlie, but tonight after a whole fucking week of feeling like a pariah, I'm done with it. "You look to be doing just fine." I raise my eyebrows. "You have a thriving business. You have no one trying to run you out of town, and if talk is still right, you have your choice of girls lining up to pick up those pieces." I shake my head, knowing I'm probably hitting him below the belt. "You lost Jennifer that night. You weren't the only one who lost her. But I lost more than just my best friend. I'm the one who lost it all." I point at my chest. "Me, not you." I exhale. "And trust me, every single time I turn a corner, someone is always there to let me know exactly what I did that night. I don't need it coming to my fucking house." I turn on my feet and walk to the door, opening it, but it's being slammed before I can step inside. His hand is over my head, stopping me from opening it. His chest is to my back as I close my eyes, telling myself he's going to go away if I don't move. But the anger in me makes me turn to look at him. "Go away." I push at his chest, and he moves back, but he's a lot bigger than me. "Why can't you just go away?" I shout at him, going to push him again when he grabs both my wrists in his hands, pushing them into the door beside my head. My chest rises and falls as we stare at each other with hatred. "I hate you," I whisper. "I hate you."

His head comes even closer to me. "Not as much as I hate you," he retorts, the both of us pant, and I don't know who does it first. I don't think either of us is ready for what is to come. I know I'm not.

Nine

CHARLIE

I HOLD HER wrists in my hands by her head. As she tells me she hates me, my heart feels like it's going to explode in my chest. I know I shouldn't be here. I knew the minute I got up from my couch, after finishing half a bottle of whiskey, I shouldn't be here. I was on my way to the crash site. But instead, I looked up, and I was here, seeing her on her swing. And for the first time ever, she met me head-on for the fight. I watch her, my eyes staring into hers. "Not as much as I hate you." I feel like I've just been in a horse race. Both of us look like we are ready to go to war but with each other. I don't know who moves first; I don't know what the fuck is happening before my lips are on hers. My tongue tastes the whiskey on her lips as I kiss her with the hatred I have for her, and she kisses me with the hatred she has for me. My hands let go of her wrists as they move up to place my palms on hers. As our fingers link together, she grips my hand as the kiss deepens, and we both fight with each other. She loosens her hold on my fingers, and I do the same as she untangles her fingers from mine and lets go of my hand, and I do the same. One hand wraps around her head, the other around her waist. While her hand goes to my head, her fingers grip my hair, not letting me move. Before she moves her hands down, she wraps one hand around the back of my neck while the other wraps around my shoulder. Her back arches in my arms, and her tits press deeper into my chest.

My hand moves down to her ass, grabbing a handful and pushing and squeezing it. She moans into my mouth as I move her away from the door. My heart tells me this is the most fucked-up thing I've ever done in my life, while my head tells me this is what I need. There's the war raging in my head as I pick her up, and she wraps her legs around my hips. I pull open the door as I try to kiss the ever-loving shit out of her. It's hard, it's wet, it's heated. It's everything you think two people who hate each other would feel. We move our heads side to side as I walk into her darkened house, the moonlight guiding me where I want to go. The moonlight guiding me to a place I shouldn't be going.

I walk into her bedroom, which I've been in a couple of times over the years when I had to help her move things. Never, never more. "Fuck," I swear, letting go of her mouth to trail my lips to her neck, where I suck in deep. She arches her back and unwraps her legs from my hips.

"Fuck is right," she hisses out before she gets on her

tippy-toes and bites my jaw, making it shoot right down to my dick that has never, ever been this hard before. Our mouths attack each other again, but this time it's not just our mouths. Her hands go to the bottom of my shirt, and she bunches it up as my hand goes to her little white tank top, pulling the little spaghetti strap down her arm and then covering her breast with my hand as I roll the nipple between my finger and thumb. She lets go of my mouth to moan, giving me a chance to bend and suck her nipple into my mouth. Her hands are frantic, trying to get under my shirt. She pulls it up and over my head, my mouth letting her nipple go as she pulls it off.

Not a word is spoken between the two of us. The only sound coming out of us is heavy breathing. I kiss her again and again as my hands go to her hips and slide into her shorts. I pull them and her lace panties over her hips, and they fall to the floor, pooling around her feet. She's standing in front of me naked as her hands go to the button of my pants. My eyes watch every single move as the sound of the zipper being pulled down echoes in the room.

I don't think I take a breath as she moves the flaps of my jeans, and her hand slides into my boxers as she grips my cock in her hand. My mouth hovers over her as she moves her hand up and down, my hand slides down her stomach, touching her neatly trimmed triangle as my hand slips through her slit, and I slide a finger into her. She sighs out a deep breath as I slip another finger into her. She bites my lower lip before she moves to my neck, sucking in deep. My eyes close as she moves her mouth to my nipple, sucking it into her mouth before biting right next to it. I hiss out as she moves away from me and drops to her knees. I should stop this. I should move out of her touch. I should do a whole bunch of things. But I don't do any of them.

I'm stuck, my feet stuck to the floor as if it is quicksand.

I feel her hands moving to my waist as she pushes my jeans over my hips, freeing my cock, and then sinking her mouth onto it. I open my eyes, watching her try to take me all in her mouth. My eyes lose focus on her as she bobs her head away from me before taking me to the back of her throat. I have to close my eyes, or I'll come. My hand comes up to her head, gripping her hair in it and pulling her away from my dick before I bend and kiss her. I pull her up to stand before moving her backward to the bed. The back of her knees hit the bed, and she falls back. I kick off my boots before getting rid of my jeans as she moves back on the bed. Our eyes watch each other as I put one knee on the bed and then the other. Her legs open for me as I crawl between them. "Charlie," she says my name.

"Shut up," I order her, and she tilts her head back.

"I hate you," she hisses at me. "I've never hated anyone as much as I hate you."

"Good," I snap, grabbing my cock in my hand. "The feeling is definitely mutual." She puts her legs over mine, her hand going to my ribs as I bend to kiss her. It's hotter than it was outside. It's even got more wetness to it. I push her as she falls to her back, her hair fanning around her. I move my cock up and down her slit as her legs move up and over my forearms while I push them back as I slam into her. Her neck arches as her mouth opens, but nothing comes out. I give her a second to get used to the feel of me. I give myself a second to close my eyes, knowing what is coming, but it doesn't come. I slide out of her and then slam back into her harder than the first time. Moving my arm to beside her head, I put my head beside hers. I pull out and slam back in, and she gets tighter than she was before. I thrust my hips into her with abandon. The sound of our skin slapping against each other drowns out the pants that we both heave out.

Her mouth is near my ear as she moans out, making me lift my head to look at her. Her closed eyes make me more pissed off. Why? I have no idea. "Open your fucking eyes," I hiss at her, pulling out to the tip of my cock, making her moan as she grips my ass with her nails, scoring me. "Look at me."

"No," she hisses right back at me.

"Now!" I slam into her and then pull out as she slowly opens her eyes.

"There, are you fucking happy now?" She moves her hands up from my ass to my back, her nails scoring into my skin.

"No," I whisper, "I'm not happy." I fuck her harder than I've ever fucked anyone in my life. The rage of her being back in town, the rage from my life becoming a shit show. The rage from being here with her and wanting to be here is more than I can even take. I push it away and let the anger seep back in, but it doesn't come as easy as I want it to come.

She arches her back, her hands gripping my shoulders, holding on as I put my other hand down on the bed near her head. Holding her head in my hand, I fuck her with abandon, transferring all of my hate to this moment. I feel her getting tighter and tighter around my cock, and I can't even breathe as my hips piston in and out. Then she lets go. The moan comes out of her in a grunt as she moves her head away from me and my touch. "No fucking way," I growl, pulling her head back to me and kissing the shit out of her. The kiss is heated as she fights back at me. The hatred in this kiss is one for the books. It's when I feel my balls getting tighter that I let her mouth go, the sound of my heavy breathing louder than her moan as I bury my face in her neck at the same time as I bury my cock inside her and let go. My eyes close, and all I can see is Autumn. All I can see is her staring at me. I tighten my eyes even more, and still, all I can see is her. I wait to see if it changes, if Autumn is the only one I see or if it'll be Jennifer.

I collapse on top of her as her legs fall to the bed. The hands at my shoulders fall to the side and away from me. I move to her side, sliding out of her and falling to my back, looking up at the ceiling. I place my hand on my stomach as I try to get my breathing under control. At the same time, my eyes get heavier than they have ever gotten. I close them for a second or at least that is my plan. My plan is to get up and get the fuck out of here. But here is the thing with plans—they can change on a dime. Trust me, I should know. My plan was to come here and find out when she was leaving. It was not to kiss her, it was not to fuck her, and it was not to feel what I was feeling. *It is time to make another plan, and this time stick to it.* That is the last thing I think before my eyes close, and then it takes so much to open them, so I just rest them. *For just a second,* I think to myself, and that is the last thought I have.

Ten

Autumn

THE ALARM MAKES my eyes fly open because it's not the soft bells that I normally have. No, not this. This is a blaring, "get the fuck out of bed, the house is on fire" alarm. I feel a hardness that was plastered behind me move away and turn, then a couple of things crash to the floor. "What the fuck?" someone mumbles, and I close my eyes again, thinking this is a dream. Actually, a nightmare, when I feel the bed beside me move and then the covers shift. I hear him stumble, but I'm too afraid to actually open my eyes again. I hear movement in front of the bed where his jeans were. "Where the fuck is it?" I hear him growl as he searches the floor for it and the alarm turns off.

I lie here watching the wall, hoping he gets dressed and gets the fuck out of here without me having to look at him. "Oh my God," he says. Then I feel him sit on the end of the bed, and I make the mistake of looking down at him. He's sitting there with his head in his hands as he leans his elbows onto his knees. "What a clusterfuck," he mumbles, and all I can stare at are the nail marks down his back. He shakes his head before he gets up, snatching his boxers off the floor and covering his perfect ass. It's a shame that he's got it all. He slides his jeans up, bending to grab his shirt. I can spot the bite mark I left next to his nipple, along with a little purple mark on his neck. He covers his perfect six-pack, and his eyes snap to mine, and he sneers at me, "Stop looking at me."

"Nothing to look at," I counter. "I'm waiting for you to get the fuck out so I can get up." He bends down to put his boot on before going to the other one. "Can you do that outside?"

He looks up at me, his stare piercing my soul. "This changes nothing." He stands up and puts his hands on his hips.

"You mean us having sex?" I pfft at him, trying to pretend that it's okay. People have one-night stands all the time, and then they wake up and hate themselves. I think I'm doing a fine job of that, if you ask me.

"Whatever it was." His teeth are clenched as he talks to me. "It was."

"Nothing." I toss the cover off me and get up. His eyes sweep my body as I lean forward, grabbing the sweater I keep at the end of the bed. "It was under nothing." I stand by the bed, trying not to vomit everywhere. "I was drunk." He turns his head to the side. "I hate you just as much today as I did yesterday." I can see him bite down, his jaw getting tight. "Actually, a little more."

"Good," he snaps, "we're on the same page." He turns to walk out of the room, or maybe he's about to storm out. I don't fucking care at this point. He came here, and now we both have to deal with what we did.

"Just so we are on the same page," I say, and he stops but doesn't turn around. I look at his back as I say the words. "We had unprotected sex last night." I can see his hands ball up beside him, his shoulders getting tight. "I better not catch anything from you."

He whips around to look at me, anger all over his face. "And I'm supposed to believe that you're clean?" He rolls his eyes. "Fucking please."

"Believe it, don't believe it," I say. "I don't give a shit. I just know I'm clean." I point at myself. "You, on the other hand"—I make sure I look him up and down—"who the fuck knows."

"Yeah, and how do you know that?" He folds his arms across his chest.

I point at him. "Because, unlike you, this was the first time I've had sex in eight years." I ignore the look of shock on his face as I turn to walk to the bathroom. I don't want to hear whatever shit he's going to say, so I slam the door behind me. Leaning my back against it, I look down at my hands shaking as I slide to the floor. At the same time, I hear the front door open and then slam. I close my eyes and try to make the nausea pass by breathing in and out slowly.

Closing my eyes, I hope it makes the nausea go away, but instead, all I can see is Charlie over me. Yelling at me to open my eyes, his eyes looking into mine as he

NATASHA MADISON

fucked me. I shake my head to stop the images as I get up and walk over to the shower, turning it on before taking the sweater off and seeing a reflection of myself in the mirror. I avoid even looking at myself before stepping in and washing away the smell of sex and Charlie. Two things I never thought I would say in the same sentence. I even wash my hair since he touched it. Every single inch of me washed twice, for good measure.

I wrap one of the towels around myself before stepping out and wrapping my hair. I walk out of the bedroom, taking one look at the bed and ripping the cover off to the floor before the sheets follow it. Gathering them in my arms, I move over to the washing machine and stuff the sheets in and then the cover. I set it on heavy-duty wash before going to the kitchen and starting my coffee. Grabbing the mug, I walk back into the bathroom to start blow-drying my hair. I ignore even looking at the bed, just like I avoid looking into my eyes in the mirror.

But now I'm standing in front of it as I take the towel off my head, combing my hair, moving to the side and seeing the reddish-purple mark. My hand drops the comb as my fingers come up to touch it, and I immediately get sick to my stomach. I lean over and vomit out the coffee I was drinking. I dry heave for a few minutes before I stand back up, trying not to think about the fact I just fucked my best friend's boyfriend. Sorry, scratch that, my dead best friend's boyfriend.

The whole time I'm getting ready, I think about how stupid I was last night. How it took one touch from him to light my body on fire. How it took a kiss and for that one kiss I forgot I hated him, but how it took one minute to make me hate him even more.

I put some concealer on the mark on my neck before getting dressed in white jeans, grabbing a light denim-blue button-up shirt, pulling up the sleeves, and tying the front in a knot before grabbing my white sneakers. I make my way to the dryer and put the sheets in there and hang the quilt up.

I get into the office later than I have in the last week. I pull open the door and step in to see my father behind the desk. "Hey there, sweetheart," he greets me, and I smile at him. He looks a little tired today, more so than yesterday.

"Hey yourself," I reply, walking over and bending to kiss his cheek. "What are you doing here?"

"I work here." He laughs. "I would ask you the same thing."

I sit in the chair in front of the desk. "Same," I tell him as he looks over the invoices in front of him, closing the book so he thinks I won't see them.

"Did you eat?" I ask, and he leans back in his chair.

"You know I'm the parent in this relationship." He chuckles, folding his arms over the book in front of him.

"Is that a yes or a no?" I raise my eyebrows, waiting for him to answer me.

"I was going to grab something when I came in," he admits. "I wasn't feeling so hot this morning."

I get up right away. "I'll go get you something from the bakery," I tell him. "What do you want to eat?"

"Something light," he says, leaning back and taking

money out of his pocket. "Here."

"It's on me. It's not every day that you can buy your father breakfast." I make a joke out of it. "I'll be back."

I'm about to walk out of the room when he calls my name. "Autumn, this was outside for you." He picks up the white envelope, and I grab it, seeing my name written in the middle in black writing and underlined twice.

"Thanks, Dad," I say, holding it in my hand. "I'll be back." I turn and walk toward the front of the bar and head to the bakery. Walking in, I'm greeted the same way I was when I got here. "Morning, Ms. Maddie." I smile at her as she walks out of the back with a tray of donuts on it to refill the front display case.

"Morning, Autumn," she returns. "What can I get you?"

"I'll have two yogurts with granola and fruit," I say, and she nods, going to the back to get my order. I open the white envelope in my hand, finding the folded white piece of paper, pulling it out, and the card dropping to my feet. My heart speeds up when I see it's the same card I got yesterday at the bar.

The back of my neck tingles when I pick it up and then unfold the paper.

Autumn,

I would love to talk to you and get your side of the story.

Clear up some facts.

Call me at your earliest convenience.

Darren

I tear up the letter and walk over to the garbage can

in the corner, tossing the letter and the card. My hand shakes as I move my fingers watching the papers fall into the can, the pieces falling away. I turn in time for Maddie to be there with my white bag. "Here you go," she says. I walk over, pretending everything is okay as I open my wallet and take out my cash to pay her. "I threw you in a donut on the house." I smile at her. "You need to fill out a bit."

I laugh at her remark. She was always saying I was sticks and bones anyway, so I'm not sure why she noticed it more now. "Thank you." Grabbing the bag, I leave her the rest of the change for a tip.

I'm walking out of the door with my head almost down when I bump into a hard shoulder. "Oh my goodness," I say, looking up. "I'm so—" The words are stuck in my throat when I see the woman in front of me. Waylon's mother, her bleached-blond hair styled perfectly. Her makeup just right, the string of pearls around her neck, and more at her ears. Her outfit is slacks and a knitted sleeveless shirt with the matching sweater tied around her neck.

"I don't believe it." The snarl is more than I remember it to be. "What the hell are you doing here?" I'm sure there are people all around waiting for this showdown.

"I live here," I reply, putting my shoulders back, trying to show her I don't care what she thinks of me.

"I heard you were in town, but I was hoping you would crawl back to that rock you've been living under for the past eight years." Her voice is venomous.

"Got tired of that." I try to garner all the strength I

can. "Decided I shouldn't be the one hiding my face anymore. I did nothing wrong."

"The minute my son started dating you, I knew you would be trouble," she hisses, and it takes everything in me not to roll my eyes. If anything, I made her son a better person. I mean, he was downright horrible at the end, but I want to believe that at the beginning, he was better, and it was because of me. "He could have had anyone he wanted, yet he picked you." She looks me up and down. "He probably felt sorry for you."

"Not as sorry as I feel for myself," I tell her, "having to endure the memories that I loved a man who was—"

I don't get a chance to finish the sentence. Her hand flies up so fast, she snatches my wrist in her hand, jerking me forward. "Don't you dare say another word about my son."

"You best take your hands off me, Mrs. Cartwright." I pull my hand free, making her move forward a foot. "People are already watching, wouldn't want the Cartwrights to have to bury another story." I walk around her, leaving her standing there and trying not to look around. But the curiosity gets the best of me, and when I do, I see I was not wrong. People have even filed out of the diner to get a good look at this showdown. My eyes go to the mechanic shop and seeing even Brock is coming out of his shop with a couple of his guys.

Brady waits for me at the door of the bar with his arms across his chest, his jaw tight, and I see the vein in his forehead looking like it's about to explode, along with the rest of him. "What was that?" he asks, his eyes then going back to Mrs. Cartwright, who is acting as if we didn't just almost get into a fistfight in the middle of Main Street. She turns to smile at a couple of people, waving her fingers at them. There's a smile on her face, and all I can think is she's just like a wolf in sheep's clothing.

I try to get my body under control before I talk. "She was just welcoming me back to town," I joke with him. "Said if I ever needed to borrow a cup of sugar, to come on down."

I walk into the bar with him right on my heels. "You shouldn't have to do this every single fucking day."

"Sooner or later, people will get tired of it and move on." I look over my shoulder. "Hopefully, sooner rather than later." I try to steady my heartbeat as we walk.

"We would understand," he says, and I stop walking, turning to look at him, seeing him with his hands on his hips, "if you decided that you wanted to leave. If this is too much for you…"

My eyebrows go up. "I don't know how else to say this." I stand tall. "But this is my home, and I'm. Not. Fucking. Leaving."

Eleven

CHARLIE

I WALK OUT of my house, coffee mug in my hand as I make my way across my backyard to the office. My eyes go to the red barn as I see some of the horses being brought out to start the day.

Pulling open the glass door and stepping into the office, I see Lilah sitting behind the desk. "Good morning, Charlie." She smiles at me. She's been working for me for the past five years. As soon as she turned eighteen, I hired her. Six years ago, she was a client here when the boy she was dating brutally beat the shit out of her and threw her onto the road from his moving truck. A passerby saw her on the side of the road, thought it was a mannequin, and stopped before he ran her over and saved her life. All of that because she beat him at a horse race. She was in a coma for two weeks. They didn't think she was going to make it. It was a slow recovery. But she eventually came out of her shell. She needed a job, we needed someone to handle the phones and schedule appointments, so it was perfect. She also handles all our social media since she is the only one who understands it: the right place, right time. She is still quiet; the only way she lets you see a piece of her is when she's riding her horse. The confidence she has, the ability to ride and keep a handle on her horse. She rides better than most girls I know, and I grew up with girls who rode every single day since they could walk. She is also the only person I let handle skittish horses. Something about her and her touch soothes them.

"Morning, Lilah." I walk past her desk, and she looks up from her computer screen. "Anything I need to know?"

"Not really," she says right before the phone rings, and her hand reaches out to grab it. "We got a busy couple of months coming up." Putting the phone to her ear, she answers, "Mustang Creek Ranch." She turns her eyes back to the computer screen. "How may I help you?"

"Music to my ears," I mumble, taking a sip and walking to my office in the back, passing the wall of memories on the way. I'm not even fully in my office when I hear Emmett walking in from the back door. "Good morning, Emmett," I greet him before he even walks into my office, and I round my desk at the same time he fills the doorway.

"Yeah," he mumbles. He's wearing light-blue jeans that are already filthy from the dirt, and I still have no idea why he keeps wearing the lighter colors, with a black shirt tucked into his pants in the front, showing off his big country belt. His cowboy boots have seen better days, and by that, I mean they are old as shit. "You're late."

I pull out my chair and look down to see that I'm two hours late. "Slept in this morning," I lie. "Didn't know I had to clock in with you."

"Slept in?" He calls me out on the lie right away. "You haven't slept in since I got here." He pulls off his yellow-and-white gloves, tucking them in the back pocket of his jeans. He studies me and I put on my fake face, which he probably knows at this point. The two of us have worked side by side over the years, and he's become one of the only people who I would confide in. He knows the pain I feel. He knows the signs of when I'm having a bad day. He knows the signs of when all I want is to give up, and he's made it a point to be there every step of the way. I can't tell you the number of times I got up in the morning and found him sleeping on my couch because he knew it was going to be a bad night. I can't tell you all the times he's seen me break down and curl up into a ball. I can't tell you all the times he literally picked me up and helped me walk.

"First time for everything." I sit in my chair, hoping he just turns and walks out of the room. But when I start the computer and look back up, he's still there watching me. "Is that what this meeting is about?"

"I'm calling bullshit." He narrows his eyes at me. "But I don't care enough to get on your ass about it. Especially with that shit on your neck." He points at my neck, and my hand comes up. The red-and-purple mark that I saw when I came home right before I stepped into the shower. I'm pissed at myself for how it got there, then pissed at myself when I closed my eyes and my cock got hard thinking about it.

"Thank you, I guess." I chuckle as I take a sip of the hot coffee, actually thankful he isn't going to ask any more questions because, truth be told, I'd have to lie to him. That's something I have never done, except for two seconds ago, but that was not really a lie. I did sleep in, just not in my bed.

"We have five new horses coming in today," he reminds me. "Should be here in about an hour or so."

"Sounds good. I'll be out there when they get here," I tell him. "Then if you're nice to me, I'll buy you dinner." I wink at him, trying not to laugh at the face he gives me.

He pffts. "Fuck that, you want to do something nice, give me a day off."

It's my turn to pfft at him, putting one hand on the armrest. "Last time I forced you to take a vacation, you stopped talking to me for a whole month." I point at him. "And then came back to work after two days where you told me to get fucked."

He shrugs. "I could do with a day off here and there." I can see the boredom all over his face as he says it. He has no family and came to us when he returned from serving two tours overseas. He was in foster care most of his life, enlisted when he turned eighteen, and finally had enough. My family adopted him since my cousin, Ethan, took him under his wing when he got out. Now he's in his thirties and refuses to date anyone or have any ties to anybody. I know he gets laid, or else he would be a bigger pain in the ass. The question is, who is he having sex with? I've never seen him with a girl, not once in the past ten fucking years.

"Then take a day off." I pick up my cup. "Take two days off."

"Now you're just fucking with me." He turns on his boot and storms to the door. "Also heard from a couple of people that Autumn just almost got assaulted"—the blood drains from my face—"by Mrs. Cartwright in the middle of Main Street." My heart beats when he says who it was.

"I don't know why you would think I care," I say tightly, ignoring the way my heart laughs at me. "The only thing I want to know about Autumn is when she is getting the fuck out of Dodge."

"When are you going to give it up?" he asks me, but he doesn't wait for me to answer. "That girl did what needed to be done, and she has been paying for it ever since." He doesn't wait for me to answer, and it's a good thing because I don't have an answer. All I can do is swallow down the lump in my throat.

I wait until I hear the back door shut before I close my eyes and let go of a breath I was holding. But closing my eyes doesn't help, because all I see is Autumn, but not the Autumn from before, the Autumn writhing under me. Arching her neck as she took my cock. The thought makes the coffee in my stomach lurch.

Showing up at her house wasn't something I planned to do, storming to her, also something that wasn't planned. Fucking her, definitely not what I planned. Never in my wildest dreams would I ever think about fucking Autumn. Then if that wasn't bad enough, I spent the fucking night. I collapsed on the bed beside her, opening my eyes and seeing the dark—not knowing where I was for a second—and then seeing her sleeping on her side, legs to her chest, shivering. I moved her as I covered both of us and then fell right back to sleep. It was to rest my eyes for a second, but the next thing I knew the alarm was blaring and I opened my eyes and saw her head. I was hoping to get out of there before she woke up but who was I kidding, the fucking alarm would wake the dead. I don't want to think about last night and I most definitely don't want to think about the shit show that was the morning after. Sadly, all I can do is hear her words in my head, *Because unlike you, this is the first time I've had sex in eight years*. She was lying, she had to be lying.

I don't have a chance to sit down and think about it more when my phone beeps in my back pocket, and when I take it out, I see the text is from Emmett.

Emmett: *Arrived early.*

A man of few words, I get up, finish my coffee, and rush outside. The sun hits me right away as I make my way over to the barn, seeing the trailer is being unloaded. "It's going to be a good day, boys," I declare when I get close enough to them. "It's going to be a good day."

"Who are you?" Rowan, one of the ranch hands, asks.

"He got laid last night," Emmett says, trying hard to hide the smile, so he looks down but not before I glare at him. "You want to keep shit a secret, don't come to work branded."

"It's a bite." I rub where I know exactly the fucking mark is. I can still feel when her teeth bit into me and then sucked in.

"Yeah, from a vampire," Rowan jokes. "I wouldn't go back if I were you."

"Trust me," I mumble, "I'm not going back there ever a-fucking-gain." I clap my hands. "Now, if we are done talking about where I put my dick last night, how about we get to work, boys?"

"I never want you to say that sentence again," Rowan grouses with a look of disgust over his face. "I don't ever want to think about where you put your dick." He looks at Emmett. "Just thinking of his dick, I might be sick." We both laugh at him as he turns and walks toward the barn, shaking his head the whole time.

"You scared him," Emmett says. "Good job." I nod at him, walking to the fence and leaning on the top rail, watching the horses being unloaded. One of them catches my eye right away. She's light brown, almost tan, her eyes look around like a deer in headlights, and she's jumpy with every single noise that is going on around her. Walking around the fence and going into the yard, I go straight to her. She backs up two steps, her eyes on me. "It's okay, girlie," I coo softly, holding out my hand. "I'm not going to hurt you." She lets me get close enough to her to pet her muzzle. "That's a girlie." I get closer to her.

"I guess you picked another one," Emmett notes, and I

look over to see him on his horse. "I was told she was the most skittish of the whole bunch. We might have to get Lilah in here for a bit," he says, almost annoyed that she has to come out. He tolerates certain people, but Lilah isn't one of them. I don't know what about her gets under his skin. Whenever she's around or we have to bring her in, he's the first one to leave and not be bothered talking to her, yet he's the last one there watching her.

"You aren't skittish," I whisper to her, "are you, girlie?" I look over at Emmett. "Goldilocks."

We spent the rest of the afternoon unloading the new horses and getting them acclimated in their new stalls. When the sun goes down, I walk out of the shower and head over to the kitchen. Opening the fridge, I look at what to make myself for dinner. I settle on grilling a steak and some veggies. Twisting open a bottle of beer, I stand here and wait for it to be ready, looking over at the barn and wondering what Goldilocks is doing.

I sit down at the island to eat my steak, ignoring how quiet the house is and how the silence is now almost deafening. Whereas for the last eight years, all I wanted was the quiet. I rinse off my plate and put it in the dishwasher before I walk out of the back door. My routine every single night is going for a walk after dinner. Except this time, I stop by the barn before I head for my walk. The sun has set, and the stars twinkle in the sky. The sound of crickets fills the night air as I walk through the grass toward the red barn. Walking in and going straight to her stall, I find her with her ass in the corner of the stall as she faces out, looking around. "Hey,

Goldie," I say, "you having a good night?" I open the gate and walk in. "Yeah, me neither," I tell her, walking to her side and rubbing her neck. "It's going to be okay. It's going to be okay." I stand in her stall and stay with her for I don't even know how long.

Walking out and heading to the woods, I move with my head down as I walk the trail until it goes off the path. I don't even know where I am until I look up and I'm staring at her house. The whole house is dark in the night. Not a light is on, but I see the swing moving.

She sits on it, not like she was lying down yesterday. No, today she's sitting, holding her knees to her chest as she lays her head on them. The bottle of whiskey sits beside the swing. It's exactly where it was this morning when I took off. My feet move before I have a chance to think about why I'm even here.

She must hear me walking toward her because her head comes up, and I see her glare. "What the fuck are you doing here?"

Twelve

AUTUMN

I LISTEN TO the sound of crickets chirping nearby, the taste of whiskey on my lips as I lick them. I wonder if I should take another pull of the bottle. It's been a fucking day and a half, to say the very least. I got home and immediately took a hot bath, hoping it would make it somewhat better, but it didn't. Walking outside and seeing the bottle of whiskey beside the swing was a sign I should drink my sorrows away. So I took a couple of pulls and the tears fell, freely. I replay the day, starting with the shit with Charlie to the letter and then running into Mrs. Cartwright.

I was adamant to my brother and my father that I wasn't going anywhere. I was being as brave as I could be in their eyes, but the minute I got home and was able to let it out, I did. This is my home and where I want to be, but it doesn't mean it is easy for me. It also doesn't mean that I belong here. Maybe I don't, and perhaps

I'm just dragging out the inevitable, but I'm not going anywhere for the moment. Doesn't mean I wouldn't like to crawl in a hole and just bury my head. Doesn't mean it isn't killing me a little staying here. Little do they know how I'm breaking inside more and more. I thought there was nothing left to break. I must have been wrong.

I hear the rustling of leaves and look up, his eyes on me as he walks toward me. All I can do is glare at him. In another fucking T-shirt that molds to his chest, and now that I know what is under it, my hands itch to touch him. His jeans hang on to his hips as he walks toward me. "What the fuck are you doing here?" I put my feet down and wipe the tear away, but another one joins it. "You have got to be fucking kidding me," I say louder, my voice almost echoing in the quiet night. "Can you, for fucking once, just let me be?" He stops in front of the railing, and I walk over to it, putting my hands on it and spreading them on the railing. "Like, just let me fucking be." I can't help the tears that come down my face. "I get it, you hate me. Trust me, I get it. But can you fucking for once just go away and let me be?" I again don't wait for him to say anything. "This is the only place I can fucking breathe." I lift my hand to my house. "It's my safe space. Leave me to my fucking safe space, Charlie." I take a deep inhale. "Please just leave me to my fucking safe space." I start to walk away. "You can spew all your hate in the street like everyone else does," I say softly, "you don't have to come to my house to do it."

I take one step forward when he speaks, "What did she tell you?" I close my eyes, not surprised he heard about the scene in the middle of Main Street.

I turn in my spot. "Why do you fucking care?" I ask. "Is it because you weren't there to witness it and add more fuel to the fire? Is that why you care?"

"I asked you a question." He ignores what I just said and focuses on his own question.

"Is this what you came here for tonight?" I ask. "To get the lowdown on what went on with Mrs. Cartwright?" He just stares at me. "It's the same shit it always is. Just like you, she hates me, wants me to crawl back into a hole and die, yada, yada, yada."

"What did you expect when you came back here?" He folds his arms over his chest, and I can see his arms get bigger.

"I expected for everyone to have moved on a little. I expected to be stared at and pointed at. Trust me, I wasn't expecting to be anyone's friend, but I wasn't expecting this," I admit. "I told the truth."

"Yeah," he snaps, "a little too late, don't you think?"

"I don't have to take this shit," I declare, hoping my voice doesn't crack. "I really fucking don't. I was scared shitless of doing it!" I shout at him, not willing to go back to that memory. "I could have kept my mouth shut and then none of this would be happening to me. But I didn't. I stood up and challenged them, told the truth about the whole family, and what did it get me?" I shake my head. "But, hey, it's not the first time I've been strong-armed and pushed around." I see his eyes flinch. "I'm just not going to stand here as a willing participant anymore." I turn and head to the door. I hear him rush up the three steps as I open the door and walk in, hoping he doesn't follow me, but then feeling him in the house. "What do you want from me, Charlie?" I ask him softly. "I literally can't give you anything else, because I don't have anything left to give." I wipe away a tear. "You can turn back around and go back where you came from."

I walk toward my bedroom, hoping he just goes away, when I feel his hand grab my wrist and turn me around, my back toward the door of my bedroom. His eyes stare into mine. Not saying a word, he bends his head and his lips crash onto mine. My mouth opens in shock, so he has the chance to slide his tongue inside. His hand lets go of my wrist, so I raise my hand to touch him but secretly stop myself, putting my hands up beside my head. The kiss I tried to erase from my memory is now alive and better than I thought it was. His mouth moves from one side to the other to get the kiss to go deeper, his hand now cupping my ass as I arch my back into him. I should stop this. I should push him away. I should do a lot of things, but what I don't do is that. Instead, my hands go to the hem of his shirt as I push it up so I can feel the heat of his skin.

My nails graze against the bottom of his stomach and his muscles contract as he pulls me away from the door and toward the bed. The bed I made as soon as I got out of the bath, a bed I was sure was never going to have Charlie Barnes in it again. A bed that has only had Charlie Barnes in it. His hands move from my ass to my sides as he pulls the tank top up and over my tits, letting my mouth go just so he can rip the shirt over my head. He tosses it to the side before grabbing my face and kissing me again. My hands work on his shirt now, moving it up, and he lets my mouth go so he can reach behind him and pull it off. I lean in, biting his nipple and hearing him hiss, my teeth mark still there from last night. Something flutters inside me as I lean back in and bite the same spot until he growls, and I'm picked up and thrown on the bed. He puts one knee on the bed. His hands go to my hips to rip the shorts down and then the panties, which are also tossed to the side, before coming back up to my face. I think he's going to kiss me, but he bites my jaw. "Got your mouth on me yesterday," he mumbles as he licks down my neck toward my nipple, stopping to suck it into his mouth. "Didn't give me a chance to use mine."

I watch him open my legs, my knees falling to the sides as his head bends, and he devours me like I'm his last fucking meal. I get up on one elbow, watching him lick up my slit toward my clit, flicking it with his tongue before going back down and sliding it inside me. My eyes close as I take in the feel of him. My hand comes out to run into his hair as his finger slides in with his tongue, hitting my G-spot before sliding his tongue out of me and moving up to suck my clit between his teeth. It's all I need for me to fall over the edge. Gushing over his finger, I moan out his name, "Charlie." But he doesn't let up, not Charlie. Instead of pulling his finger out, his finger just speeds up. I can't even help the pant coming out of my mouth, moving my hands through his silky hair, gripping it in my hand. "I'm going to come again," I admit. His eyes look up at me as his tongue flicks my clit from side to side. His fingers fuck me faster and faster until I let go again, this time bigger than the last time. Bigger than when I do it to myself, bigger than it's ever been. "It's…" I close my eyes, feeling it rushing through me. My hand loosens his hair as I move my elbow and lie down in the bed.

He slides his fingers out of me, one hand lying beside me, the other up by my head. My body feeling like it's floating on air. My eyes watch him move off my bed, thinking he will grab his shirt and leave. But instead, with his eyes staring into mine, he kicks off one boot and then the other. His hand moves to the button on his jeans. My eyes watch his hands, seeing him pull the zipper down. My heart beats even faster than it was two seconds ago when I had my second orgasm in less than three minutes. His hands push the jeans down, and then he stands there in black boxers, the outline of his cock filling out the front of his underwear. He pulls his boxers down, his cock springing free. My eyes watch him move one knee onto the bed and then the other, his cock in his hand.

"On your knees," he orders me, "ass up, face down." I must be moving too slow for him because he grips my hips and turns me over himself. "Hands stretched in front of you." He picks up my hips as I put my forehead to the bed and stretch out my hands in front of me. I'm about to say something to him, but he rubs his cock up my slit once before he slams into me. The sound of us both groaning fills the room. He stays rooted inside me for a second, his hands gripping my hips harder before he pulls out slowly, then slamming back into me.

I grip the sheets in front of me as he mercilessly pounds into me. It's so fucking good I can't help but moan out, "Yes!" His hands grip me even tighter as he lifts me off my knees, and his balls hit my clit over and over again as he fucks me. I can't do anything but hang on as he takes me over the edge again. My eyes close to ride it out, my hips now moving to meet his thrusts. I hear him hiss from behind me when he slams into me one last time before he gives me small little thrusts, until I feel his chest on my back at the same time as his fingers let go of my hips.

He slides out of me and collapses beside me as I move my knees and hips to the side. Neither of us says one word to each other. Neither of us do anything but trying to catch our breath. I lie here looking at the wall, my eyes getting heavy, probably from the crying I did after work. I should probably kick him out of my bed, tell him to leave now before we have another confrontation like this morning. I'm about to tell him to get out when I feel him curl into me. His legs tangle with mine, his face almost in my neck, and I hear him softly snoring. I close my eyes, taking in his warmth. The only thing going through my mind is that he'll be gone by the time I wake up.

Thirteen

CHARLIE

MY EYES FLICKER open when I feel something tickle my nose. I feel weight on my stomach and then feel the heat from a body beside me. I blink a couple of times, looking down to see Autumn's head on my chest, her arm over my abs, and her leg hooked around mine. My arm under her body holds her close to me. I put my head back and look at the ceiling, trying not to hate myself but failing fucking miserably.

I look over at the side table, seeing there isn't even a clock on there to tell me what time it is. I look out the side window, seeing the sun is just coming up, so I have to get the fuck out of here before the alarm goes off again and wakes her up. I think about how to dislodge myself from her. At the same time, I want to turn into her and wake her up in a different way. My cock agrees with this plan while my head screams at me to get the fuck out.

I slide away from her, slowly pulling my arm from

under her. It takes me a full five minutes before I walk over to the end of the bed, grab my boxers, and slide them on. This is somewhat like it was yesterday morning, but we aren't telling each other how much we hate each other. I grab my T-shirt, putting it on before picking up my boots and walking out of the bedroom. "Next time, get dressed outside," she mumbles. I turn my head to look at her as she turns over from where she was lying, which was on top of me not five minutes ago, as she puts her hand under the pillow on the other side of the cover, just barely covering her, as my eyes go to her perfect arch of her back and up to her neck.

I take one final look before walking out the back door and slamming it. The struggle to go back in there and let her know this is never going to happen again is real, but instead, I go to sit on the step and put on my boots. Walking down the steps toward the path that goes to my house, my head is down, trying not to look over my shoulder. But right as I get into the forest, I make the mistake of looking back. I don't know what I'm expecting, but nothing is there for me. Just the swing moving softly front to back, with the whiskey bottle right beside it.

Kissing her last night, I tasted it on her lips and knew I should have stepped away, but just like the day before yesterday, the pull to her was something I couldn't understand. Seeing her standing there with tears running down her face, begging me to just leave her be, but because of the asshole that I am, I just pushed her even more. I didn't even know why I was doing it; I just knew it was happening. Hearing her say *I literally can't give you anything else because I don't have anything left to give,* I felt like I was kicked in the stomach. The air left my body, making it harder and harder to breathe. We were all broken from that night, something I don't think I ever admitted.

I walk through the forest, replaying last night in my head. The night before when I went to her, I was drunk, and when I slid into her and closed my eyes, I was expecting to see Jennifer, but not with Autumn. With her, I closed my eyes, and all I saw was her, which pissed me off. So last night I went to her without alcohol in my system, with her hips in my hands, slamming into her, I closed my eyes, and again, all I saw was her. Her staring at me, her moan ripping right through me to my dick, down my balls and back again. I have never fucked anyone as hard as I've fucked her before. Never has there been almost no foreplay, yet my dick was harder than stone. Never has there been someone who I want to go again with as soon as I finish. Never again have I struggled the way I'm struggling with Autumn. I'm usually in and out, with the promise of maybe calling them the next day but not actually doing it. That is what I'm used to. That is what I've become, but with her I'm not that person.

I walk into the clearing, making my way past the barn and toward my house. The sound of gravel crunching makes me look over to the side, seeing Emmett arriving while I'm walking up the steps to my house. I turn the handle, and at the same time, my phone blares from my back pocket. Taking it out, I turn off the alarm as I walk into the kitchen, tossing the phone on the counter before walking to the bedroom.

I pull off my shirt, smelling her around me as I toss it into the laundry basket before I add my jeans and boxers to it as soon as I take off my boots. Stepping into the bathroom, I turn the water on, and the cold immediately hits me as it warms up. I put my head back, letting the water wash over me. I get out, grabbing one of the white plush towels from the side to wrap around my waist. Then I grab another one and open it to dry my hair before tossing it on the hook beside the shower door.

Running my hands through my wet hair, I look into the mirror and wonder if I should shave or not when I see the bite mark. My hands come up to touch it as I look at it in the mirror. My cock stirs, and I drop my hand. I ignore the way my heart sped up seeing her teeth marks on me. I ignore it all when I turn and walk into the closet, grabbing a pair of boxers followed by a pair of my work jeans and a black T-shirt with the barn name written on the back of it. The socks are next, followed by the boots as I step out of the closet and into the bedroom. The bed hasn't been made in two days, but it also hasn't been slept in in that amount of time either.

My eyes go to the bedside table where the clock tells me it's almost seven and also where Jennifer's picture is in a frame. She is looking at me, smiling, and I walk over to the frame, picking it up. My finger rubs her cheek through the glass as I think about one of the last moments we were together.

"Hey, baby," I said when I walked into the house. The

smell of something baking in the oven filled the whole house.

"In the kitchen," she called, and I walked down the small hallway to the kitchen, not seeing her there, but then she popped up. "Hey." Her whole face lit up when she saw me. "Guess what I'm making."

"Whatever it is," I replied as I walked around the counter to her. My arms circled her waist, bringing her against me. Her arms wrapped around my neck. "It smells good." I buried my face in her neck. "Although, not as good as you smell." I nipped her neck, and that made her squirm in my arms.

"Charlie," she said breathlessly, and if I closed my eyes tight enough, I would always remember it. "Do you know how happy you make me?"

"Not as happy as you make me, baby." I kissed her lips. "Dance with me." I turned and played our song on my phone, putting it on the counter.

"Anytime, anywhere," she said as she swayed side to side. "Forever."

"Anytime, anywhere," I say to the picture. "Forever." But I avoid looking her in the eyes. I put the picture down before turning and making my way to the kitchen.

I put the pod in the coffee maker before grabbing a mug and putting it under the spout and pressing the button. My phone rings from the counter, making me walk over and I see it's my father.

"Hello," I say, putting the phone to my ear, "it's not even seven."

He laughs on his side of the phone. "I've been up

since five," he tells me and then stops for a second, like he's wondering what to say next. "What's going on?"

I pick up the mug of coffee, bringing it to my lips and taking a sip. "What are you asking me?"

I turn to head to the barn, wondering if maybe Emmett said something but also knowing that he wouldn't. Pulling open the door, I step outside. The sun is now high in the sky as I walk down the steps I just walked up. "I'm asking you if you are okay."

I stop mid step. "Why would you be asking that?" I say, my voice tight, and I have to wonder if he heard about Autumn and me. Not that there is anything with Autumn and me, but just that we were together. My stomach lurches, the guilt rushes through me, and I think I'm going to be sick. "Why wouldn't I be okay?" My voice is low, almost a whisper.

I hear him taking a deep breath in. "A couple of things." His voice is soft but tight at the same time.

I grip the handle of my mug even tighter. "Which are?"

"Well, for one"—my neck tingles with anticipation and nerves—"I heard that Autumn is back in town and—" I want to be surprised he's heard, but I also know that not a lot of things happen here that he doesn't know about. It's the way the small-town life works.

"You heard right." I cut him off before he even finishes, not wanting to discuss Autumn with him or anyone else. "There is nothing to say on that topic," I bite out, hoping it's the end of this part of the conversation.

"Okay, we'll table that for later," he backpedals, and

I shake my head.

"We aren't tabling anything for later," I say between clenched teeth, "because there is nothing to discuss about her. At fucking all."

"I heard you two had a confrontation." My eyes turn toward the barn and straight to Emmett, who is drinking his coffee by the fence. His eyes are on Lilah as she races around the fenced area with her horse. She moves side to side on her horse as she pushes her harder and harder.

"Emmett tell you that?" I ask.

"Actually, he didn't." My father tries to cover for him, or maybe he didn't. It's a small town, and anyone could have seen us talking to each other. Gossip spreads faster than a wildfire in a small town. "The other thing is." I put the coffee down on the counter before I reach a hand out and brace myself by gripping the side. "It's almost the anniversary." My eyes close, and I'm expecting to see Jennifer, but it comes out black. There is nothing, no vision of her... nothing. Not a smiling face, not a sad face, nothing but blackness. "I think we should do something to celebrate her life."

"I don't know," I say softly.

"I know you don't." His voice comes out just as soft. "It's why I'm bringing it up now. We can talk about it when your mother and I visit in a couple of weeks."

"Yeah, fine," I say, just to get him off the topic. "Let's do that." Knowing I'm not going to agree to do anything they want to do.

"I'll let you have that play also," he states, picking up on that. "Heard you got a new friend."

My hand loosens from the countertop as I reach for my cup again, knowing the conversation about Autumn and then Jennifer has ended, at least for now. "You been hearing a lot of things for someone who doesn't live in this town." I make the joke, and he laughs at it.

"You should know how this works by now." I turn to walk out the door. "Eyes are everywhere in a small town." I walk down the steps and wait for him to say the next thing I know he needs to say because he trailed off, and he always does that when he's thinking of how to break the next piece of news to you. Like you have to brace for something. "I want you to be happy, Son." His voice is filled with worry.

"I'm happy," I lie to him, lie right through my teeth, "as a clam." I decide that it's time to end this conversation. "Okay, Dad, as much as I love this heart-to-heart, I have to go and check on the new horses."

"Is that your way of telling me to fuck off?" He chuckles.

"I would never." I smile. "Tell Mom I love her."

"Will do," he agrees. "See you soon. Love you."

"Right back at you," I say, disconnecting the call, putting the phone in my back pocket, and going to the fence where Emmett stands. My eyes are on Lilah as she stops racing her horse. She brings her to a trot, leans down, rubs her neck, and whispers something to her.

"Morning," he greets, looking over at me. The scowl all over his face.

"Morning," I return to him, raising my cup and watching a couple of the ranch hands bring out the new horses.

"You need to tell her she's not allowed to be riding her fucking horse alone without anyone here." He motions with his head toward Lilah. "It's a security hazard."

"A security hazard," I repeat the words because I don't think I've ever heard that sentence before in my life.

"Yeah, like if she fucking falls and breaks her neck, she's going to sue your ass, and then I'll be out of a job." He tries to play it off, but my eyebrows just pinch together.

"You mean safety hazard," I tell him, trying to hide the fact I'm joking. "Just got off the phone with my father." I look over at him. "You been telling tales?"

His eyebrows pinch together before he glares at me. "You think I have time to be sitting around, twirling my hair, and talking about you?" His voice is low as he shakes his head. "You better check your sources." I nod at him, not saying a word. "Could be the fact you walked into your house in the morning after spending the night God knows where." I don't turn back to look at him. "I see the cat's got your tongue." He turns his head toward the fence. "I have things to do"—he turns to walk away from me—"and it's not sit here and discuss the shit you are up to."

I watch him walk away without saying anything because, frankly, there is nothing to be said. The last two nights were a mistake, a mistake I will never repeat again. At least that is what I plan to do.

Fourteen

AUTUMN

I MAKE THE mistake of looking out the window and seeing him walk away. His head is down, probably in shame that he spent another night with me. I close my eyes so I don't have to watch him walk away and make sure when I turn my head on the pillow. Opening my eyes after a second, I see the dent from his head on the pillow beside me. I turn on my side, grabbing the cover and pulling it up to my neck, which is a mistake because I smell him all around me.

Tossing the cover off me, I get up and strip the bed again for the second time in three days. I toss the bedding inside the washer while I walk to the kitchen, making myself a coffee before heading back to the bathroom and starting the shower. The mark on my neck has faded a bit, but not enough that I don't need to cover it up.

I leave my house an hour later when the sheets are back in the dryer. I have another pair of blue jeans on with a baby-blue-and-white striped linen button-down shirt that is rolled up to my elbows. My hair is half dry since my shower, and all I did was run a comb through it. I get to the distillery and see I'm the only one here, so I hit up the bakery.

Walking in and spotting a couple of people, I avoid eye contact, as usual, focusing on the line in front of me, getting my coffee, and getting to my desk to tackle the past due invoices. I hold my hands in front of me, trying not to let everyone see they are shaking with nerves as I step to the counter. "Morning, Autumn."

"Morning, Ms. Maddie." I smile. "Can I have one sugar donut and a cup of coffee, black, please?" I reach in my purse to grab my wallet as she rings me up, and I hand her the five dollars. The rest of the change is put in the glass tip jar by the register.

"Sure thing." She turns and walks to the paper coffee cups, filling the blue cup and then putting on the white lid, walking to me and setting it down in front of me before she grabs the donut and hands me the blue bag. "See you tomorrow." I nod at her, grabbing the bag and the coffee in one hand before walking out.

I keep my head forward as I walk, not making the mistake I did yesterday. I take the keys out to the bar and open the door, locking it after me before making my way to the distillery office. Switching on the lights, I see the whole floor light up as I walk to the office. Putting my purse in the chair in front of the desk, I pull out the desk chair and sit down.

I flip open the laptop and turn it on as I pull off a piece

of donut and pop it in my mouth. The sugar hitting my tongue makes me smile before I flip open the little tab to take a sip of the coffee. "Good morning," I tell myself before turning to the side, taking the ledger book off the cabinet, and opening it.

The white envelopes are all stacked one on top of each other, all of them stamped with the red past due mark. I close my eyes and take a deep inhale before pulling out the white paper and unfolding it. Seeing the amount past due, I grab a pen and write down the amount. I do the same thing when I go through the whole stack, then look at the total. "Fuck." That's the only thing I can say, leaning back in the chair.

I pull up my bank balance and see I have just enough to cover it all, but then I won't have anything left to help do all the things I want to do to bring new people in. As I go through the stack of bills again, I hear footsteps coming from the back and look out the window to see Brady coming in.

"Hey," he says, picking up my purse and putting it on the corner of the desk before sitting down in the chair. "What are you up to?"

"I'm up to these." I pick up the stack of white papers. "It's a lot worse than I thought it would be." He just nods. "I've been thinking."

He puts his head back and groans, "That is never a good thing." I fold my arms in front of me.

"Well, you don't even know what I'm thinking." I tap the desk. "But here is what we are going to do. I called the Morgans." I mention the distribution company we used to use some ten years ago.

"They dropped us," he reminds me.

"Yes, but that was then, this is now. Time has passed, and I found out the old man has retired, and his son is in charge." I tilt my head to the side. "Then I think we should offer a tasting menu for businesses." His eyebrows pinch together. "We have that room off the bar. We can get some tables in there. Have companies come in and do their parties here. Get bachelor parties and bachelorette parties. Couples' night with the chef. There are a bunch of things we could do."

"I never thought about that," he admits.

"Then there is bringing a cook in from five to ten every night." He shakes his head. "Too bad, it's happening and I have interviews next week. Small menu, I'm thinking burgers, fish and chips, a good cut of steak with a side, and a sample of whiskey. We can work on the menu with the cook we hire." He leans forward. "We also do a five-to-seven two-for-one. After work people drop in before going home."

"They have to come in." His voice goes high.

"If you offer them two-for-one, trust me, people will come in. Maybe not in droves, but as time goes on, word of mouth." He puts his head back, looking up at the ceiling. "Listen, we have to try. If we don't try, then they win. Also, Brady, I was thinking since my samples were such a hit, I think we should add whiskey flights to the drink menu. It's relatively inexpensive to order a few flight sets for now. If business picks up, we can invest in more."

"What are you going to tell Dad?"

"I'm not going to tell Dad anything," I admit. "He has other things to worry about than worrying about this." He nods. "I also am going to be working nights. You need some time off to sleep. You look like shit."

He laughs. "Wow."

"When was the last time you slept eight hours?" I ask him, and he smirks.

"When was the last time you slept eight hours?" He raises his eyebrows. "You look like shit." He gets up from the chair, and we both burst out laughing. "I'm going to test the last batch we made, see if it's ready."

"Good, Bryan should be here any second anyway." He turns to walk out, and I look down at the bills, going through them and making a spreadsheet to see which ones are the oldest to the newest.

I'm finishing my coffee when I hear a knock on the door and look up to see Bryan. "Hey." I get up, smiling at him. He's wearing a button-down dress shirt with blue pants, his blond hair pushed to the side, and his brown eyes looking at me. The smile on his face goes big when I get up and walk over to him. "Bryan." I hold out my hand to shake his. "I'm Autumn."

"Autumn," he replies, his voice deeper than I thought it would be, "nice to meet you."

"Thank you for coming in today," I tell him.

"Of course," he says, looking around. "I've never been here." He puts his hands on his hips as he looks around. "Heard about it but—"

"I can give you a tour, if you like." I move out of the

office with him, going over the story of how we started. He listens to the story as we circle back to the office. "I know that you closed the account with us."

He avoids looking at me as he looks down to the side. "I'm not sure what was said as to why the account was closed." He turns back to look at me.

"I can imagine what was said," I tell him, and his eyes go big. "It's no surprise that the Cartwrights might be behind it." I don't give him a chance to admit it or deny it. "But it's been close to eight years, and, well, business is business. It's also time to move on, don't you think?" I don't know why I put in that last part. I just know that I'm over all of this. The hatred that seeps into your soul until you don't even know who you are anymore.

"I agree. I know your product," he admits. "I have to agree it's some of the best whiskey out there. What are you looking for exactly?"

"I'm looking to get my product on the shelves of liquor stores, as well as in restaurants. Sort of exactly what we had before." I explain to him exactly what I want. "I have a product I know is far more superior than what is out on the market. It's a family-run business, and I guarantee once they try our whiskey, they won't go back."

He puts his hands in his pockets. "You aren't going to take no for an answer, are you?"

"No, I won't." I fold my arms over my chest.

"Good, then neither am I," he states, shocking me. "I'll take the contract. We will start with twenty cases. Usually, the deal was twenty percent, but since I'm going to have to do this personally, I will have to do it for twenty-five." I can't believe my ears. Twenty cases is a lot more than zero.

"Are you serious?" I ask him, and he smirks.

"Yeah," he replies, pulling out his hand for me to shake, "we have a deal."

"Only if we can revisit the terms in six months." I put out my hand, and he chuckles.

"We have a deal." He shakes my hand, and I feel his warm one take mine. The smile is so big on my face it hurts my cheeks.

"Thank you." I take my hand out of his. "You won't regret this."

"I don't think I will either. We'll be by tomorrow to pick up the cases." He turns and walks out of the door.

I put my hands on my head and silently scream before the door opens again, and he comes back in, shocking me. The dread now creeps up my body. "Hey," I say as he gets closer. "Did you forget something?"

"What?" He shakes his head. "No." He grins. "It's just, that was business." He points at the door. "And now I'm not here for business." I watch him. "Now I'm here for personal business." I roll my lips. "I want to know if I can take you out."

"What?" The shock rips through my words.

"I want to take you out," he announces. "I'm very persistent also."

I can't help but smile. "Is that so?"

"That is so." He takes a step forward, his voice going soft. "I'd like to take you to dinner."

"I don't know," I counter him, "the town and all that."

"How about I pick you up or you meet me at my house, and I'll cook for you?" I think about all the reasons I should say no, but then I think, *why the fuck shouldn't I do this?*

"Okay," I say softly, "you have a date."

"Good, how about tomorrow? That way, you can't change your mind." I laugh now. "I'll text you my address."

"Sounds like a plan," I reply, and this time he winks at me before walking out the door.

"So how did it go?" Brady walks back into the distillery from the bar.

"He took twenty cases." His eyes about pop out of his head. "Twenty-five percent instead of twenty commission, but it's not zero."

"Fuck." He runs his hands through his hair. "I can't believe you did it."

"And he asked me out," I say, and he rolls his eyes, "so high five." I hold up my hand.

"I am not high-fiving my sister for having a date." He slaps my hand away, making me laugh as he turns and goes back to the bar. "Proud of you," he tosses out right before he walks out of the door.

Six hours later, I'm behind the bar looking at the eight people who are in tonight. All of them from out of town, not one face I know, which is fine by me. I have just kicked Brady out of the bar and told him to go home. I'm walking around the bar to make sure everyone is okay when Darren walks in the door again. He takes a look around before heading to the bar and sitting on a stool.

I make sure everyone is taken care of before going back behind the bar. "What can I get you?" I ask him, tossing a napkin down in front of him.

"I'll take the special blend," he orders. I turn to pour in two fingers in the glass before walking over and putting it on the napkin in front of him.

"Fifty bucks," I tell him and he tries not to laugh.

"It was twelve bucks the other day."

"Inflation," I inform him. I expect him to get up and walk out the door, but he doesn't. Instead, he takes out his cash and puts three twenties on the counter. "You can keep the change." I start to walk away from him. "I would like to ask you some questions." I raise my eyebrows as he takes out his notepad.

"Thought I made it pretty clear to you I wasn't interested the last time," I remind him and look up when I see someone coming in the door, and everything in my body stops dead. It can't be, but as he gets closer and closer to the bar, there is no mistaking that my eyes are not playing tricks on me. He comes straight to the bar, standing between two stools, looking at me, and the only thing that comes out of my mouth is his name, "Charlie."

Fifteen

CHARLIE

I LEAN AGAINST the bar, looking at the blood rush out of her face, her lips looking like they are going to tremble. "What are you doing here?" She looks at me and then at the man in front of her.

"Was out for a walk, decided I would come in and have a drink." I pull the stool out and sit down. "This is where you get drinks at, isn't it?" I look around the bar at some of the people sitting down, and I have to admit, I've never seen them in my life.

She walks down the bar, and I take her in. The past couple of days I've only seen her in shorts and a tank top. "What can I get you?" She stands in front of me with her button-down top loose around her.

"I'll have the house whiskey blend," I tell her. Turning, she nods and walks down the bar to get me my order, placing it down in front of me on a white napkin. "Thank you," I tell her, picking it up and bringing it to my lips as she walks away from both of us sitting at the bar and makes her rounds. She comes back to fill two drinks before going back to the table. It's a lot fuller than it's been in the past couple of months. Actually, the past years, to be honest. I left my house after dinner, my feet going to the crash site and then turning off course to her house. The house was dark, as always, but I knocked twice before I walked around to the front, seeing her car wasn't there. Before I knew it, I was making my way to town, telling myself I was just going for a walk, but also lying to myself. I have no fucking idea as to why I'm here, but I'm here.

"Can I get you anything else?" she asks the man sitting beside me.

"I have two questions, three at tops, and then I can get out of here, and you never have to see me again," he replies. Something about what he says has the hair on the back of my neck standing up. "You were the one who came forward and started the investigation into the Cartwrights." The hair on the back of my neck stays frozen in time as my body turns to stone.

"No," Autumn snaps, "I'm not doing this. I don't want to answer your questions. You need to leave."

"It's two questions." He tries to make his case.

"The woman is telling you to go," I speak up from my stool and turn, his beady eyes looking at me. "You asked him to leave before?"

"Yes," Autumn says softly.

"Then I guess you should go." I turn back to the guy, who picks up his drink and finishes it in two gulps, hissing.

"See you around," he tells her as he walks out with his pad.

"Thank you," she says, and I finish the whiskey in my own glass.

"Didn't do it for you," I retort to her. "Brady's been busting his ass to get people in here for the last couple of years. It would suck that it would be all for nothing."

She nods at me. "Well then, thank you for Brady." She turns around.

"Who is he?" I want to kick myself for asking her. It's none of my business. I need to get the fuck up and get the fuck out of here. I had a plan for tonight, and that plan had nothing to do with fucking Autumn.

"His name is Darren." She walks back over to where I'm sitting, I start turning the glass in my hand. "He's a reporter for a New York magazine called *The Future and The Past*." My hand stops moving and so does the glass. "They are doing some special on the accident involving Waylon Cartwright." Her voice trails off. "He came in a couple of days ago, and Brady kicked him out." My eyes focus on the glass in front of me as I try to get a handle on the anger roaring inside me. "Then he sent me his business card."

"What did you tell him?" I hiss out the words.

"Nothing." I can see the tears well in her eyes. I push the stool away from me, and the noise makes everyone stop talking and look over at me. "I didn't tell him anything." She takes one more step toward the top of the bar.

I don't say a word to her. Instead, I turn on my heel and march out of here. My hands ball into fists by my sides as I walk down the street and head to where I should have just gone to begin with. The echo of my heart beating fills my ears, and it's the only thing I hear as I make my way to the crash site. The last time I was here was when Autumn first rode into town, stopping by the tree where another wreath sits. Sitting down and closing my eyes, I remember the days after the crash.

I sat in my closet, my back against the wall because it was the only place where I could still smell her, as if she was still here with me. The shirt she wore the night before was in my hands, soaked with the tears that fell onto it while I held it to my face. The light turned into darkness in a blink of an eye. "Honey." My mother came into the closet. It felt like she left me alone for five minutes, but it was two days later. "Jennifer's parents are here." I looked at her, confused, not sure why she was telling me this, as she came to kneel in front of me. "We have to choose something for her to wear."

"I should have married her." The words left my mouth as I stared at my mother, my eyes itching from the dryness, or maybe it was because I hadn't slept since I got home. Not a wink. The minute my eyes would close, I would be right back where my heart stopped. I would be right back where my hell started. I would be right back there, and without her by my side this time. "I wanted to marry her, Mom." The dryness in my eyes was no more as the tears slowly started to roll down my face. "I love her, Mom." My mother shed her own tears. Not saying a word, or

maybe she did, it didn't matter because nothing anyone had to say to me during that time I wanted to hear. There was nothing I wanted to hear except for Jennifer calling my name. Mom sat beside me with her arm around my shoulders as she kissed my head, and I wept for the only woman I would ever love.

My father came in not long after, helped me get dressed, and led me out for the first time in a week. Sunglasses on as I stood there in my black suit, watching her coffin, begging for her to come back to me. Begging for her to just kiss me one more time. Begging at one point to be with her. If she wasn't with me, I didn't want to be here. I was so angry at the whole fucking world. Angry with my grandfather for telling me she was gone. Angry with myself for not protecting her when she needed me to. Angry with myself for going out that night. Angry at the world.

I sit by the tree in a daze. "I'm sorry." I put my hand on the tree like I always do before I get up and walk back home. Seeing that it's almost two o'clock in the morning, I walk through the trees and expect to see Jennifer's face. I always see her face when I walk back home as if she's walking home with me.

My head down, focusing on seeing her face so much, I don't even notice I'm walking toward the back of *her* house. She's sitting on the swing, one leg up, one leg on the porch as she pushes it back and forth.

I wait until I'm at the bottom of her steps before I speak. "You keep my name out of this." I walk up the steps and see that she's wearing the same shirt she was tonight, but her jeans are gone. "You keep Jennifer's name out of this," I hiss as I stand by the swing. "You don't bring up anybody else but you."

"Okay." Her voice is defeated. "Whatever you say, Charlie." I walk to the side of the swing and sit down. "For the record…" She looks at me. "I was never going to talk to him to begin with. I don't want any of this." I stare at her for a second, willing her to look at me, wanting to see her face, but all she does is stare straight ahead.

"Look at me," I tell her, and all she does is shake her head. My stomach dips, my hands shake to touch her, my body fighting it all. "Autumn," I snap, and she gets up.

"Go home, Charlie." My hand flies up to grab hers, and I pull her to me. "I won't say anything."

My hand lets hers go so I can grip her hips and turn her to face me. Opening my legs for her to stand between them, I look up at her, and she looks down at me. "It's a shame," she says softly, "how you can be so beautiful on the outside but then so ugly inside." The words get lodged in my throat, and I pull her down on me. She puts one knee beside my hip and then, with the other, straddles me. She plays with my hair. "Such a shame," she repeats, as if I'm not here, as if she's talking to herself. Before she bends her head and kisses my lips softly, she closes her eyes like she doesn't see me.

"Open your eyes," I tell her as I grip her hips on top of me.

"No," she retorts, leaning forward and sliding her tongue out on my lower lip before she slips it into my mouth. My eyes close as I let her kiss me, my hand moving from her hips up her back. Her hips move up and down over my covered cock. My hand slides over her shirt to the front, to the buttons, as I open one and then another until it's hanging open. My hand comes up to push her bra down, and my mouth leaves hers as I bend to take her nipple into my mouth. She moves up to her knees, her hand going to the button of my jeans. I sit up to help her, and when she wraps her fist around my cock, I let go of her nipple. Wrapping an arm around her waist, I lift her at the same time as I get up. I push one side down and then the other before sitting down. She moves her panties to the side, her eyes watching me hold my cock for her to slide onto it.

Her head goes back when she sinks down onto it. One hand goes to her neck, gripping it in my palm, forcing her head to come back and for her to look at me. The other goes around her waist as I help her ride me. "Autumn," I say her name, watching her face the whole time, seeing her close her eyes and never once open them. No matter how much I ask her to open them, she doesn't. I lean down, biting her nipple as she arches her back, pressing her tits into me. My hand roams up her spine to the back of her head, pushing it forward toward my mouth as it comes down to devour hers. The kiss is brutal and rough, and I can't get enough of it as she comes all over my cock. I'm not too far behind her, thrusting my hips up and planting myself in her as I come. My head goes back as she buries her face in my neck and collapses on my chest. I close my eyes, thinking that again, for another night, nothing has gone according to my plan.

Sixteen

AUTUMN

I BURY MY face in his neck, which is the wrong thing to do because all I can do is smell him all around me. The musk reminds me of a time I didn't hate him. The first time I met him and thought to myself that he might be the hottest man I'd ever seen. With a megawatt smile and dark-blue eyes, you would be lucky if he smiled your way. I'm reminded of this right before I remember this Charlie isn't that one. This Charlie is a man who hates me. Is a man who I hate. Is a man who no matter how many times I tell myself I can resist him, I don't. He is the perfect example of a wolf in sheep's clothing.

He wraps his arms around me, one around my waist and the other around the tops of my shoulders, as he buries his own face in my neck. I need to move away from him, and I will in a minute, when his body's heat warms my bones' coldness. I'm about to disengage myself from him when he gets up, and my legs wrap around his hips instead of getting down. His cock still buried in me, still hard, making me feel a fullness I've never felt before. A fullness, even if I don't want to remember it, I will.

He carries me into the house, making his way to my bedroom. "I have to put the sheets back on the bed," I say softly from his neck.

"Where are they?" he asks me, his voice softer than I've ever heard.

"In the dryer," I tell him. He pulls me off him, putting me on my feet, the cool hitting me as soon as he steps away from me.

"I'll go get them," he says, turning, not waiting for me to say anything. Then I wrap my linen shirt closed in the front to warm myself. I hear him open the dryer as I sit on the bed, hooking my feet on the side of the bed frame, wrapping my arms around them, and my chest pressing into them. He walks back in and stops when he sees me.

He dumps the covers on the bed, and I get up. The two of us make the bed in the darkness, the light from the moon guiding us. I don't know if he's going to stay or not. I also don't care. The whole day catches up with me. He walks back out of the room toward the laundry room as I put the pillows in their place and comes back with the quilt. I pull the covers back as I shrug off the linen shirt, slipping into bed with just my panties on. Facing the other side of the bed, I curl into a ball as my head sinks into the pillow.

I don't know what he's going to do, if he's going to stay or not. My eyes stay open but not looking for him. I hear his boots hitting the floor, followed by the clashing of his belt buckle before he walks to the other side of the bed and slides in. My heart speeds up as I watch him lie on his back, looking up at the ceiling, one hand on his chest, the other folded under his head.

I should close my eyes and fall asleep and wish him gone by morning. I should turn and give him my back. I should have never started this shit with him, whatever it fucking is. Even knowing all that, instead of doing what I should do, my mouth opens. "I wasn't going to talk to that reporter." I don't know why I tell him this, but I do. It won't change what he thinks of me, but I still want it to be known.

"We'll talk about it later." His voice is as soft as it was before. "It's late." He turns his head to look over my way. We stare at each other until I make the move to turn and give him my back. Placing one hand under my pillow and closing my eyes, I wait for sleep to come and take me, when I feel him around me. His arm slides under my pillow with mine while his other arm falls over my hips. The lone tear slips out of my eye, sliding to the pillow before sleep takes me.

The alarm wakes us both up in the morning, and when I open my eyes, I see we've moved in the four hours. My head is now on his chest, my arm over his abs as he curls up, so my arm falls to the side before he gets out of bed, heading toward the blaring sounds. He turns the alarm off as I hear him start to get dressed. After the sound of the zipper, I wait until I hear the sound of his boots being put on before I speak, "I have a date tonight, so you can't come over." I can hear him stop moving.

I hear him stand and make the mistake of looking down the bed at him standing there, his face like stone. "Why would I care?"

I don't let the words hurt me. There is nothing he can say that can hurt me anymore. "I care"—I toss the covers over me—"that people might find out you show up here at night." I stand here in my panties and nothing else, knowing I should cover myself up. "I don't know why I should care." I hate that I'm admitting this to him, of all people. "But I do, and I don't need you showing up here in case someone is here." I fold my arms over my chest, both of us now glaring at each other.

"Don't worry about it," he growls before he turns on his boot and storms out, making sure he slams the door before he walks out. I put my head back, looking at the ceiling before closing my eyes. The stinging comes to my nose as I push the tears away. I look out the window at the same time as he disappears into the forest.

"Fuck you, Charlie," I say to the empty room, wishing I'd said it to him before he slammed out of my house. I look over at the bed and think about stripping it again, but I've washed the sheets for the last two nights, and after the exit he just had, I doubt he'll ever show his face here again. So I go to the bathroom, start the shower, and ignore how pissed I am that I let him have the last word again.

Even when I get dressed and snatch the gray T-shirt dress off the hanger, putting it on, I'm mumbling to myself, "He's a dick." I walk back to the bathroom, combing through my hair. "He has a big dick, but he's also a giant fucking dick," I tell the mirror, "and I hate him." I look down at my vagina. "And you need to stop being a traitor when he's around. We hate him, and that includes his dick, fingers, and his mouth. You've been sleeping for nearly eight years, and now you want to wake up. Wrong time, wrong place, definitely wrong fucking person."

I slide on my white sneakers, grabbing my black bag as I head out the door. "Asshole." I'm still mumbling as I get in my car and head toward town, parking at the same time my brother gets there.

He gets out of his truck with the baseball hat on his head backward as he waits for me to get out of my car. "Morning," he greets me as I slam my door.

"Whatever," I say to him. "I'm going for a coffee and some donuts," I inform him as I start to walk away.

"Are you going to get me anything?" he asks, and I look over my shoulder at him standing there with his hands on his hips.

"No, because a gentleman would have offered to go and get me coffee."

His eyebrows pinch together. "Are you okay? Is it that time of the month?"

"Ugh." I turn and walk away from him, raising my hand in the air and flipping him the bird.

"I'm going to go with a yes on that one." He laughs. "Get me a donut."

I walk over to the bakery, this time on my way there, a couple of people smile my way and I have to wonder if I'm in another dimension. Especially when one of the women smiles at me and says, "Good morning, Autumn." I stop in my tracks. If she hadn't said my name, I'd think she was talking to someone else.

"Morning," I reply to her as I look around to see if I'm actually awake or it's a dream, but she's already halfway down the block before my feet move toward the bakery. I walk out with a cup of coffee in each hand and a bag filled with four donuts, going around the building to the back where the door will probably be unlocked.

I make my way to the office where Brady sits down behind the desk, going over the bills from last night. "We had a great night." He looks up, and I nod at him.

"It was," I tell him, putting the coffee down in front of him. "You're welcome."

"Um, thank you," he says. "Just checked, and Bryan emailed that they will be here by one thirty to grab the cases."

I take a sip of the coffee. "That check should help." I sit down in the chair. "Finally, some good news."

"How was last night?" he asks me, grabbing the bag of donuts and snagging one. "What time did you end up closing?"

I do not end up telling him about the reporter. "I closed up at around eleven." His eyes go big. "We had a group of six, who were from out of town, and started talking to each other about where they were from, then they started buying each other drinks." I shrug. "Left a good tip also."

"Which you didn't take," he points out.

"I took a twenty so I can get gas and buy my donuts."
I point at the bag. "Priorities."

"You still need to live," he reminds me, taking another
bite of the donut while I reach out and grab my own. The
sugar sticks to my fingers as I take a bite of the fluffy
goodness. "We should offer sweets," I suggest to him,
and he glares at me. "You know, when you are sitting
around chatting and drinking as a woman, and you're just
a touch tipsy, you want to have that piece of sweetness."
He puts his head back, and I try not to laugh at him. "I
can't work late tonight," I tell him, and he just looks at
me as I chew my piece of donut. "I have a date." I wiggle
my eyebrows, "First date in eight years." I try to make a
joke out of it.

"That's not true," my brother refutes, and I just stare
at him.

"When I came to visit you that one time, there was a
guy at the bar who was trying to date you." I look at him
confused. "He came in every single day, stayed all day
long just to talk to you."

"Are you talking about Clint?" I ask.

He snaps his fingers and points at me. "That's him."

"He's eighty-four," I gasp, "with a wife."

His head goes back, and he laughs. "Oh yeah, he was
trying to get you to do the polyamorous thing."

I glare at him. "Yeah, because you taught him that
stupid word. You know his wife came in to have a talk
with me." He slaps the desk. "It's not funny. She said
we should split the chores; she didn't even care that her
husband asked me out."

"At that age, I'm pretty sure she just wanted to get rid of him."

I can't help but belly laugh. "You are not wrong." I'm taking a sip of my coffee when my phone beeps from my purse.

Putting the coffee cup down and licking the sugar from my fingers, I pull the phone out and see the text from a number not saved in my phone.

Unknown Contact: here is my address, 151 Second Street. Come at five. Can't wait to see you.

"Everything okay?" Brady asks me. "Your face got a little pale there for a second."

"Yeah." I push away the dread that is starting to creep up. "Bryan was confirming." I put on a fake smile. "Let's get to work," I say, trying to avoid the fact that going out with him scares me to my core.

Seventeen

CHARLIE

I WALK OUT of my house and bypass the office, going straight to the barn. My hair is still wet from the shower I took not twenty minutes ago. The sun is high in the sky, birds flying in and out of the dense forest all around me.

"You look like you're in a great mood," Emmett says to me when I step into the barn. I look over at him as he sits on top of the desk, papers in his hand while he writes, clipboards hanging behind him in five rows across and down. It's where all the ranch hands go to find out what needs to be done for the day. It's Emmett's office of sorts. We gave him an office next to mine, but he never, ever steps foot in it. Instead, he grabbed the desk and placed it here in the barn. "It's going to be a good day."

"I'm fine," I lie to him. I'm pissed. Actually, I'm past the fucking point of being pissed. I just don't want to think about why I'm so pissed. It's another lie I just told myself. I've been lying to myself a lot these days. "Why aren't the horses out yet?" I look around and see most of them still in their stalls. "It's a full day. The horses need to be out there getting prepped."

He picks up the mug of coffee from beside him. "It's not even eight," he tells me. "They always eat at this time and then are taken out."

He just stares at me while I look around, seeing a couple of the ranch hands chatting and laughing in the corner. "There are people just standing around doing nothing." I point at them.

"Why don't you go in your office and do paper things?" He puts his mug down. "Then come back when whatever it is that crawled up your ass is out."

"Nothing has crawled up my ass," I hiss at him. "Have we evaluated all the horses twice?" I ask him, and he chuckles.

"If you want to do it, go right ahead." He smirks. "Seems you have the time."

I turn around and head to the stall where I was thinking of going first. "She's ready to be taken out," he announces, and I unlock the gate.

She just stares at me. "Hey," I greet her, my voice going low, "come on, let's get you out of here." I hold up my hand, and she retreats from me. "I'm not going to hurt you," I assure her, not moving from my spot, leaving it up to her to come to me. "I'm going to get you out there," I say as she takes one step forward, her tail whipping behind her. "Atta girl," I coo to her as she takes another step to me, finally nudging my hand with her muzzle. "What's up, pretty girl?" I rub up her nose as she stares at me, letting her smell me and get used to me. "You ready to go out?" I hold her lead rope in my hand and walk her out of her stall.

"Feeling better?" Emmett asks me, still sitting on his desk, but now all the clipboards behind him are gone, so I know the jobs have been handed out.

"I'm fine." I walk toward the fenced pen on the side of the barn.

"Word around is that you were hanging out in town last night." My back to him, the hair on my neck stands up.

"I went for a walk," I state, and it's not exactly a lie. "Jesus, when did people start giving you a play-by-play of my life?"

"And a drink, apparently." I hear his boots hit the floor and then hear them approach me as he stands beside me. "Not a friendly one either."

"People need to mind their fucking business," I hiss at him, "and not worry about what I'm doing."

"People are also saying she's fixing to change the state of the distillery." He continues talking. "Even some of the old folks who are holding grudges are thinking of going in to have a drink."

"They should." It's the only thing I say to him before I walk out with the horse. My thoughts go right back to her, where they shouldn't be. The last thing I should be doing is thinking about Autumn. "It's nice out, isn't it?" I ask Goldilocks, who walks slowly beside me. "It's going to be a warm day." I look around, spotting one of the ranch hands. "Can you get me a saddle and bridle?" I ask. "I'm going to take her for a walk."

"Sure thing, boss," he says, turning and walking back into the barn. Emmett stands there staring at me as he drinks his coffee. He looks to the side when the ranch hand comes back out with the tack in his hand. "Let me help you," he offers, tossing the saddle on her back as we strap it on her and bridle her. She moves a bit, not sure what is happening, as I put one foot in one of the stirrups before hoisting myself up on her.

She backs up five feet. "It's okay, girl," I say. "We're just going for a walk. You're going to like it." I nudge her side a touch as she walks forward, heading to the edge of the property. She is scared to go into the forest, but I lean down. "It's going to be okay," I tell her as she walks, and the branches snap under her hooves, I go down the trail where we take all the other horses. "See? I told you it would be fine," I reassure her as we make our way back. "I won't lie to you."

I get off her when we get to the fence, walking her back to the barn. "She needs water," I say, walking into the barn and going to her stall. "I'll be back after dinner," I tell her as she walks over to the pail where the water is.

I walk out of the stall, leaving her with one of the hands as he takes off her saddle. Walking to the next stall, I do it all over again, making sure all the horses get their exercise. By the time I walk the last horse in, the sun is setting and the only one left in the barn is Emmett. "Hey," I say, walking with the horse to his stall, "everyone gone?"

"Yeah." He leans back in his chair, his feet up on the

desk. "Need help with him?"

"No," I reply, and he takes his feet down and stands up.

"Then I'm going to get out of here." He grabs his keys off the hook behind him. "A couple of us are going for a drink." I turn my head to him. "Want to come with us?"

"No," I snap, turning back and going to grab some fresh water. He just nods at me as he walks out.

I put the water down in the stall before making my way to my house. As I walk up the steps, I get angrier and angrier with every second that passes. "I have a date tonight." I hear her voice as I step into the shower. The minute she said the words, it was like someone threw ice-cold water over my head, and the blood inside me also turned to ice. She got out of bed—which was a first. Usually, she waited for me to leave before she did that. And, apparently, she hated me so much she washed the sheets each time. When I saw her standing there in just her barely there lace panties, my mouth watered right away and my cock stirred in my pants, obviously not picking up on the fact it wasn't the time. Every single step toward home, I got edgier and edgier.

Getting dressed and making my way to the kitchen, I check to see what I'm going to eat even though I have no appetite. I take out one of the prepared meals I ordered for the week, nuking it for a couple of minutes, grabbing a beer, and taking a pull of it. I swallow the food only because I know I need to get something inside me, then finish the beer and head out.

The minute I start making my way toward the path, I

hear her voice in my head.

"I don't know why I should care, but I do, and I don't need you showing up here in case someone is here."

I ball my hands into fists as I make it to her house, not even pretending that I'm not going there. I should just go to see Jennifer, but my head and my feet are not on the same page. My eyes find her house in the darkness, as I walk up the steps and sit down on the swing and wait for her. Which is the dumbest thing I think I could be doing. I should get the fuck out of here and not be waiting for her to come back from her fucking date.

Every single noise has me looking to the side to see if she's home. My hands are on my knees as I think of every time we were together since she's been back. I think of the fact that last night, she refused to look me in the eyes. I think of the fact that she washes her fucking sheets every single time we've been together. I think of the fact that every single night instead of getting dressed and getting the fuck out of there, I stay. I climbed into bed with her last night and then curled into her when she gave me her back. I shake my head, not wanting to acknowledge what is going on.

I push up to my feet, the swing moving back and forth as I walk to the back door and turn the handle, expecting it to be locked, but instead, it opens. I walk into her house. "Autumn," I say her name, wondering if maybe something is wrong with her car and she's already home, but no one is home. I close the door behind me and shake my head. "She left her fucking door unlocked," I hiss out as I walk to her bedroom. My eyes do a sweep of the room to see that she made the bed already, not sure if she washed the sheets. I smell her perfume in the air, and I clench my teeth together, thinking about her getting ready for her date and putting it on for him.

Turning back toward the living room and sitting on her couch, I lock my eyes on the front door. Feeling so off-balance, I literally think I'm going to trash her whole house while I wait for her. The possessiveness in me feels so unnatural as my leg moves up and down, the nerves in me unbearable.

I hear the crunch of gravel and see the headlights shine into the house before they go off, and the sound of a car door closing. I wait to see if another one will close. But the only sound is the one of her walking up the front steps and then the key going into the lock before the door opens and shuts right behind her.

She takes two steps into the house, putting her purse on the table, not even noticing I'm here. She makes her way to her bedroom when she looks over at me, and yells as she jumps back, putting her hand on her chest. "Jesus fucking Christ," she hisses, "you scared the shit out of me."

I take her in, wearing a pair of green shorts that show off way too much leg, with a tight white T-shirt that falls just above the waist, showing off her stomach. Her hair looks ruffled, and that just pushes me off the edge. I fly off the couch. "Did you fuck him?" My voice is lethal as I cut the distance to her, close enough I can smell her. Close enough to make me lose what little control I have left. "Did you fuck him?" I roar out, my head moving toward her, and two things happen at the same time. One, her body shakes in front of me, shaking so much it's a wonder she's even standing. At the same time, she turns her head to the side, closing her eyes as if she's shielding herself from me, as her hands come up to protect her face. The action makes me take a step back, my heart feeling like it's going to come out of my stomach. "Did you think I was going to hit you?" My hand shakes that she would think that. I'm a lot of things, I know I am, but I would never, ever hit her.

Her hands go down as she opens her eyes, and her head turns back to look at me. I can see the fear written all over her face, and I'm expecting the worst answer. I'm not expecting the answer to knock me right to my core. "Wouldn't be the first time a man put his hands on me."

Eighteen

Autumn

I STAND HERE in the dark, shaking like a leaf on a windy day when the storm is rolling in. Never in my wildest dreams did I think I would come home and find him waiting for me. The anger rolling off him like I've never seen before, and I've seen him be fucking angry. "Did you fuck him?" He gets off the couch and makes his way to me. Standing in front of me, his body tight, his face comes so close to mine that I can feel him breathing on me when he roars out, "Did you fuck him?" On reflex, I turn my head to the side and hold up my hands, waiting for something to happen. My eyes are shut tight for a couple of seconds when he whispers, his voice cracking, "Did you think I was going to hit you?"

My hands go down as I open my eyes, and my head turns back to look at him. My heart pounds in my chest so hard it's a miracle I'm not having a heart attack. There is anguish on his face as he asks me the question, but is he ready for the answer I'm about to give him? Am I ready for what is to come next? "Wouldn't be the first time a man put his hands on me."

His face pales as he takes a step back, as if I just struck him. "What the fuck?" His words are a whisper.

I don't even notice the shaking has not stopped. I don't realize anything standing here in front of this man who has made it a living hell for me for the past eight years. The man who hurt my soul, he just didn't pick up his hand to do it. He did it with his words and by turning his back on me. "Shocked?" I ask him, my shoulders going back as I stand in front of him. The man who was kind, who was caring, who if I was having a bad day would go out of his way to make me smile. The man who will never see me as anything other than the woman who ruined his life. He just stares at me, his eyes moving back and forth, his mouth still open in shock. "The first time Waylon hit me was in this room." I can't believe I'm telling him this secret, a secret I've buried deep inside me. "It was after we had dinner at one of his parents' fundraisers. Apparently, I wasn't enthusiastic enough. He grabbed my arm so tight and twisted it, I thought it was going to pop out of its socket."

"Autumn." His hands go to his hair, and he pulls it in his own hands.

"He blamed it on the alcohol, saying that he was drunk." I shrug. "I was naive. What could I do?" I'm not asking him to answer this question since I've been asking myself this for the last eight years. "He was Waylon Cartwright, his parents were the most influential people of the town, and I was the daughter of a widower, who was running a family business that was successful, but we were not Cartwrights." I swallow down the bile that wants to come up, but I'm doing this. "You were right," I say softly, "I didn't kill them but, in the end, it's because of me they died." The air in the room goes still. "That night, the night of the accident." I watch his face, like stone. "I asked him to open the door to the cabin so I could go to the bathroom. He was already agitated because of the fight he was having with his parents about him not doing anything with his life. And, of course, I was to blame for this since I was working with my brother and father. Again, I was making him look bad. He followed me into the bathroom, and I looked at him and begged him not to drive. Told him I would drive." The scene plays over in my head. "He told me to shut the fuck up, no one was asking me. He took my head in his hand." I hold the side of my head he gripped. "Fisted my hair in his hand, and then proceeded to knock it against the wall"—my hand drops from one side as the other one comes up to touch the place where I had the stitches— "so hard that I felt the burn as the skin tore open. I knew I would need to go to the doctor. I also knew I would have to come up with another story about it. I also knew that was the last time he would ever put his hands on me." Charlie puts his hands on his knees as he hisses out, his breathing coming as if he just sprinted five miles without stopping. "I don't think he would have fought me on it since the sex had dried up, as he said. Obviously, then he told me he didn't know why he put up with me since I wasn't even good at fucking. Which is also why he was constantly going on trips with his brother, so he could get his frustration out."

Charlie stands up. "Autumn." His face ravaged, his voice breaking, but I'm too far gone to stop.

"So I wasn't driving that truck, but I also should have said something to you, to Jennifer, to anyone. I should have done what was the right thing to do. For that, I will forever live with the guilt that I lived and she didn't. Not him, he got what he deserved. But I should have saved her. I should have been the one sitting next to him. You would have kept her safe." He takes a step to me, and I hold up my hand. "But just so you know, I died that night also. I'm breathing, but inside I'm dead. There is nothing left for you to destroy." I thought his face was ravaged before, but I was wrong. "I took your verbal punches over and over again, just like I did with Waylon. Unlike with him, I guess I deserve yours."

"Don't you dare compare the two," he hisses at me. "I'm nothing like him." He turns on his heel and storms out of the room toward the back door. The door slams so hard as he walks out of it the window shakes. I watch him walk through my yard to the darkness of the forest, disappearing as if he was never here.

"This is the end of it," I tell the empty room. "There is nothing else left to do." I walk to the door and turn the lock. "Whatever it is that we were doing is over." I look out into the darkness one more time before going to my bedroom. I strip out of the shorts I chose for the night. I pull the shirt over my head before I go to the bathroom and wash my face, the tears mixing with the water as I replay the scene with Charlie over in my head. "I'm nothing like him" are the only words I hear over in my head.

Slipping a T-shirt over me, I pull the covers back, sliding between the cold sheets, laying my head on the pillow. My eyes land on the empty pillow beside me as I'm taken back to the day my life would really never be the same.

"Did you hear?" My brother walked into the office while I was doing the paperwork as I looked up at him.

"Autopsy came back." His eyes stared into mine. It was six weeks after the accident, six weeks since that fateful night. The bones healed, but the guilt was eating me alive. I held my breath as I waited for him to tell me what I've known, what I've been dreading. "No alcohol or drugs in his system." The air sucked out of me. "I guess those court cases suing for wrongful death will be dismissed now." My hands pushed against the desk to stand, but my knees gave up, and I fell back on my ass. Two weeks after the accident, a couple of people started chattering about suing the Cartwrights. Jennifer's parents were some of them who wanted them to take responsibility for the accident, something the Cartwrights refused to do.

"That can't be," I said the words that shocked my brother. "That can't be," I said over and over again until my brother came to the side of the desk and squatted by my chair. "There is a mistake."

"What are you saying?" He looked at me.

"I'm saying that he was drunk. I know he was drunk."
There, in the office, I told him that Waylon had swapped out the water in his water bottles at my house before going to get everyone else, filling them up with vodka instead. "It's not right."

"What are you going to do about it?" he asked me, and I looked at him.

"I have to make it right." That was the only thing I knew. Little did I know that making it right would ruin everything around me.

With my father and brother by my side the whole way, I went to Jennifer's parents and told them what I knew. They went ahead with the court case, but it kept being postponed and pushed aside. Something that smelled like the Cartwrights' doing. The case brought forth by three victims' families was the biggest thing that this town saw after the accident. I was called as a character witness for the Cartwrights. I was to go up there and tell the world how amazing Waylon was. Except I didn't, I went up there and said the truth. Everything from that night, that he was drinking vodka instead of water.

After my shocking testimony, the trial turned into an absolute shit show. Jennifer's attorney knew the Cartwrights were as dirty as they came. He believed they were withholding evidence, so he filed an immediate request for Wallace and Margo Cartwright to produce Waylon Cartwright's legitimate autopsy report. The courtroom went into an uproar and, of course, their attorney objected, as he stated that his clients had the same autopsy report that was filed at the coroner's office.

Shocking everyone, especially the Cartwrights, who thought they were above the law, the judge granted the request and ordered Mr. and Mrs. Cartwright to produce their copy. You didn't need to be a doctor or an expert to see the major differences between the Cartwrights' copy of Waylon's autopsy report and the report filed with the coroner's office.

And lo and behold, it was all there in black and white. Waylon was indeed intoxicated. His blood alcohol level was three times the legal limit and now the entire town knew about it. The judge even ordered the Cartwrights to produce Waylon's medical records to confirm that his blood type matched the legitimate autopsy report.

But of course, the blame was placed on the medical examiner, who—according to the Cartwrights—was not only incompetent but he chose a "low-level lab" that mixed up their son's test results with someone else's, and when they received a copy of the report, they didn't bother to read it since the medical examiner said the results were negative for alcohol and drugs.

And now that they knew he was drunk, they blamed me. He drank alcohol because of me. I wasn't good enough for him. I couldn't make him happy, and I should have made him stop drinking. Mrs. Cartwright even spread the rumor that I was giving Waylon several bottles of whiskey from my family's bar. That's funny, considering he only drank vodka, which eventually was his downfall.

The truth of the matter was, the Cartwrights paid the medical examiner off because they knew Waylon was drunk. There was no financial trace of it. However, it was rather ironic that the medical examiner abruptly retired, sold his house a month after filing the autopsy report, and no one has seen hide nor hair of him since.

The Cartwrights were well aware of Waylon's habitual drinking, and like everything else in their life, they disregarded it. Rumor was, Mrs. Cartwright made an emotional plea and requested that they refrain from desecrating her son's body by performing an autopsy on him. I heard she put on quite a show too. She even wiped her "tears" with her silk handkerchief while clutching her Tiffany pearls. However, because Waylon was the driver and it was an ongoing investigation, her request was denied. As soon as she received that news, those fake tears dried up like the Sahara Desert. This was also probably why Waylon was cremated a week after the autopsy was performed. They didn't need to wait on the results because they already knew what they were going to be.

The blackmail the family had done over the year was all brought to light because of me. The government contracts to build everything from the roads to high-rises were all done with an inside person who would tell them the bid to put out or would make sure there would be no other bids brought to the table.

Slowly, the cards came tumbling down.

I expected some pushback, but I wasn't expecting the onslaught that would come my way. The Cartwrights might have taken a dip in the status department, but there were still people who stood by them, which meant I was public enemy number one. And after me was my family, who were in the direct path of their ammunition. I shouldn't have left. I should have stayed and bore the brunt of it, but I couldn't take it, and the last straw was when Charlie showed up at my house, drunk off his ass, and he stood there and blamed me for it all.

A couple of days later, I left with every intention to return, but one day turned into one month turned into one year, and so on. Now, here I was, still living in the shadow of being the woman who sullied a good man's name. But tonight, all the secrets have come out. I have nothing left to give, not to the Cartwrights, not to the people who hate me, and not to Charlie Barnes. Especially not to him.

Tonight was the end of whatever the fuck was happening between us. It was the end of us hate-fucking each other. It was the end of me paying penance for something I'd already been paying for secretly. It was the end of the road for all of it. I would get up tomorrow and try to rebuild the company my father was proud of. I would bring it back to how it was before everything happened, and then I would leave, just like I did the last time. But hopefully this time I would do it in one piece and not shattered.

Nineteen

CHARLIE

I STORM INTO my house, slamming the door as hard as I did Autumn's, wondering if any of the windows will shatter. Not caring if they do. As I walk over to the cabinet on top of the fridge, I grab the bottle of whiskey, not even waiting until I'm sitting on the couch before I take a pull from it. Putting one hand on the counter, with the other one holding the bottle in my hand before I take another pull, I try to block out her voice, try to block it all out, but the words come to me louder and louder each time.

He took my head in his hand, fisted my hair in his hand, and then proceeded to knock it against the wall so hard that I felt the burn as the skin tore open. I knew I would need to go to the doctor. I also knew I would have to come up with another story about it.

Another story, the words feel like I'm being kicked in the stomach, sucking all the air out of my lungs. I take three gulps down, hoping it dulls the way my body feels, but instead, her face flashes through my mind. The way her whole body shook while she said, *But, just so you know, I died that night also. I'm breathing, but inside I'm dead. There is nothing left for you to destroy.*

I take the bottle of whiskey, pulling more gulps. My eyes look at the bottle in my hand, right before I pull back my arm and pitch it across the room. The light on over the stove is dim, so I can see the golden liquid drip down the wall, just like the tears that poured down her face. My head hangs down, *I took your verbal punches over and over again, just like I did with Waylon. Unlike with him, I guess I deserve yours.*

I put my head back, but it feels so heavy I have no choice but to let it fall in front of me, before I turn and make my way to my bedroom. As I collapse on the bed, my hand goes to my chest as I turn my head to the side, the guilt hitting me like a freight train head-on, crushing me and taking me under.

All the times I saw them fighting, and we would always make jokes about it. The way he would reach out to grab her and yank her to him. The times he would hiss at her, and she would avoid looking at everyone. The times they would walk in and you would know they were fighting, since they would sit apart, and he would say she was having a hissy fit. All of it flashes in my mind, making it harder and harder to breathe. I turn to the side, seeing her face in my mind, her face and no one else. Nothing comes in but her face as I remember the last time I saw her before I found out she left town.

I was drunk, so fucking drunk, it was a wonder I wasn't falling all over the place. The day in court, listening to her on the stand tell everyone how she knew he was drunk that night. The floor I was standing on felt like it opened up, and I fell into the dark hole. I avoided even looking at her until it was the anniversary of their death. Two years since Jennifer was taken from me.

I walked to her house, held on to trees to help me not fall on my face. Walking up to her door and balling my hand into a fist, I pounded over and over again. She opened the door, the light from the hallway on, and I could see her face. Her eyes swollen from crying, the tip of her nose red. I wanted her to hurt even more than she did.

"How could you do this?" I asked her. *"How could you do this to Jennifer?"*

"Charlie." Her voice came out in a whisper. *"I never wanted this to happen."*

I should have listened to her, but I didn't. I was so wrapped up in my grief I didn't care about anyone else's. "All of this time, you fucking knew."

"I know," she admitted. *"I was waiting until the results came back."*

"You fucking knew he was drunk!" I roared in her face. *"You did this."* My face went closer to hers. *"You could have stopped him."*

"I tried," she said, *"I tried to get him to give me the keys."*

"You didn't try hard enough." My words were like a knife stabbing her again, the wince on her face should

have had me step back, but instead, the rage took over. "It should be you in that grave, rotting in hell with him." That was the last thing I said to her before I turned and stumbled into the forest. Collapsing on my knees in the middle of the forest, I lay on my side, wishing for the pain to go away.

I get up in time to make it to the bathroom before I throw up, closing my eyes, seeing her there. Not Jennifer. Autumn. Her face white from me yelling at her, every single time I had a chance. Every single time I could spew hatred her way, I did. Sharpening my knife each time, not caring that I was leaving her with the pain she was in. Ignoring all of the signs. Falling back on my ass as I put my back to the wall, I want to go to her.

But I don't. I sit in the bathroom with my head back, and my eyes closed until I hear the alarm coming from behind me. Pulling it out and turning it off before placing it on the floor beside me, I don't move from my spot on the floor. Not moving one inch. My body is glued to the floor, feeling like I've been run over. No, that isn't right. I feel like I'm being buried by the guilt that runs through me.

The phone rings from beside me, and I look down and see Emmett calling me, but I don't pick it up. I just sit with my head back, seeing her face, Autumn. How the first time I met her, I was taken aback by how beautiful she was. How her smile lit up her whole face. How she used to make little jokes with me, and we used to laugh with each other. Waylon hated that, so I stopped doing it. He didn't mind after I started dating Jennifer, but by then, it had shifted.

The knock on the back door has me turn my head to the side, my phone ringing again. I wish everyone would just leave me alone. I don't have that because the back door is opened, and he hisses, "What the fuck is that smell?"

He walks in, and I can hear his boots crunch the glass from the bottle. "Charlie," he calls, moving through the house, his footsteps coming closer to the bedroom, and then finally, he's standing outside the door. "What the fuck is going on?" He's wearing jeans and a T-shirt with the barn name on it.

"Nothing," I say, my voice monotone, but my head screams *everything*.

"You smashed?" He puts his hands on his hips as he glares at me.

"No," I answer him honestly. "Wish I was," I admit to him.

"Get up and get your ass in the shower." He doesn't entertain me. "Get your head out of your ass."

I laugh. "I wish I knew how," I retort as he shakes his head.

"You have five minutes to get up and get in the shower, or I'm calling your grandfather," he threatens me. "I'm not cleaning that mess in the kitchen, but I'll make you coffee."

I think about his threat, knowing that he will absolutely call him and then he'll definitely head down here and kick my ass. Then he will probably find out what I've been doing and kick my ass even more. I turn on my knees before getting up and pulling my shirt over my head, looking down to see her teeth mark barely there and suddenly wanting it there. I kick off my boots and get in the shower, with the cold water hitting me first. As I close my eyes and picture her in my arms, the pressure in my chest makes me reach up to rub the ache.

Fifteen minutes later, I'm dressed and walking out of my bedroom, seeing that he cleaned up the mess and that my coffee is on the counter. Picking it up, I head outside to start my day. Walking to the barn, I find him sitting on his desk, and he looks up at me as if he hadn't just seen me fifteen minutes ago. "Morning," he greets.

"Morning." I take a sip of the coffee. "Thank you for—"

"I'll add it to the list of things you owe me for." I nod at him in agreement. "That list is getting longer and longer."

I smirk before I take another sip of coffee. "I'm good for it."

"I don't know about that. You going to ride her today or not?" He motions with his head toward Goldilocks, and I just nod.

"Figured," he grunts. "Get out of here. I have work to do."

I finish my cup and put it on his desk before going to Goldilocks and smiling when her tail whips side to side. "Morning, girl," I greet, grabbing her reins, and noticing she's already saddled. "Let's go for a walk, yeah?"

I walk to the edge of the fenced area before climbing on her and making my way to the trail. "It's a nice day,"

I tell her as she slowly makes her way. "You like it here, right?" She trots over a log. "I have a friend I'm going to bring to meet you." I smile as the tears sting my eyes. "To be honest, I don't think she's my friend. At least she shouldn't be my friend, but I'm going to make her be my friend again." I chuckle. "That is if she doesn't leave before then." The thought of her leaving town makes me grip the reins in my hands tighter. "You'll like her, she's pretty, like you. You have the same hair color." I pet her neck. "She hates me, but you... she'll love you, and that's going to be enough for me. If I can get her to smile at you, I'll take her hating me." The tear escapes the side of my eye. "I'm going to try," I vow out loud, "I'm going to try."

We walk for over four hours, and when we get back, she drinks for a solid five minutes. "Good ride?" Emmett asks when I get back.

"Yeah," I say to him as he stands there looking at me.

"A couple of guys and I are going to have a drink tonight. You want to join us?" Emmett offers.

I stare at him. "Drinks where?"

"At Brady's place." He mentions her brother as if I won't know it's Autumn's place also.

"Sure," I agree, shocking him a bit. "Meet you there."

I spend the rest of the afternoon in my office, going over the schedule and interviewing another therapist to add to the ever-expanding company. I take another shower, and at eight o'clock, I get up and make my way to town.

I park my truck in the back, next to her car. I get out

and walk in, seeing it's more crowded than it's been the last few times I've been here. Definitely fuller than it was the last time. I look around the room, my eyes going to her behind the bar serving a group of women sitting on the stools. Light music plays in the background, something that has never been done before. I look to the right, seeing most of the tables full as I spot Emmett and a couple of the guys. I walk over passing Brady. "Hey," he says, "you want something to drink?"

"Yeah," I reply and then look back at the bar, "but I'll go to the bar and get it myself."

"Um," Brady starts, and I'm sure he's heard about Autumn and me, "listen—"

"It'll be fine." I slap his arm and make my way to the bar, her eyes coming to mine as soon as she looks up. Shock fills her face but she puts up a shield. "Hey," I greet when I stand on the side of the bar.

"Hey," she says softly, tucking her hair behind her ear. I see she's wearing a short white tank top with blue jeans, her sweater wrapped around her waist. "What can I get you?" she asks me, avoiding looking at me.

"The house blend is good," I remark, and she nods as she walks over to the other side, grabbing a glass and filling it before coming back to hand it to me. "I'm going to be sitting over there." I motion with my finger to my group of guys. "Do you want me to pay for this now?"

"I can start a tab." She outstretches her arms on the bar top. "Emmett has one going also."

"Sounds good." I pick up the glass and head over to the guys, who look surprised to see me here.

I sit down next to Emmett, listening to them talk, but the whole time, I keep looking over at the bar and seeing her smile with the girls. She gives them a different smile than she gave me, but then again, she doesn't hate those girls like she hates me, and they haven't made her life hell for the last eight years. The whole night, I'm constantly looking over at her. Every two minutes, I feel my eyes go to her. "You got your head out of your ass?" Emmett asks from beside me as I look at Autumn. I pick up the drink and bring it to my lips, not answering him because I don't owe him an answer. The only one I'm going to owe that answer to is Autumn.

Twenty

AUTUMN

I WATCH HIM sitting there with Emmett and a couple of the ranch hands, and my whole body feels like it's on fire, literally burning up. "Are you okay?" Brady asks, and before I turn to look at him, Charlie turns his gaze over to me. We lock our eyes for what feels like an eternity before I look at Brady.

"I'm fine. Why?" I ask him, my hands a touch shaky.

"You look all flushed and shit," he notes, putting the tray down on the bar top.

"I'm fine," I lie to him. I'm not fine. I'm the opposite of fine. I was fine this morning when I walked in here, but then people started coming in. A table of two, then a table of six, and by the time I looked around the bar, it was almost full. I honestly couldn't believe my eyes, but then he walked in. The man who I thought, after everything was said and done, would never want to be in the same room as me. But then he walked in the door, and I felt the air being sucked out of me.

"You sure you're good?" he asks, looking around. "I'm okay with you leaving."

I raise my eyebrows at him. "Um, how are you going to serve…" I turn and count the number of tables, and when I look at Charlie's table, he's still looking at me. I try not to let it get to me, but how he looks at me is different from the last couple of times. "Fifteen tables plus the half-full stools."

"I would handle it." He rolls his eyes, and I laugh. "Do you want to switch it up?" His eyes go to me, then to the four women sitting at the bar, laughing at something.

"No." I shake my head. "The last thing we need is for you to—"

"I'm not doing anything." He feigns innocence. "I'm just trying to help you out."

"Be a doll"—I fake smile at him—"help me out by going back and checking on your tables and getting more orders."

He taps the bar top for a couple of seconds before grabbing his tray and turning on his way.

I walk to the far end of the bar. "Are you good?" I ask a couple of men who came in and sat together. They let me know they are in town for the week for some convention or something in the next town over, but all the hotels were booked.

"I'll take another one of the house blends," the man says, lifting to finish the rest of his glass, "neat."

"Will do." I grab his glass while the guy next to him says he's fine.

I step to the group of four girls, who have been drinking white wine this whole time. "Can I get you guys anything else?" I ask them with a smile on my face.

"We were thinking of trying some of the whiskey," the blond one says, "but we don't like anything strong."

"Give me a second," I tell them, going over to fill the other order before returning to them.

"I have something," I tell them. "It's a blackberry mint mojito, but instead of rum, it's bourbon."

"Oh," the brunette chirps, "let's try it. Can we do a taste sample of it?"

"You sure can." I nod at them, going over to the shaker and filling it with blackberries, mint, sugar, and bourbon, before covering it and shaking it well. I take the cover off and strain it into four little tasting glasses. I turn and place them in front of the women, who look at the drink that turned pink because of the blackberries being shaken. "Let me know what you think."

I feel him before I see him. My heart rate picks up, and my stomach tightens. I turn to the side, watching him lean against the side of the bar where Brady was just standing. I watch the women pick their glasses up, and then one of them looks over at Charlie, and her eyes light up. I mean, I'm not surprised. He was always turning heads whenever we walked into the room. "He's a tall glass of water," the woman states, bringing the glass to her lips, and her friends laugh at her.

"I don't think that's how it goes." The blonde shakes her head. "You've been in this town for a day, and all of a sudden, you are country."

"It's been thirty-six hours," she fights back, "and I'm moving here."

I just stand here folding my arms over my chest. "You know, they don't have one drive-through coffee shop," the third woman says, "and I checked to order something last night and it said unavailable." She puts her hand on her chest, thinking about the horror of it. The four of them have driven down from New York to see, as they said, the South. I don't even know what that means but I do know if any of them think they are going to move here, it'll be over in three days... tops. She puts the glass to her lips and takes a sip of it. "Oh, this is good." She finishes it. "So refreshing and it's not strong." The rest of them take a sip and they all open their eyes.

"Oh, I'll have one like that." I nod at them as they all order one before turning and walking to where I was making the drink, which is right next to Charlie.

I look at him, taking a deep breath in. "I'll just be a minute," I say, rinsing out the shaker and not looking at him. I make four of the drinks and hand them to the women. "Cheers, ladies." I smile, trying to tell myself that it's going to be fine.

I walk back over to him, and now he's leaning on one elbow on the bar. "Hey," I say to him, "what can I get you?"

"Hey," he tosses back, "nothing. I was just coming to see how you are."

His words shock me so much I have to blink my eyes a couple of times. "Hey, Charlie," Brady says, coming up to his side, "do you need anything?"

"No." He shakes his head. "Just talking to Autumn." I'm not the only one shocked by this, so is Brady; it's no surprise to anyone that Charlie hates me. It's especially not a surprise to Brady, who ran interference when he showed up at my house two days after I moved out. A conversation I have yet to know what was said, nor did I want to know.

"Um," Brady starts, looking at me and then looking at Charlie. "Okay," he says, not sure about what is going on. He doesn't have a chance to say anything because someone raises their hand in the air to get his attention.

"It's okay," I reassure him, and he pushes off, but not before he gives Charlie a look of warning.

"Can I get a glass of water?" he asks me and I nod, turning to go get him a glass before filling it with water. "I'll be back." He pushes away and walks back to his friends. I let go of the breath I was holding, needing to move my feet.

I walk around the bar, heading to a couple of tables and asking them if everything is okay. I take a second to look at the almost full bar, and I can't help but feel a bit proud of it. Brady hands me the tray before walking to the back of the bar and going to the women. I make my way around the bar and try to act normal when I head to Charlie's table. He sits there with his back against the booth and his one ankle on his other knee. "Can I get you guys anything?"

"Just the bill," Emmett says, smiling at me.

"I'll take care of it," Charlie quickly offers, "you can get it next time."

"Thank you." He gets up, and I walk over to the bar area, grabbing a pad and heading back over to him with his bill in my hand.

"Here you go." I hand him the bill, and he takes it. Our fingers graze each other, and the back of my neck tingles. "You can go and pay Brady." I quickly turn around and head to the rest of the tables. They slowly trickle out, and when I look back, I see the group of four women are a little bit gone with the wind as they laugh at Brady saying something. I spot Charlie sitting on a stool at the far end of the bar.

I look at my watch, noting it's just past midnight, and the women are the only ones left. "Okay, last call," I announce, walking behind the bar, and the girls all groan.

"Where does one get a taxi?" The blonde leans into the bar, and I have to close my eyes.

"Where are you staying?" I ask, and she shrugs before reaching into her purse and taking out a card with a B&B address.

"Here."

Brady grabs the card before I do. "I can get them home." He looks at me.

"I'm sure you can," I say. "Why don't you close the tab and get them out of here so I can close up?" I walk toward Charlie. "It's last call."

"I'm good," he replies, picking up his glass of water and bringing it to his mouth. I grab the rag and walk around the bar to see Brady trying to wrangle the girls, who are all wearing stiletto heels as they wobble.

"Have fun." I hold up my hand as he props one of

them up while holding the door open.

I wipe down the table, the whole time my body knows that he's right around me. "You going to sit there all night?" I ask him as I walk to the next table. "I'm tired, and I want to close up."

"What can I do to help?" He walks toward the back of the bar, putting his glass in the bin.

"I don't need help," I tell him as I wipe down the tables.

"I'm staying until you're done," he declares, "so you might as well just tell me what needs to be done."

Our eyes lock on each other as I try to figure out what his game is. Like what the fuck is going on right now. This back-and-forth is giving me whiplash and I for one do not want to be in this game with him. His eyes penetrating into mine and I know that he's not going to give in. "Fine." I toss him the rag. "Clean down the tables."

"Got it." He walks past me and his smell fills my nose. All I can do is picture me on top of him, sitting on him on the swing, with my face buried in his neck. I walk around to the bar as I place the glasses in the dishwasher. "Tonight was good, right?" he asks from across the bar.

"It was," I confirm, "busier than we've been in a while." I make sure the bar is clean.

"Lots of new faces in town." He tries to prolong the conversation.

"Yeah," I agree. "I went to the bed-and-breakfasts on the outskirts of town, offering their clients a two-for-one discount on their first round of drinks." His eyebrows shoot up. "I didn't think it would be this successful, to be honest."

"That's a great idea," he admits, walking over to the sink and rinsing off his rag before hanging it over the sink. "Are you done?"

"I am." I nod as I walk toward him. "You can go out the front."

"I'm parked in the back." He looks down at me. "Right next to you, so why don't I walk you out?"

"Fine," I concede, turning and walking to the back of the bar, turning off the lights, leaving us in the dark before I push through the swinging door and head into the distillery part of the building. Going to the office, I grab my bag before walking out. The whole time he's beside me, my body itching for his touch, but knowing the last thing I need is to fall under his spell. I flip off the lights before arming the alarm and then stepping out. He stands by my back as I lock the door, and when I think he's going to leave my side to go to his truck, he shocks me even more by walking me to my car. "Um," I mumble, not sure what else to say. "Thank you." I finally look up at him as he stands there way too close to me, so close if I lifted my hands, I would be able to feel his chest under his T-shirt. I would be able to see the bite mark I left on him the last couple of times we were together, and I suddenly wonder if it's still there. "For—"

He takes a step closer to me, and I stop talking because I can only watch him bend his head. I can't even move; my body is still as his head covers the light from the moon, and he moves his head to the side of my face, kissing my cheek. "You look good tonight, Autumn," he says softly in my ear. "I'll see you tomorrow." He kisses my cheek one more time before he steps back and opens my door for me to get in. I quickly get into the car, and when I turn back to look at him, all he says is, "Drive safe." Then the door is shut in my face.

I watch him in the rearview mirror walk around to his truck, my heart lurching, my hands holding the steering wheel while my head spins. "What the hell is happening?"

Twenty-One

I GET IN my truck and look over at her sitting in her car. Her eyes stare straight ahead while her hands grip the steering wheel. I wait in my truck for her to snap out of it, and all I can see is her shaking her head and mumbling something to herself before she backs up and makes her way home.

I pull out of the parking lot, and instead of going home, I follow her to make sure she gets home. She pulls into her driveway, and I park outside on the street. She gets out of her car and holds on to the door while she looks over at me. I put the truck in park before I get out and leave it running, walking around to her. "Are you okay?"

"What the hell are you doing?" She folds her arms over her chest.

"I'm making sure you get home safe." I stop in front of her and look down at her. The breeze makes her hair fly onto her face. My hand comes up with hers as I tuck it behind her ear, wanting to bend down and kiss her lips but also knowing I haven't earned this yet. From now on, the only kiss I'm taking from her is when she wants to give it to me. It's also not going to be a hate-fucking kiss.

"What game are you playing, Charlie?" I step into her, my hands going to her hips.

"I'm not playing a game," I tell her. "I'm trying to make up."

"For being a dick and an asshole?" she questions, and I can't help but chuckle.

"That's putting it lightly," I say softly. "I'm so sorry. I want to think of other words to say, but there isn't anything I can say that will erase the hell that I brought down on you." One of my hands goes up to touch her face. "There is not enough time on this earth that can make up for it, but I'm going to try to show you that I am."

"You don't have to show me anything. We can just avoid each other." The thought alone makes me angry. "Maybe if we do run into each other, we can be civil with each other."

I'm not going to lay out that we won't be avoiding each other, and I've decided quite the contrary to that statement. So instead, I bend down and kiss her cheek. "Okay, Autumn." My hand drops from her face. "Now get inside so I can go home." She stares at me for a second more before she steps away from her car door and slams it shut, turning to walk up the steps. As I watch her strut, my cock stirs in my jeans. "And don't let me catch you outside on that swing."

She turns around. "I've been just fine for the past eight years, Charlie." She clenches her teeth. "I think I'll be good."

"Should I turn off my truck and meet you on the swing, then?" I ask her, and she doesn't answer me. Instead, she just storms up her steps and slams her front door.

I turn and head to my truck, turning it off before walking around the house, up the steps, and sitting on the swing. She comes out five minutes later and groans when she sees me. "Can you just go away?" She's changed out of her jean shorts to one of her white tank tops and her tight light-gray sleep shorts. A long sweater hangs open, and she wraps it around her middle when she sees me.

"Not until you are in your bed," I say, and I want to pull her to me and have her sit on top of me so we can make out. Fuck, I've never wanted to kiss someone so badly in my life, which makes me feel a little guilty. "You going to come over here and sit with me, or are you going to go to bed?"

"I'm going to ask you to leave, then I'm going to sit on the swing and decompress."

I swallow down the words that want to come out, which are *I have a better idea to make you decompress*, but instead, I move over on the swing, and she comes over and sits next to me. "Honestly, Charlie." She looks over at me, and I put my hand on the back of the swing. "I don't have the energy to fight with you. I'm mentally exhausted." She sounds tired, and I want to kick myself because I'm probably one of the reasons she's so tired.

"I don't want to fight with you," I say, my thumb rubbing her shoulder. "I just want to make sure you're okay." I turn to look ahead at the darkness of the night. I don't know how long we sit on the swing, neither of us saying anything, when I look over and see her closing her eyes. "If you want, I can carry you inside." I get up, and she turns to look at me, her eyes filled with sleep.

"I'm good." She gets up, taking a step toward the door. "Good night." She turns and looks at me over her shoulder.

"I'll just stay here a while to make sure," I state as she opens the storm door, "unless you want me to come and lie down in bed with you?" I know if I go into that house, I'm not going to be able to keep my hands off her. I know the minute I get into her bed, I'll want to sink into her. Even though it'll be amazing, I want more than that. I also know we are both not ready for whatever it is that this is going to be. "Lock up," I say as she walks inside, and I hear the lock click. I sit here and wait thirty minutes, and when she doesn't come out, I get up and make my way to my house. Sliding into bed and laying my head on the pillow, I don't expect sleep to come and take me as fast as it does. When the alarm rings in the morning, I reach over, finding the bed empty but wishing I was waking up with her.

Instead, I'm in the middle of the bed, thinking about her. I get up and look out at the sun coming up, making the sky look like it's pink. I step into the shower, my hand gripping my cock as I think about her. It takes me no time before I'm moaning out her name in a release. I get dressed in jeans and a white T-shirt before grabbing my mug of coffee and heading out to the barn. Emmett gets there at the same time as I step into the barn, and he stops in his tracks.

"You're here," he says, and I just stare at him.

"Where else am I supposed to be?" I bring the cup of coffee to my lips.

"It's just that the past couple of days you're usually getting back home at this time." I raise my eyebrows.

"You keeping track of me?"

"It's hard not to see you coming back when you walk through a fenced area and head to the house." He points at the door that shows where I would walk by. "Slinking home with your head hanging forward, regretting whatever or whoever you just did."

"No regrets," I say. "At least not lately."

"Is that so?" he asks me, walking over to the coffee maker and starting the coffee. "That's interesting."

"Nothing about it is interesting," I inform him, "and it's also none of your damn business."

"You literally just made it my business by answering my questions." He chuckles as he pours himself a cup of steaming coffee.

"Are we going to be gossiping all day long?" I ask, and he shrugs.

"It's Saturday, so not much to do on the weekend. We can gossip."

"How about we get to work?" I turn on my heel and walk to the stall that's become my habit of checking on first thing in the morning. "Good morning, beautiful girl." She is lying on her side. "Aren't we being lazy this morning?" I put the mug down on the floor before opening the stall and going to pet her. "Did you have a good night?" I ask her. "I did." I walk over to grab her pail of water, walking out with it and heading over to get some fresh water.

I muck her stall before taking the hose to wash some of it out when I hear my name being paged. "Charlie, Charlie." Emmett's voice fills the barn and the outside of the barn. "You have someone here for you." Instead of clicking disconnect, I hear him slam down the phone.

I walk out of the stall, putting my gloves in my back pocket and seeing Emmett standing there with a man. "What's up?" I ask him. The guy turns around, and I see it's the man from the bar.

"You got someone who would like a word," Emmett says, standing next to me.

"Hi, Mr. Barnes," he greets, "my name is Darren Trowel." He reaches out his hand to give me a business card, and I look down at it. "I'm a reporter for a New York magazine called *The Future and the Past.*" I look back up at him. "We are doing a special article on the Cartwright accident, and I'd love to ask you some questions about it."

"Sure," I say, surprising Emmett, who just looks over at me. "Why don't you come to my office?" I turn and walk toward my office. He follows me in there, and I can see the snide smile on his face.

I walk around my desk, tossing the card on top of it, as he takes a seat in the chair. "What exactly is this article about?" I pull out my chair and sit down.

"Well, Mr. Barnes," he starts, "we're doing a follow-up, sort of a 'where are they now' piece." I don't say anything. I just wait for him to talk. "How the accident changed your life. What hardships came from it. We also would like to know its fallout with Autumn Thatcher." I cross my hands. "There was speculation that she lied under oath. We were wondering about the events that led up to the crash. Things that haven't really been discussed."

"Kind of hard to lie about an autopsy that was performed twice, don't you think?" I ask him, trying to keep my anger in check and not freak out and give him anything. "They did a private one, and we were lucky that the coroner never flushed out the blood that was collected at the morgue when he was brought in. Then the court found out about the discrepancy and requested another one."

"Right," he says, ignoring my point. "Do you think she did it as a vendetta against the Cartwrights?"

"Is this a piece about how our lives are since then or is this a piece about how wrong the Cartwrights were?" I ask him the question, waiting to see what he says. His body gets tight for a minute, and then he relaxes into it.

"We are just trying to get a different angle of the story," he explains, and my skin prickles at the back of my neck. A bad vibe is just rolling off him, and something definitely feels off about him.

"I'll tell you what, Mr. Trowel." I pick up his card. "How about you email me the questions you want to ask me, and I'll have my attorney look at them, and then I'll get back to you." Disappointment registers all over his face as I put the card down and start to get up.

"I would think that with everything Ms. Thatcher did to you, you would be willing to give your side of the story."

"Ms. Thatcher wasn't the one driving the truck," I remind him, my teeth clenched together tight. "I'll look forward to hearing from you." I hold out my hand, and he shakes it before walking out of the office and down the hallway to the front door. I stare out the window at him getting into his rental car, and only when he's out of the parking lot do I take the phone out of my pocket and scroll down to the number I'm looking for.

He answers after half a ring. "Charlie," he says and I can see the smile fill his face.

"Hey, Pops," I reply, and he must sense that my voice is tight. My grandfather is Casey Barnes, who owns CBS Corporation, which is one of the top security companies in the world, with contracts with the military that are top secret.

"What's up, big man?" he asks, and I turn and walk back to my desk.

"Someone came in here," I state, and I know right away the smile on his face is gone. "A reporter, Darren Trowel," I read his name off the card.

"What did he want?" he asks, and I sit back in my chair.

"He's doing a follow-up about the accident."

"What?" he hisses out. "Did he ask you questions?"

"Oh yeah, but the questions were more an accusation on Autumn and if she had a vendetta." My voice gets tight. "It was fucking strange, and I did not get a good feeling about this article."

"Send me his contact information, and I'll run a check on him." He gives me a deep sigh. "But from what you said, I don't like it."

"That would make two of us."

"Has he spoken to anyone else?" he asks, and my stomach burns at the memory.

"Yeah, he went to talk to Autumn," I say, "but Brady put him out on his ass, and the next time, she told him to leave."

"Persistent," he notes. "Let me see what I can find."

"Sounds good." I take a picture of the business card and send it to him via text.

"You sound different," he immediately says, and I shake my head, chuckling.

"I sound the same." I take a deep breath in.

"No, you sound... I don't know how to explain it."

"Well, I have work to do." I don't want to get into it right now. "Let me know what you find."

"You got it. When are you going to come and visit Grandma and Grandpa?" He mentions my great-grandparents.

"I'll come soon. Got to go. I love you," I say before I hang up the phone on him.

I'm putting my phone in my pocket when it pings with a text, and I can't help but laugh.

Pops: *You know that I can find out things, right?*

I answer him right away.

Me: I don't have anything to hide.

I put the phone back in my pocket and walk out toward the barn. I don't have anything to hide, but I also have something I want to keep to myself. At least for now.

Twenty-Two

AUTUMN

THE SUN HITS my face, making my eyes flutter open and then quickly close for a couple of seconds before I blink them open again. I sink more into the bed as I look out the window at the blue sky, spotting a couple of birds soaring high in the sky before disappearing from view. I stretch my hands out from under the covers before I toss the blanket off me, lying still for a couple of seconds before I get out of bed. Sleep's still in my eyes as my body moves slowly toward the end of the bed where I grab the sweater. My brain screaming for coffee makes me walk to the kitchen and start the process. Once the coffee is brewing, I take a couple of steps over to the back door and step out into the warm air. I walk over to the swing. Sitting down and curling my feet under me, I think about the past couple of days and how amazing work has been.

Yesterday, the bar was practically full. Tables filling

up from all the promos I've been doing. The men who were in the other night came back with about forty men from their trade show and all requested the sample menu, which then led to a couple of them buying bottles to ship home. Something I didn't even think about doing but now is at the top of my to-do list tomorrow when I get back in. By the end of the night, my feet were aching in the best way, and I had a smile on my face from ear to ear when I saw how much we made. It wasn't mammoth, but it was something to help, and if every single day there is a little more and more, I could see the light at the end of the tunnel. That as well as how every day there were a few more smiles that came my way than scowls. I mean, the scowls will always be there, but now it is six scowls to four smiles. I'm calling this a win, considering it was zero for ten from shortly after the accident to when I got back home.

The only thing that kept me on pins and needles all night was looking at the door every other minute, expecting Charlie to walk in. But he never came in. Even when I was sitting on the swing that night, my eyes would stare into the forest looking for movement, but again he never showed up. I should be happy that he's moved on and isn't out to make my life hell, but something nagged at me. Especially since the night before he stayed to clean up with me and then drove home to make sure I was okay. It was a little glimpse of the old Charlie. The Charlie who I always told Jennifer she was lucky she had. The Charlie who oozed sex appeal without even trying. The Charlie I would call first because I knew he would answer and be there for me.

I'm almost done with my coffee when I see him walking out of the forest. He's staring straight ahead, wearing jeans and a white T-shirt, his hair longer than I've ever seen him wear it. Knowing how soft and silky it feels under my hand makes my fingers tingly. His eyes are on me the whole time he makes it across the yard. "Hey," he says when he gets close enough, "I was hoping you would be up."

"Is that so?" I try to get my heart rate to return to normal, but whenever he's around me lately, it's like he's the air I need to breathe, which makes me hate myself a little bit more.

"I was wondering if you were busy." He smirks at me, the Charlie smirk that you always want to see.

"I'm on my way to go to lunch with the pope," I retort. He throws his head back and laughs. A full-on laugh I haven't heard since that fateful night. A sound I didn't know I missed, yet now that I heard it, I want to hear it again. The lightness in his eyes is mesmerizing as he stares at me.

"Well, if I could maybe persuade you not to go to lunch with the pope, there is someone I want you to meet." All I can do is stare at him; my eyebrows pinched in confusion. "Why don't you get changed?"

"Who am I meeting?" I ask, standing up and walking over to the steps. With him on the step below, we are face-to-face. It would take nothing for me to wrap my arms around his neck and lean into him and take the kiss I want, but know I can't ever get.

"There is this horse we got." The minute he says the words, I can't help that my face beams as my eyes go big. "I'm assuming you are okay with that?"

"I mean, it isn't the pope," I joke with him, "but I think he can take a rain check. I heard he's a bit busy on Sunday anyway."

He puts his hands on my hips, and I stop breathing. "If he gets to spend time with you, I bet he'll take what he can," he says softly, his eyes going from mine to my lips. My mouth opens a bit as the tip of my tongue comes out to run across my lower lip. Both of us just stand here until he closes his eyes for a second, then opens them back up. The hunger and need are still in them, but it's a different look than he's given me. "Go get changed." His hands squeeze my hips. "I'll wait for you here."

"Okay." I turn around and head inside, putting my mug in the sink before walking to my bedroom and taking off my sweater. I grab a pair of blue jeans and a sleeveless black high-neck T-shirt, tucking it in the front, before brushing my hair and brushing my teeth. Putting on my old worn boots, I walk out and see him sitting on the swing. His arm is outstretched across the back, and all I can think of is cuddling up in his arms, which is silly since I've never cuddled with him. Sure, after we fucked it out and we turned on our side, neither of us wanting to face the other, I would always wake in his arms.

His head turns to me. "You look nice," he compliments, getting up from the swing. "You ready?"

"As ready as I'm going to be." I put my phone in my back pocket as I follow him down the steps toward the forest.

"Do you work today?" he asks as we walk over to his barn.

"Yeah, I have to be there at five."

"I'll make sure to get you fed and back by then," he assures me, his hand grazing mine as we walk, his index finger hooking onto mine. The heat from his hand fills me as we step out of the forest and into the clearing, heading toward the red barn.

I stop walking when I see the big house across the way. I put my hand up over my eyes to see it clearly. "That wasn't here the last time."

"No." He shakes his head. "We built it a couple of years ago. It's where I live now." My stomach lurches as I look at the house, shocked that he moved. "I'll give you a tour," he mumbles as we walk into the side barn, and I follow him down the concrete hallway to a stall. "Hey there, girl," he says softly. "This is Goldilocks," he tells me before turning back to talk to the horse. "Brought you a friend." He holds up his hand, and I see the most beautiful horse I've ever seen. She's a light blond with a white mark down the front of her forehead. He turns to me. "I told her about you." My body moves back a touch as he talks to her and then looks back at me. "She's a bit skittish," he cautions, "but once she trusts you, she's fine."

I step to his side. "Hi there," I say softly, and he reaches for my hand and lifts it with his.

"She won't hurt you," he says as she makes a little noise and takes a step back.

"I won't hurt you," I assure her, and she looks in my eyes, almost to my soul. "I promise." She takes a step to our hands.

"Do you want to take her out?" he asks, and I just smile up at him.

"Will she let me?" I ask.

"Only way we will find out is if we try," he states, and I can't contain my excitement as he opens the stall and walks in to grab her bridle. I see she already has a saddle on and everything.

"I haven't ridden in over eight years," I admit as we walk out with the horse next to him.

"It's just like a bike," he says, and when we are in the fenced area, he holds out his hand for me. I put my hand in his as I put my foot in the stirrup and then get up on her as I hear him. "You be good with her," he tells the horse. "She's special." My chest tightens at his words as he looks up at me.

"I'm going to go get my horse, and we can go out on the trail." I nod as he turns and jogs back to the stable.

"We're going to be just fine. I'm scared too," I admit, and she bends her neck to eat some of the grass.

A minute later, he's walking out with a brown horse, stopping and getting on it with ease as he trots over to us. "You two look good," he says, and I just smile. "Let's go that way." He points to the side as we follow him.

"How are things?" he asks once we start on the trail.

"That's a loaded question, Charlie Barnes." I try to make a joke of it. "How are things with me?" I shrug. "I've had better days," I say softly, "but then again, I've had worse days." I swallow down, knowing he knows what I mean.

"How are things with the bar and stuff?"

"I'm not sure," I answer him honestly. Because even though it's been better, is it good enough? "I'm hoping we can crawl out of the hole. But I'm not sure."

"What are you talking about?" he asks, and I look over at him.

"Don't pretend you don't know," I bark out, and his head snaps over to look at me.

"I can honestly say I have no idea what the fuck you are saying." His voice is tight.

"We are practically bankrupt," I start. "My father is dying, and the only thing I want to do is make sure he knows that everything is going to be okay."

"He's dying?" he says in a whisper.

"It's why I came back to town," I say, looking ahead, blinking away the tears that threaten. "No matter how bad I thought it was going to be, it's a million times worse." I see him hanging his head. "And now I'm just trying to get things going again."

"I'm sorry, I can't imagine how you feel." I just nod, the lump in my throat is the size of a softball. "What do you mean, you guys are almost bankrupt?"

"Cartwright," I say the name I wish I never had to say again. "Apparently, their reach is long-lasting. We lost our distribution, and the bar is bringing in no money. We haven't produced anything since I've been back, and I've been coming up with ideas on how to get people in the door."

"How?" he asks, and I say the ideas I've come up with, including the ones of having the out-of-towners buy some bottles from us. "If anyone can turn it around, it's you."

"It's also my fault that all of this is happening," I admit. "If I would have just shut my mouth."

"Then the families who suffered wouldn't get the justice that they deserved, and it would all be a lie."

"Nothing good came from that day in court," I remind him, "not one thing."

"I'm sorry," he says softly, and I look over at him, "more than you will ever know. More than I can ever explain."

I swallow down the lump in my throat. "The only thing that matters is making sure my father knows we are okay. The only thing I want is for him to know that, whatever happens, the business is going to be okay and we are going to be fine." The tear falls. "And I'm going to stay until then."

"Then what?" He doesn't look at me while he asks the question.

"Then I go back to my place, I guess." He stops his horse from walking, so Goldilocks also stops.

"This is your home." He looks up at me.

"I don't know where my home is," I admit. "Maybe in all of this I'm going to find my home."

"Your home is right here," he repeats, "right fucking here."

"Once upon a time, I thought it was." I pick my hand up and wipe away the tear. "I'm not so sure anymore."

"I am," he declares, his shoulders back. "I'm not sure of a lot of things these days." His voice comes out shaky. My body gets tight waiting for the rest of his statement, except it's nothing that I thought it would be. The words that come out of his mouth send me jumping off a cliff, but this time, there is water there to catch me falling and not just an empty black hole. "But I do know that this is where you belong."

Twenty-Three

CHARLIE

SHE LOOKS OVER at me with her eyes filled with tears, and it makes me angry. Angry that she hurts so much. Angry I was one of those people who made her cry. Angry because I can't do shit about it until she gives me a hint that she wants me to do something about it.

We ride the horses all day long, and when we finally get back to the barn, it's after four in the afternoon. "What a day." She dismounts the horse and walks over to the side as she pets her neck. "You were so good." She puts her forehead against her neck. "The best."

"Let me get them settled, and I'll feed you," I say, and she shakes her head.

"I have to get going, get ready for work. Shower. I'll get something on the way." I try not to be disappointed that she's leaving. But I am. I wasn't ready for the day to end.

"Okay, let me put them away, and I'll walk you back

home." I start to walk to the barn.

"That's okay, it's a ten-minute walk."

"I said I'm walking you back home," I say, trying to be cool about it, but failing when her eyebrows shoot up. "Just to make sure you are okay."

"This going to go faster if I agree?" she asks, and I nod. "Then hurry up. I've already taken up all your time, and I don't want you to waste any more time with me."

"Let's get one thing straight," I say, grabbing the reins from her. "I was exactly where I wanted to be today."

"Oh." She looks up at me, her lips parted, and I swear I can taste the kiss.

"Exactly, it was what I wanted to do with my time. And now I want to put the horses away, get them some water, and then I'm going to walk you home." I don't wait for her to say anything to me as I walk into the barn and stop when I see a couple of the ranch hands there with Emmett. "What are you doing here?"

"Just going over a couple of things," Emmett replies. "Do you want me to take care of them for you?" He motions with his head toward the two horses.

"Yeah, I'll be back in thirty minutes."

"Take your time," he says, looking over my shoulder at Autumn. "Be good."

"Yeah." I'm irritated by his comment. I walk out and see her standing there looking at my house. "You sure you don't want to have something to eat?" I ask, and she shakes her head. "I have a shower you could use."

"Wait?" She turns to me. "You have a shower in your house?" She bites her lower lip. "You fancy." She chuckles at her own joke, and I grab her around her neck, just like I used to do way back when. But this time it's different because I don't let her go. My hand hangs off her shoulder as we walk to her house. I stop at the bottom of her steps as she walks up them. "Thanks for today. It's one of the best days I've had in a while," she admits and then looks down at her feet as she twirls her fingers nervously.

I walk up the steps to her, my hands reaching up and holding her face in mine. "There are going to be more of those." My thumbs rub her cheeks, and I lean down, my lips aching to be on hers, but I move my head to the side to kiss her cheek above my hand. "I'll make sure of it."

She doesn't say anything. She just nods at me before turning around and walking into her house. I stand here for a second before turning and heading home. Emmett isn't there when I get back, but the horses are taken care of, so I head to my house and step in my own shower. I slide on a pair of jeans and a fresh T-shirt before grabbing a steak from the fridge and walking over to start the grill. Sitting at the island, as I eat the steak and salad I threw together, it dawns on me that I hate eating alone. Have I always hated eating alone, and I've just realized it, or have I started to hate it now since she's been back?

I try to think of the last time I went to see Jennifer as I look around the house, getting up and cleaning up a couple of things—putting things away, checking my mail, and doing shit I don't want to be doing but doing it so I don't go to the bar. An hour later, I finally give in and head to the bar instead of staying away from her. I walk over there, and when I step in, I see that it's half full, and for a Sunday, that's a great turnout. I walk over to the bar and sit down. She glances over from the group of men she is serving, and she looks surprised to see me. I can't wait for the day when she's expecting me to show up and not that me showing up throws her off. "Hey." She tosses a coaster in front of me. "This is a surprise," she admits.

"Don't know why." I tap the bar top. "I'll have a soda water."

She nods. "You got it." She walks over and fills my glass, bringing it over. "On the house." She laughs as she looks around. "I'll be back. I sent Brady home, so I'm riding solo."

"You need help?" I ask, and she shakes her head. "Of course not," I mumble as she walks away. Slowly, people start paying their tabs. I see it's close to eight and wonder if she'll drive me home and then come in with me.

I'm thinking this when the stool beside me is pulled out, and when I look over, my mouth hits the floor. "Well, I'll be—" I say, and the man sits down beside me and looks over at me. His eyes look like he's lived ten lifetimes. "—damned."

He chuckles, his hair longer in the back at the nape of his neck and on the top. "Aren't you a sight for sore eyes?"

"What can I get you?" Autumn says and then stops when she sees who it is. "Brock?" she says his name in a whisper. From her reaction, I'm guessing this is the first time they have come face-to-face.

"Saw you were back in town. Then heard you were

staying back in town," he says, putting his hands on the bar top. His hand looks rough, his knuckles look like they are healing from being torn to shreds, his fingers tainted with grease, which means he probably just came from his shop down the street, a shop he inherited from his father. "Wanted to see if the rumor was true."

"It's me," she says, putting her hands on top of the bar stretched out to her sides, "in the flesh. Can I get you something to drink?"

"I'll have what he's having." He motions toward me with his head, so Autumn takes off and comes back and puts the glass down in front of him.

He picks it up and holds it up. "To old times." He clicks my glass with his before taking a sip and then grimaces. "There is no alcohol in this." We both laugh at him. "What is this?"

"Soda water," I say, and he looks at the glass like it's the most disgusting thing he's ever tasted in his life.

"Why?" He shakes his head, and Autumn walks to the end of the bar and pours him some whiskey in a small tumbler before handing it to him. "Now, this is a color I like." He takes a sip and then sighs. "Tastes like heaven." He looks over at Autumn. "So what's new?"

"Same old, same old," she says, her answer guarded. I would imagine she's still pissed at him for lying when the accident happened. He sided with the Cartwrights. Why? We had no idea; I didn't care enough at the time to question it. After the accident, it seemed the four of us all went our separate ways. All four of us with our own journeys to go through to heal. Everleigh was here one day, and then when the truth came out, she was gone. From the rumors around, Brock let her go and quickly moved on with someone else, but it was over before the ink was dry on the marriage license, the only thing left is their eight-year-old daughter, Saige. "What about you?"

"Same old, same old." He looks in the glass, bringing it to his lips and taking another sip. "You look good." I glare at him, wondering where he is going with this. He finishes the rest of the whiskey, getting up, and taking a twenty out of his pocket and putting it on the bar. "I guess I'll see you around," he says, then slaps my shoulder. "Fuck, it's good to see you." He squeezes me before turning and walking out of the place.

"Eight years later," she says, her voice soft, "and we are all still living with the demons from that night." She takes a deep breath in. "I hate him."

"Brock?" I ask, and she shakes her head.

"No." She looks at me. "He did what he did for a reason. One that is his own. The only one who was to blame for that night is Waylon, yet he's the only one who seems to have escaped it all." She grabs a rag from the sink. "Coward until the end."

She stays silent for the rest of the night, her mind elsewhere, and when she closes the bar, I kiss her cheek and turn to walk toward my house. I watch her drive out of the parking lot before I turn and make my way home, walking straight up the back steps and into the house.

The next day, I get up and wonder what she is doing all day, and finally, right before dinner, I make my way over to the bar. I'm rounding the corner when I catch her walking out, and she shakes her head while smiling. Something in me settles, and I don't know what it is. All I know is that all day I felt like I was on pins and needles, and now, seeing her, it's like it's all gone away. "Hey," I say, and she turns her head my way. She's wearing a skirt with flowers on it and a white crop T-shirt that stops right above her waist, showing just a touch of that skin I vowed I would spend the night worshipping if I got another chance with her.

"Hi," she says, her voice breathless.

"Where are you going?" I ask as we stand in front of the door to the bar, and I see there is a slew of people.

"Brady told me to go home," she mumbles, "even though he's swamped, and I'm going to leave just to teach him a lesson."

"Good," I say. "Have dinner with me?"

She looks at me and then looks down. She does that when she's nervous. "I don't think that's a good idea." Her voice is soft as she looks around.

"Why not?" The question comes out harsher than I want it to.

Her eyes sweep the street again. "Well," she hesitates, and my stomach gets tight as she avoids my eyes.

"Are you dating that guy?" I take a step closer to her, my heart beating out of my chest. I look down at her, wanting to kiss her more than I've ever wanted anything in my whole life, but also knowing that I have to gain her trust. I vowed I was only going to kiss her if she wanted me to kiss her, and that is what I'm going to do, even if it kills me.

"No," she quickly answers me, "Bryan and I are just friends." Even the name makes me want to ball my hands into fists and punch a tree.

"We're going for dinner," I say, not giving her a chance to refuse while I grab her by the elbow and proceed to walk to D'amores restaurant.

I pull open the door, and the aroma of fresh-baked bread hits you right away. The tables are all covered with white linen tablecloths, and the servers wear tuxes. It's a fancy place, and the two of us look like we are dressed to go to a diner and not here. "Can I help you?" the hostess asks.

"A table for two, please," I say, putting my hand on the base of Autumn's back when she grabs two menus and motions for us to follow her. A server is beside the table, pulling out a chair for her to sit in when we arrive.

"Thank you," she says softly to the server and gives him a shy smile as I sit in the chair in front of her.

The hostess hands us each our menu and then places the wine menu on the side of my plate. "Would you like still or sparkling water?" the server asks us.

"I'll have sparkling," I reply, knowing she won't answer first.

"I'll have the same." She looks up at him before taking a look around the room. I can literally hear the whispers from the people around us.

I ignore them as I open my menu and look over the specials. "The pasta is homemade," I inform her, and when I look up, I see that she's pale. "Relax," I say, and she just stares at me.

"I don't know if I can do this," she whispers softly, and I reach out my hand and put it on hers, making sure more people stare and whisper, also not giving one fuck about who is pointing and who is whispering.

"You can do this." I smile at her. "You can do anything." She has to be quite honestly the strongest woman I've ever met.

"I'm not sure about that." She opens the menu and avoids looking around.

"Hey," I say. She looks up at me and has the biggest tears brimming the bottoms of her lids, and I want to get up and pitch my table across the room. "We'll go."

"No," she mouths. "If I do that, they win. Everyone wins."

I couldn't be prouder of her. "Then we eat, and I'll take you home, and we can have dessert at my house." I don't mean it like that, and the minute I hear the words, I want to kick myself, but then I see her eyes gloss over in lust, and I just smirk at her. "I didn't mean it like that, but with the way your face just changed, you can take it however you want."

She silently giggles, bringing her hand to her mouth as she looks at the menu. I order a plate of pasta and she does also. "Just focus on me," I say when she looks like she's about to crawl out of her skin. "Focus on me and nothing else."

"Easier said than done." She grabs a piece of fresh-baked bread when it arrives and puts butter on it. The whispers slowly die down like I knew they would. A couple of people even stop and say hello to us on their way to their table, which makes her feel a little bit more at ease.

I hurry through dinner, knowing this is probably killing her but also knowing she did nothing wrong. I pay the bill, and then I'm about to slide my hand in hers when we walk out. I head back to her car when she stops in her tracks. My eyes go from her face that had a soft smile on it to whatever she is looking at that made her stop.

The Cartwrights are walking down the street. Mr. and Mrs. Cartwright, heads held high, arm in arm as they walk, followed by their son, Winston, and his wife, Harmony. They look around, and the minute they set their eyes on Autumn, their faces twist into a sneer.

"Jesus Christ," Winston hisses from behind his parents, "I thought she would be gone by now."

"Winston," Harmony chastises from beside him, avoiding looking at us.

"Well, what do we have here?" Mr. Cartwright says, looking at Autumn and then back at me. "Didn't think we'd find you hanging around with scum."

"I'd watch your mouth if I was you." I step in front of her to block them from even looking at her. "Only scum I see standing on the street are the three people in front of me." My arms cross over my chest. "The ones who live in glass houses." I can feel her shaking behind me. "The ones who still think their shit doesn't stink, but the minute they walk into the room, it reeks of shit."

"Watch your fucking mouth." Winston steps before his father to stand in front of me, and I have to look down at him.

"You think you scare me?" I stare into the eyes that are exactly like his father's and his brother's and laugh bitterly. "I was friends with a devil in sheep's clothing and didn't know." He grinds his teeth. "But you guys knew"—I point at him—"knew that he was a no-good piece of—"

"Is that any way to speak of the dead?" Mrs. Cartwright holds a hand to her throat.

"Is the way you just spoke to Autumn any way to speak to a woman who was the victim of your son?" I hiss at them, wanting Winston to put his hands on me, secretly begging him to do it so I can beat the ever-loving shit out of him. I stare at Winston. "You guys are a joke." I turn and look at Autumn, who is trying to breathe, but knowing she's about to lose it and doesn't want to do it in front of them. "Let's go." I grab her hand in mine as I shield her and walk away from them, stopping next to Mr. Cartwright. My voice goes very low so only he can hear me. "And if I find out that you pull any more shit on her, you'll have to deal with me and my family." I smile. "And between you and me, I would love nothing more than to drag your name through the mud." He turns his eyes toward me. "Again." I walk away with her hand in mine and her head looking down at the ground. "Don't do it," I say. "Don't give them the satisfaction." She looks at me, and I hold out my hand. "Keys."

She lets go of my hand to reach into her purse and hands me the keys as she gets into the car. I pull out of the parking lot, going in the opposite direction of her house. She looks over at me. "Where are we going?"

I know I should take her home. I know she should go back to the place she feels safest, but there is somewhere else that I want her to feel safe in. "My house."

Twenty-Four

"MY HOUSE," HE says, and I turn my head forward, watching the street, holding on to my purse in my lap as if my life depends on it. My whole body feels like I've been run over. My day started out so fucking good, better than good. It had been such a long time since I had gone riding, and then doing it again with Goldilocks was therapeutic in a way. It was strange to describe, then I went from the best day to sitting down with Charlie at dinner. In. Front. Of. The. Whole. Town. I thought I was going to throw up the whole time. However, even though I didn't want to crawl out of my skin by the end of the meal, I still wanted to get the fuck out of there.

Nothing, and I mean nothing, could have prepared me for running face-to-face into the Cartwrights. I was also unprepared for Charlie to handle it the way he did. The last thing I wanted was for him to be swept up in this. I look over at him, seeing him gripping the steering wheel with both hands, so tight that his fingers are white. He keeps wringing the steering wheel, while his jaw is tight, as if he's biting down on his teeth. "Are you okay?" I ask softly, and all he does is shake his head.

I don't say anything as he pulls up to his house, a house that is bigger than I ever imagined him having but also fitting for him. The lights on in the front show you the four columns that hold up the porch covering in the front. A huge double-wide door with a window is set in the middle, with the same windows on each side. Two rocking chairs are on the left side and then on the right side is a little sitting area. Lights are on in the right-hand side of the house while the left-hand side is dark.

He turns off the car and gets out. My hand goes out to open my own door, and I step out. Charlie waits for me at the front of the car, which he parked right next to his truck. He reaches for my hand, his fingers intertwining with mine as he walks up the two steps to the porch and to his front door. Placing his finger on the handle, the sound of the lock opening makes him turn the handle, and he steps in first. "Welcome to my home."

I take a step into his home, and I turn to him. "Charlie," I say his name, "I'm so sorry."

He slams the door, and I jump at the sound. "What the fuck are you apologizing for?" He looks like he's about to throw something.

"You shouldn't have—"

"I shouldn't have what?" He takes a step toward me. "I shouldn't have protected you?" He doesn't wait for me to answer him. "I shouldn't have put them in their place?" He grabs one of my hips as I swallow down a lump, but I can't say anything. "I should have punched him in the fucking face is what I should have done." His voice is low and tight. "That is what I should have done."

"They aren't worth it," I whisper. "It's not worth it." I don't want anyone else to be at the mercy of the Cartwrights, and even though Charlie and I have created a truce, it doesn't mean I want him wrapped up in this.

"It's not worth it," he agrees, stepping even closer to me, "but you are worth it." His hand squeezes my hip. "Do you want a tour?" he asks, and I look up at him, wanting to thank him for dinner and for what he did with the Cartwrights before getting the fuck out of here. I don't want to see where he lives. I don't want to see any of this because I fear that I'll want to know more and shouldn't want to. His eyes never leave mine. "This is the foyer, as my grandmother calls it." He smiles, the tightness of a minute ago gone, his features relaxed. "That's the dining room I never use." He points over his shoulder, and I move to the side to look at the big, long table with dark chairs. "And that's the office." He motions in front of me with his chin. "Why I have an office in here I have no idea, but I wasn't part of the floor plan process."

I can't help but laugh at him as he softly takes my purse out of my hand and places it right next to the door before resuming the tour. "That leads to upstairs, where there is a game room and three other bedrooms." He points at the staircase against the wall next to the office before sliding his hand into mine again as he walks slowly past the staircase toward the archway that leads to a hallway that goes right and left. "This is butler something," he says. "Again, I've never used it." Then he steps into the living room with a vaulted ceiling. The room feels so big yet so cozy. The vast kitchen has cream-colored cabinets and a massive island with a light brown countertop and cream-colored stools, making it not stuffy. The stainless-steel appliances are top-notch, including the eight-burner stove and the double-wide industrial fridge. "This room is the one I use the most," he admits. "Well, this and the bedroom." I walk into the room and look over at the living room with the massive L-shaped couch. It's so deep three people could lie down next to each other and be comfortable. "Do you want something to drink?" he asks. "I could make you a tea."

"You make tea?" I ask, trying not to make it a big deal that I'm standing in his house after the last eight years of hell.

"I have a kettle." He walks to the kitchen and opens a cupboard, taking out a stainless-steel kettle. He goes over to the big sink and fills it up. "And I have tea bags." He turns the knob on the stove, and the tick sounds until the flame fills under the kettle, then he walks to what looks like a barn door and slides it open. I see it's his pantry, which is the size of my bedroom. "I have a box of tea," he states, looking around the shelves and then finding it before coming out with a big brown wooden box. "Told you." He puts it on the counter and flips over the lid. "We have a bunch of tea." His eyes scan them. "There is lemon, ginger, and some fruit." I can't help but laugh at his description of them. "There is even sleepy tea." He picks up the pack between his fingers. "And then English breakfast, which is probably not for night. There is apple cinnamon and chai and—" He looks up. "I don't even know where they got this from."

"I'll have the lemon or ginger one," I say, and he puts down the sleepy tea one before picking up the lemon one.

"Done." He closes the box but leaves it on the counter. "Go sit down on the couch, and I'll join you." He motions to the couch. "Make yourself at home."

I walk over to the couch and sit down, putting my hands down beside me and feeling how soft it feels under my hands. I stare at the table in front, seeing pictures of Jennifer all over the room, and I get a tightness in my stomach as I look away from her smiling face. I'm about to get up when he's in front of me, bending to put a mug on the table, the string from the tea bag hanging over the rim. "There you go."

"I think I should—" I start to say, and he squats down in front of me. "Go."

"I think you should drink your tea and relax." He walks over to the side of the couch and grabs a big thick knitted blanket. Tossing it down beside me, he squats down again and pulls off one shoe and then the next one. He sits beside me, wraps his arm around my waist, and pulls me to him, reaching out and pulling the cover over me. "Relax," he says softly, and his smell fills my nose, making me close my eyes and push away all the nerves coursing through me. "What are you thinking about?" he asks, his hand rubbing up and down my arm.

"I'm worried about what happened with the

Cartwrights," I admit and push away from him. "Charlie, what you did was"—I put a hand on my forehead—"dumb and irresponsible. You know what they did to my family and our business, not to mention what they held over Brock's head."

I'm expecting him to say something, but instead, he moves to the side, grabs his phone out of his pocket, and presses something, then ringing comes out of it. "Hey," the man answers, "I don't hear from you for months and then I get two phone calls in less than two days."

"Hey, Pops," he says to his grandfather, Casey Barnes, and my eyes almost come out of my sockets. "Something happened," he says, looking at me, "thought you should know."

"Is that so?" he replies, and I shake my head, telling him not to.

"Was out to dinner tonight, and I ran into the Cartwrights." He ignores my headshaking. "Words were exchanged, along with a little bit of a threat."

"How little is this threat?" He's not even fazed by the meaning of this. I'm pretty sure if someone called me and said they made a threat, my voice would be skyrocketed to the sky. I wouldn't be acting like he just told me that it's going to be a sunny day.

"Something along the line, if he wants to fuck with anyone, he should pick on someone his own size." He smirks, looking into my eyes.

I'm expecting his grandfather to freak out, but instead, he just laughs. "Why are you calling me?"

"Just wanted to give you a heads-up in case of

blowback."

This time, Casey laughs even louder and harder. "I'll try to be ready. Call me tomorrow."

"Gotcha," Charlie says, "later." He presses the disconnect button and throws the phone on the other side of the couch. "Happy?"

"No," I gasp out. "Why would that make me happy?" I ask. He gets up off the couch, walking over to the lights and turning them all off. The room is lit with a soft light coming from the other side of the room through a doorway. "Charlie," I say his name softly as he comes back.

"Did you enjoy dinner?" he asks, completely ignoring the fact that there is a huge elephant in the room. "Next time, we should try more than just the pasta." He pulls me to him.

"Um," I start softly, trying to catch my bearings, "we should."

"It's a nice night." He looks outside. "Overall, I would say today was a great day."

I don't answer him. Instead, I listen to him breathing and close my eyes for a minute, or at least I think it's for a minute before I feel like I'm being carried. My eyes open, and I look up at Charlie carrying me through the house. The light gets brighter right before it's being shut off. "I'm sorry I woke you," he murmurs, standing in what appears to be his bedroom. "I thought you would be more comfortable in the bedroom." He walks over to the side of the bed and gingerly places me down in it.

My back rests on the rows of pillows. "I should go

home." I sit up in the bed as he puts one knee on the bed beside my hip.

The moonlight comes into his room and I wish the lights were on so I could see him as he stares down at me. "Stay." His hand comes up to touch my face, rubbing my cheek with the softest touch, and if I wasn't awake, I wouldn't know it was happening.

"It's better."

"I want you to stay with me." His voice is a whisper. "I won't touch you. I just want to sleep with you in my arms." I swallow the lump in my throat, knowing I should get up and get out of here. "Just stay with me."

Twenty-Five

CHARLIE

I WISH I could kiss her. I wish I could just taste her one more time. "Please," I whisper in a plea as she looks up at me. I move to the other side of her, laying my head down on the pillow, hoping she lies down next to me. I hold my breath with each passing second, my heart speeding up faster and faster. She slowly leans back against the pillows that never get used.

She is the first woman to be in my bed in eight years. The first woman I want in my bed. The thought makes my head spin at the same time settling the achiness I have been carrying around in my chest for the past eight years. She turns to face me. "Thank you, Charlie," she says softly, putting both her hands pressed together under her cheek, "for the ride this morning." I move closer to her, putting my hand on her hip and pulling her chest up against mine. "And for dinner."

"Anytime." My hand on her hip moves to her back as

I slide a hand under the pillow, and her head falls forward onto my shoulder. I lean down and kiss her head. I can't resist not being able to kiss her the way I want to kiss her, so I settle for this. I close my eyes and settle into my bed. For the first time in eight years, I fall asleep with a slight smile on my face.

I open my eyes when I feel something tickling my nose. My hand comes up to rub it, and I find it's Autumn's hair. I look around the room, seeing it's still dark outside. The bedside table clock shows me it's a little past 2:00 a.m. The last time I saw the clock it was a little bit after nine when I had pulled her into my arms. Now I am on my back, and she is draped over me, her leg hitched over my thigh in the middle of my leg. Her head is in the middle of my chest. I put my head back and close my eyes, taking in the heat from her body when she stirs in my arms. Her body gets lighter on me and I know that she's moved away. She picks her head up, sleep all over her face as she looks up at me. "Did I wake you?" I ask softly, and she just shakes her head.

"I don't think I've ever fallen asleep so fast." She moves her hand thrown over my abs to under her chin. "I crashed out."

"Must be all the adrenaline." I lift the hand that was just scratching, my face to move her hair away from her cheek. "I want to kiss you so bad," I say the words, and I want to kick myself. Her mouth opens in a gasp. "But I won't kiss you." I can feel her heart beating on my chest, mimicking my own. "I made your life hell for the last eight years. I blamed you for things I know weren't your fault, but I knew I had to blame someone, and you were the easy target." She looks away from me as she blinks faster. "I don't think there will ever be anything I can do to forgive what I did." I tighten my arm around her waist, making her crush onto me. "But every single day, I'm going to show you how sorry I am. Every single day, I'll try to right my wrong."

"It's okay," she whispers, and those words kill me because this is who she always was. The kind and understanding woman I forgot she was.

"It's not okay," I snap, and her neck lifts higher. "It's not okay," I repeat softly. "None of it was okay. Nothing I did to you was okay, and you are going to stop saying it was okay." I raise my voice, and her eyes open at me. "When I think back on what I said and the words that came out of my mouth, I'm disgusted with myself."

"Charlie." She moves her leg from between mine.

"Don't you fucking say it." I start to get angrier. "Don't fucking say it."

"Fine, I won't say it." She moves, and this time, she throws a leg over and sits on me. "Why won't you kiss me?"

I put my hands on her hips, making sure she doesn't move. "Because I don't deserve you. Because you are the one who will have to make that move. Because I've already taken so much from you, I'm not going to take that also." She's about to open her mouth, probably to tell me it's okay—which will piss me off more—so I put my finger on her lips. "Don't fucking say it," I hiss at her, and what she does next shocks me. She kisses my finger.

"Autumn." My hand falls from her lips.

"If I kiss you, will you kiss me back?" Her voice is so low, so soft. Her eyes search mine, her chest rising and falling as if she just sprinted here from her house. Her hands go to my face, her nails running through the scruff on my cheeks. "If I kiss you, will you kiss me back?" She puts her forehead on mine.

"If you kiss me, I don't think I will ever be able to stop." My hands trail from her hips up to her sides. "I took it for granted before," I admit. "I didn't take enough time those nights to commit it to my memory." I don't say anything else because her lips are on mine, her tongue sliding into my mouth, and it's nothing, and I mean nothing, like I thought it would be. One arm wraps around her waist while the other rubs up her back, and my hand disappears into her hair. She moves her head to the side to deepen the kiss. Her hands move down to my jaws as she rotates her hips over my cock. The both of us moan into each other's mouth, her hands move down to my neck as she lets go of my lips. My head goes straight to her neck, sucking in and then biting. "Charlie," she says my name, and her head falls back. Her hands grip my shirt and pull it up. My hands move up to help her get rid of my shirt before my own hands grip her shirt and rip it off her, leaving her in the lace bra. My hands come up to cup her tits while my head bends, pushing the lace away from her nipple and taking it into my mouth. "Charlie," she begs, her hips pressing into mine.

"I said I would hold you and that's it." I let her nipple go to look at her face, her eyes hooded over. "That's all

I wanted."

"What about what I want?" she asks, her lips plump from our kiss. "What about what I want?"

I push the hair away from her face. "Tell me what you want?" I ask. "You are the one in charge."

"I want you to touch me. I want to touch you." Her voice is unsure and shaky.

"Then touch me, baby," I urge. Her eyes drop to my lips as they part, and her hands, even though they have been on me more than once, touch my chest as if for the first time. Her eyes on her fingertips, she moves them from the middle of my chest and then up. "I need you to do something for me," I say. Her hands stop moving over my body, her fingertips hovering. "Will you do one thing for me?" I ask, and all she can do is stare at me. "I miss your mark," I say. "You bit me twice." I move my hand to where her mark was. "Here, and it's gone away. I want it back." The need to have her mark on me so I know this moment happened has to be the strongest feeling I've ever felt.

"What?" Her eyes go from me to my chest and then back to my eyes.

"Your mark," I repeat, "I want it on me."

"Charlie." She puts her hands down on my chest palms down. "That's—"

"That's what I want," I say, "your mark on me."

"But," she says, "that wasn't…" I lean forward, taking her mouth and kissing her, hard and wet.

I put my arm around her waist and turn her so her back is on the bed. "I need to taste you." I push up her skirt and close my eyes when I see the matching lace panties she is wearing. My finger comes up as I rub it up and down over her, her wetness coming through the lace. "Is that for me?" She opens her legs for me, and I move the lace panties to the side, bending my head and licking her. The moment I taste her, and she feels my tongue, we both moan. Her hand comes up to run in my hair. I slide my tongue and finger into her at the same time, and she grips my hair in her hand and pulls it as she arches her back. My eyes watch her as my tongue slides out and licks up to her clit, flicking it with my tongue before nipping down on it and sliding another finger into her. Her pussy tightens around them as I finger-fuck her, wanting to push her to the edge but not go over it. "Are you close?" I ask, knowing she is almost there.

"Yes," she pants out, and I pull my fingers out of her, but she doesn't let my hair go. "No."

"What do you want?" I ask, putting one of my hands beside her as she pants. "Tell me what you want." She stares into my eyes as I slide my fingers back into her. "Is this what you want?" I ask, and she nods. "I'll give you what you want." I fuck her with my fingers faster and faster. "But you have to give me what I want."

"Yes," she mewls, and I know she's so far gone she'll agree to anything.

"You'll give me what I want?" My thumb presses down on her clit, moving it side to side as my fingers stay buried in her.

My mouth covers hers as she kisses me with no control. She's moving her hips to make my fingers move.

"Charlie." She lets go of my mouth, her hands going to my chest, her nails digging into it. "Move your hand."

"Fine." I pull my fingers out and then fuck her a couple more times. "But only if you give me what I want." Her head moves side to side as I bury my face in her neck and bite her. "Give me what I want, baby." I move slower now, rubbing my nose against her jaw.

"Charlie," she pleads with me as my fingers work faster.

"Yeah, baby?" I say softly, pulling out and then brutally pushing back into her.

"I need you," she begs, and everything inside me snaps. I pull out my fingers and unbutton my jeans but don't even push them off my hips before I slam into her. The tightness of her pussy is even too much for me. I fuck her hard, the sound of skin slapping against each other. "Yes." She cocks her legs around my waist. "Yes."

"Gripping me so tight," I mutter between clenched teeth, "I'm not going to last long." I put my palms down beside her sides, holding myself up as I fuck her uncontrollably. I wanted to take it slow. I wanted to take my time. I wanted to savor it, but everything with her is always pushed to the edge of the cliff, and I always jump over without looking down. "I'm there," I declare when my balls get tight. "Fuck, I'm there." I slam into her, pulling out until the tip and then going again. "Autumn," I say her name at the same time I feel her pussy convulsing over me, and her head comes up to my chest, right near my nipple. She screams out my name right before she sinks her teeth into me. "Heaven." That's the last thing I say before I collapse on her.

Twenty-Six

Autumn

MY EYES FLUTTER open, and I see I'm on my stomach in almost the middle of the bed. My arms are under the pillow that feels like I'm sleeping on a cloud. The sheet and cover are covering the bottom part of me, right above my ass, leaving my bare back out. My left leg hitched up is touching his hip, my eyes roam up at Charlie, who is lying on his back beside me. The sheet at his waist, covering just a bit of him, because his leg is half out and on top of it. He has one hand over his head and the other hand on my ass. His face is turned toward me, and I take him in. He's the most handsome man I've ever laid eyes on. He's the man who walks into the room and you want to be the one he smiles at. I knew he had it all before, but now that I've been with him, I know he's the whole fucking package.

I don't get to spend much time watching him because his alarm blares into the room. His eyes fly open as he gets up to a sitting position and looks around the room toward the side of the bed, where he threw his pants after we had sex last night. His hand leaves my ass as he turns and bends over to take it out of his pants and shut it off. He puts it on his bedside table before he lies back in bed and looks over at me. His face is still full of sleep, his eyes half closed as he turns on his side, his hand coming to me as he turns me to face him. His arms hug me like a big blanket as he buries his face in my neck, where he takes a deep inhale before he mumbles, "Morning."

My arms hug him back. "That alarm is awful," I say, and he nods. "It's enough to wake the dead."

"I'll change it," he says while kissing my neck. "Do you like bells, whistles, or chimes?"

I smile as he pulls me even closer to him, and I'm already plastered on him. His cock is hard and on my stomach. "Anything but the blaring horn you have." His kisses move from my neck up to my jaw, and his arm around my waist moves down to cup my ass.

"I'll change it as soon as we get out of bed," his sleepy voice whispers in my neck, and I push him onto his back. My leg moves over his, and I straddle him. His hands go to my hips. "Or tomorrow because we aren't leaving the bed until then."

"I have to get to work," I remind him, "and so do you." I bend to kiss his neck before I sit back up and see the mark I made right beside his nipple. A mark he asked me for. A mark he said he missed. It sent shock waves through me, but then I also wanted my mark on him. "But"—I trail kisses down his chest—"I didn't do something last night that I wanted to do."

The sheet moves off us. "Oh, yeah?" He folds his arm and tucks it under his head. "What is that?" His voice trails off when my hand fists his cock.

"This." I lick from the base of his cock to the tip, then twirl my tongue around the head of it.

"Fuck," he hisses out, watching me. His other hand comes up and rubs my head as I lick back down to his balls and then back up again, before sucking half his cock into my mouth. I repeat the same movements three times, his eyes closing when I take him deeper into the back of my throat. My hand moves with my mouth as he grips my hair in his hand. "God." His teeth are clenched together, and I know he's about to lose control. "First fucking morning that I get to have you, not going to come down your throat." He sits up, his cock still in my hand as he forces my head back and kisses me brutally. "I'm going to come in you."

He turns me onto my back, his cock in his hand, lining himself up, and slams into me. Pulling out until the tip is almost out, then he takes one of my legs and throws it over his shoulder before he plunges back into me, going even deeper. "Charlie," I mutter, staring into his eyes as he fucks me, his hand moving down to my nipple as he tweaks it before he kisses me. He puts his hands by my shoulders as he looks between us, watching his cock ram into me.

"Look at how you take me, swallowing me up." His hips move faster. "So fucking tight, it's getting harder to pull out." He puts his forehead on mine. "Tell me what you want."

"Don't stop." That's the only thing I think to say. "Please don't stop." The feel of him inside me makes my body light up. I feel like every single cell in my body is alive with him. There are no words to describe how good he makes me feel. How good this feels. "Charlie," I repeat when I'm almost to the edge.

"I can feel you, baby," he says softly, "choking my cock with your pussy. Begging for me to come in you." I arch my back as he slams into me and moves side to side, my clit tingling. "Squeeze me, baby," he urges, and I contract my pussy around him. "That's my girl." He pulls out and then rams back in. "Give me one of your fingers." I hold up a finger, and he sucks my index finger in his mouth. "Now play with your pink little clit," he says, and I'm mesmerized by him. My hand goes between my legs and up. "Move your finger in little circles." He watches me play with myself as his cock thrashes into me over and over again. My finger moves more frantically as it moves side to side, my eyes closing as I take in the feeling. His thrusts are faster and shorter. "So fucking wet for me," he hisses, and I know I'm dripping all over his sheets. "I need you to hurry up and come, baby." His hips thrust into me over and over again. It happens as soon as he calls me baby, the tightness in my stomach travels to my pussy, and I come on his cock. "Autumn!" he roars out and plants himself inside me, bending his mouth to mine as we kiss slowly. "If waking up with you wasn't great enough, that might be the icing on the cake." He smiles, and I can't help but grin at him. I'm about to say something when his alarm goes off again. "Shower time." He pulls out of me and turns off his phone before grabbing my ankle and tugging me to the edge of the bed. "We are going to shower together." He wraps his arm around my waist, walking me through his room toward his bathroom. "To conserve water."

I can't say anything else because the shower is turned on me, and I'm standing under it. I should have known that a shower with him wasn't just a shower but more. He grabs the bar of soap and lathers me from head to toe. He washes me down before rinsing me off and then sucking my nipple while he finger-fucks me to another orgasm. My hands grip his cock at the same time, and when he's about to come, I get down on my knees and swallow everything he has.

I'm wrapped in a towel as I walk out of the bathroom and stop when I see her picture by the bed. My neck suddenly burns, and I have to look away from her smiling face. Charlie steps out and puts his hands on my hips. "What's wrong?" I shake my head and try not to let him see that I'm a little flustered, or I'm one second away from tears.

"I'm good." I step out of his touch. "I just have to get going."

I can feel him staring at me as I walk around his room and gather my things. I slide my panties on and then my bra before letting the towel fall away. "You're lying to me," he accuses, and I look at him, standing in the middle of his bedroom with a towel around his waist, hanging low on his hips. His chest still has a couple of droplets of water from his hair.

My eyes go to the bite mark. "I'm not lying. I have to go and you have to go, and I'd like to get out of here before people see my car still here." I look away from him to grab my shirt.

"We had dinner last night together," he reminds me, and I slip my skirt on. "Everyone is already talking about us." I look at him. "Does it bother you?"

"Yes," I answer him honestly, "it bothers me. I don't want you caught up in this shit with the Cartwrights."

"I already told you I don't give a shit about that." He turns and steps to his walk-in closet that I saw on the way out. My eyes avoid looking at the bedside table, but I can't help it. I look at her picture and mouth, "Sorry," to her.

"I'm going to go." I turn and see that he's already come back in the room, and he's caught me looking at her picture. "Thanks for last night." I almost run out of the room, going to get my boots and sitting down as I put them on. He walks out of the bedroom wearing jeans and a T-shirt.

"Autumn," he calls my name, so I look up at him and fake smile, "it's—"

He doesn't get to say anything more because the phone rings from his bedroom, giving me a chance to get up. "I'll let myself out," I say. "You need to get your phone." I walk out, looking over my shoulder at him. I want to say, "See you later," but I don't. I just take one more look at him before I grab my purse and get the hell out of here. Only when I've made my way away from his house and stop, my head hitting the steering wheel, do I let the air I've been holding out. "Well, add that to the list of why I'm the shittiest friend ever."

I think of going straight to work but then think about walking in wearing the same thing I did last night and make my way back home. "Nothing says walk of shame like going to work with the same clothes on," I mumble as I walk into my house, going to my bedroom and picking out my tight, light-blue jeans, a white T-shirt, and a pair of white runners. After putting on a little bit of mascara and walking out the door, I head to work. I arrive at the same time as Brady who looks at me. "You better be going to get coffee."

"Late night?" I ask and he glares at me.

"All this tasting menu shit has everyone talking about it. We got five different reservations for tonight. And the back room is reserved for those guys who bought cases to take home; they are coming with friends."

I hold up my hand. "High five."

"I don't see any coffee in that hand," he mumbles. "Get me coffee and I might high-five you."

"You got it." I turn and walk toward the bakery, pulling open the door and stepping in, coming face-to-face with Charlie's parents.

"Oh my goodness," his mother, Willow, says when she looks over her shoulder at me. "I can't believe my eyes." She comes over to me, not giving me a chance to do anything when she takes me in her arms. "Look at you." She lets me go and holds my arms. "Quinn." She looks at her husband. "It's Autumn."

"I see." He smiles at me and bends his head to kiss my cheek. "It's good to see you."

"It's good to see you both," I reply, my heart hammering in my chest, wondering if they went to Charlie's house and saw my car.

"Mr. Barnes." He turns his head when Maddie calls his name and holds a big bag for him.

"We're surprising Charlie," Willow fills me in as I try not to make it seem that I'm freaking out, but I'm freaking the fuck out.

"That sounds like fun," I say as Quinn joins us. "I'll let you two get to him." I step aside from them and watch them walk out the door. My eyes follow them to the SUV as Quinn smiles down at Willow and opens her door for her, bending to kiss her lips before she gets in.

"What can I get you this morning, Autumn?" Maddie asks from behind the counter.

"I'll take two coffees and a whole box of donuts," I order.

"That kind of day?" She raises her eyebrows.

"You have no idea." I take one look over my shoulder and see the SUV drive away. "You have no idea," I mumble again.

Twenty-Seven

CHARLIE

I OPEN THE back door and storm out with the coffee in my hand, headed straight to the barn. My mind on the way Autumn was looking at the picture of Jennifer when I walked out of the shower, something we both need to talk about. It also makes me think about the last time I went to visit her, something that has been less and less in the last couple of weeks.

Walking in, I spot Emmett sitting on the desk, his coffee in his hand as he looks up at me. "Well, you look to be in a fine mood." He lifts the cup to his mouth and tries to hide his smile.

"I'm fine," I snap at him, even though I'm not fine. I woke up feeling like I've never felt before. I mean, never felt before, hands down, and it just got better, until it didn't. Until I walked out of the walk-in closet and saw her staring at Jennifer's picture by the bed. I didn't even notice the picture until she mouthed something to it, and her face got white. The little happy that I had for an hour or less was gone, and I wanted desperately to get it back. I wanted it back more than I wanted anything before.

"You sound fine," Emmett fires back. "Peachy." I take a sip of my coffee. "Heard you were in town last night."

"Yeah." I walk away from him when the phone rings again from my pocket. "I live here, so occasionally I go to town," I bark, looking down and seeing it's my grandfather, and I've already ignored his call this morning when Autumn left. "I'm going to take this inside." I walk back out and head to my office, putting the phone to my ear. "Hello."

"I called you," he states, "twice."

"I know, I was in the shower the first time," I lie to him, "and now I answered you. What's up?"

"What's up?" He laughs. "You called me last night talking in code."

"I wasn't talking in code," I deny. "I called to give you a heads-up."

"Is that how you remember it?" he pushes as I pull out my chair and sit on it. "Care to fill me in on the whole situation?" I close my eyes, wondering how the fuck to word it without putting Autumn in this. I don't want her to be involved in any of this. But I know I have no choice but to say everything, so I do. Well, definitely not everything. "I'll see what I can get from my end. After everything fell to shit in court, I didn't give it another thought."

"Yeah, I've spent the last eight years with a chip on my shoulder and placing blame on someone who wasn't to blame."

"Is that so?" he questions, and I close my eyes.

"Became a man I didn't recognize," I say honestly. "I want to get back to the old Charlie."

"Not going to lie," he huffs, "not too fond of that Charlie."

I chuckle. "Well, hopefully, I can make you like the new and improved."

"Rough around the edges," he teases. "I have to go. I'll let you know what I turn up."

"Appreciate it," I say and hang up the phone. I'm about to call Autumn when I hear my name being paged by Emmett.

"Charlie, you are wanted," he announces and then I hear the crashing of the phone when he hangs it up. I shake my head, getting up and walking over to the barn. Putting my phone in my back pocket, I step out into the sun.

I think about leaving and going to get lunch with Autumn when I step into the barn and my mother shocks the shit out of me when she yells, "Surprise!" Her hands are in the air over her head.

I take a step back and look over to see my father standing there, the box of donuts on the desk and Emmett leaning against the other side of the barn. "Oh my," I say as my mother comes to me and hugs me around my waist. "What are you guys doing here?" I hug her around her shoulders.

"We came to surprise you." When my mother looks up at me, her whole face lights up like a Christmas tree.

"We're going to stay with you for a couple of days." I should be excited my parents are here, but all of a sudden, I want them gone. I don't want them here when things with Autumn are just starting. The less time she has away from me to think about things, the better it is. "Are you surprised?" she asks.

"You could say that," I reply and my father comes over to me and slaps me on my shoulder before pulling me to him. "Hey, Dad."

"Hey yourself," he mumbles.

"I can't believe you're here," I say, looking at the both of them.

"You called your grandfather last night," my father starts and now it all makes sense.

"So you guys came to spy on me?" I ask both.

"Of course not," my mother quickly refutes.

At the same time my father says, "Yup." He nods. "We want to make sure that you're okay and that everything and everyone is doing well."

"I think everyone is doing well and it was just talk."

"Did you hear about this?" My father looks over at Emmett.

"Sure did," he confirms, and I roll my eyes.

"I'm surprised he can work since he's always hooting and hollering with all the gossip in town." I glare at him.

"You look different." My mother puts her hands on her hips. "Something is different with you."

"No, it's not." I shake my head.

"Yes, there is." She turns to my father. "Quinn, do you see it?"

"He doesn't see anything"—I walk over to the box of donuts—"because there is nothing to see."

"I see it," Emmett agrees, and I turn my head. "He looks like less of an asshole."

"That, I can see," my father says, slapping my back as he grabs a donut from the box. "So what's this trouble you are in?"

"I'm not in trouble," I groan.

"What trouble is this?" My mother looks at me and then my father, the worry all over her face. "What happened, Quinn Barnes? Why did you not tell me any of this?"

"You heard the man, there was nothing to tell." He bites off another piece of donut. "I was just playing with him." He full-on just lied to my mother and even she knows that because he avoids looking at her.

"How long are you guys staying?" I ask and my father stares at me.

"Not sure yet." I inwardly groan. "Is that a problem?"

"Nope," I lie to them. "No problem at all." I take a donut, glancing over at Emmett, who is looking down at his boots, laughing and shaking his head.

"Mrs. Barnes, did you see Goldilocks?" Emmett asks, and she shakes her head. "Third stall from the end." He points down the barn. "Charlie has taken an interest in her."

"Are you fucking done?" I ask.

"Not even close," he retorts, walking with my mother to see Goldilocks.

"What's up with you?" my father asks, looking to

make sure my mother can't hear what he says.

"Nothing," I lie to him and avoid his eyes, instead taking a bite of the donut. "Just got things on my mind."

"I heard you threw down with the Cartwrights," he says, and I nod.

"Things came to light in the last little bit," I inform him. "I don't like it."

"What sort of things?" he asks, and I don't say anything. "You know that you can't keep secrets, boy." He puts his ass against the desk. "So you might as well just tell me what we are dealing with."

"They have been fucking with Autumn's family." I look down the barn to make sure my mother isn't near me. "Her family is practically bankrupt." His eyes are shocked.

"The whiskey one?" I nod. "Saw her in town just before," he shares, and my head turns back so fast it's a wonder it doesn't snap off. "She looks like she's been through it, all right."

"She has," I admit, "and I was one of those who put her through it." He's about to say something when I lift my hand to stop him from talking. "But I'm not anymore." It's his turn to nod his head. "She's got enough to deal with. She came back to town because her father is dying."

My father doesn't say anything, but I see it in his eyes, worry mixed with sadness. "We'll scope things out, but your mother is right." He stands back up. "You look different." I roll my eyes and groan at the same time. "Can't put my finger on it."

I finish my donut. "Well, I'm fine. I'm all good.

Nothing is different. And I'm happy you're here."

"So we aren't cramping your style?" he jokes, and I laugh.

"Dad, I know you are trying to sound cool, but"—I shake my head—"you don't."

"Are you seeing anyone?" he asks, and I gawk at him. "What? It's a question."

I don't even answer him. Instead, I turn and walk to my mother, but I can feel his eyes on me. When I look over my shoulder, he's standing there with his hands on his hips, trying to figure me out. "Are you done, or are you going to help?" He walks to me.

"Deflecting," he observes, "I know that game."

"It's not a game. Nothing is going on, and I'm not seeing anyone." The words feel wrong in my mouth. "At least not officially." I want to kick my own ass when the words slip out. "Or not." I try to take them back, but the only thing heard in the barn is my father's laughter.

Twenty-Eight

AUTUMN

"WHAT DO YOU think?" Brady stands in front of the desk, his hands on his hips, watching me. "Honest opinion, obviously."

I bring the small glass back to my lips and take a little sip. The amber liquid hits my tongue right away, followed by the softness of the vanilla, ending with the spice at the back of the throat. But it's a smooth transition. "I think this one is my favorite." I put it to my lips again and take a bigger sip, feeling the same thing this time. "It's really good."

"I tweaked a couple of things in the recipe," he explains, picking up his own glass and looking at it. "The color is good, not too dark, just light enough." Then he brings it to his lips and tastes his drink. "It's good."

"It is," I agree. "We should serve it tonight."

"Dad hasn't tried it yet. He always tries it before anyone."

My father hasn't been in the distillery for the past two weeks. He came in once, but he wasn't feeling so hot, so he went home. Even so, we spend most lunches together with me at his house. He's getting a touch weaker, even if he doesn't want to admit it. I try not to notice it, not wanting to think of what the outcome can mean. "Then I suggest you take a bottle over to him and let him try it out. Because I'm serving that tonight."

"You know you aren't the boss around here." He tries not to smile.

"Yeah." I set the glass down and put my elbows on the armrest of the chair, before folding my hands. "Says who?" I tilt my head, pretending to look around. "Who is going to tell me otherwise?"

"There is no use in arguing with you." He grabs the bottle of whiskey we were trying. "I'm going to see Dad."

"Good decision." I grin. "I would have done the same."

He turns to walk out of the room, stopping to look back. "I don't know if I told you this lately"—his voice gets softer—"but I'm happy you're here."

I swallow down the lump formed in my throat with his declaration. "I don't know if I told you this lately, but I'm happy I'm here also." He nods at me as I blink furiously to make sure the sting of the tears that are threatening to come don't.

"Be back soon!" he shouts as he walks out.

"I shall be waiting with bated breath." I chuckle to myself before opening the email and seeing a couple of new ones come in from some of the hotels around town. Last week, I went to visit them and pitched the idea of a distillery tour for their guests. We would do small tours of ten people, and they would get ten percent back on all sales. It was no skin off their back to put our flyer out with all the others, and in return, they would make money if people came. The tour would also include a tasting menu, which would hopefully sell some bottles at the same time. They each confirm that a group of ten is coming in next Wednesday, so I make sure I get up and write it on the board. I also brace because it's not something I mentioned to Brady yet, which should be fun since he'll be giving the tours.

The day goes by so fast that I don't even notice it's almost dinnertime until Brady comes in and puts a plate with a burger and fries on my desk. "Eat," he orders, "then get your ass out there." He motions with his head. "We've already got a couple of tables."

The chef, who is a cooking student and is doing this for free just to get his feet wet, started today. We are doing a special two-for-one for everyone who comes in from four until seven, but are keeping the kitchen open until the max of nine, depending on how busy it is, hoping to get some of the diner customers. We have started on a small menu for the first couple of weeks to see how things go. The last thing I need is to go in the red even more. "We might have to hire someone soon," I say, and he raises his eyebrows. "I said soon, I didn't say tomorrow."

"After, not now, we are going to discuss that." He

points at the calendar where I wrote my message in big letters. "Maybe tomorrow."

"You'll love it," I say, picking up a fry and dipping it in the ketchup. "It'll be fun."

He doesn't answer me, just walks out while I take a bite of the burger and groan. It's so fucking good. I finish the whole thing before going to the bathroom, washing my hands, and stepping out to see about ten tables filled with people. I see Brady running back and forth from the kitchen to the front. "What can I do?" I ask, and he motions with his head to the bar.

"I wrote down the drinks I need," he says, carrying two plates to a table of two girls, who smile up at him, one of them blushing. I get behind the bar, and in a matter of thirty minutes, Brady is standing beside me behind the bar, waiting to see who needs us. "This is good," he finally admits.

"It's still too early to tell," I warn him. "As much as I want to toot my own horn"—I look over at the tables of people who are from out of town—"we need to bring in some of the locals and spread the word that way."

"It'll come," he replies, "I have faith." I'm about to answer him when I look over at the door and spot him. My heart speeds up and not from the nerves of everyone here, but from seeing not only him, but he's with his parents, who are holding hands beside him. He looks around the bar and spots me, his face going into a smile. "I take it you'll handle that table?"

I whip my head to look at my brother. "No." My neck tingles. "You can do that."

His face lights up. "Oh, but then I won't have fun teasing you." He picks up his finger and taps my nose. "You're it."

"Brady," I hiss at him as I look over and see the three of them have taken stools at the fucking bar. Not in the front, nope, the three on the side, where it's more intimate. "I'll be back," he says to me, turning and walking out from behind the bar from the other side.

I take a deep inhale and turn to walk to them; they are customers, after all. "Hi," I greet them, looking at Quinn first, who smiles at me, then Willow—who has the biggest smile on her face—before falling on Charlie, who is looking at me with a sly smile. "Welcome." I am going to remain professional and hope like fuck his parents don't catch on to anything.

"Hey," Charlie says, "I didn't know you started serving food."

"We just started," I reply. "Something to help bring in people."

"Well, it smells delicious," Willow states, "and looks it also." I turn, grabbing three little square menus that I made and laminated.

"Here you go." I hand them each one. "Can I get you anything to drink?"

"I saw on your social media that you have a new blend," Quinn mentions and I try not to think about that he was searching me online because he found out I was banging his son and wants to make sure I'm good enough for him.

"We do." I avoid looking at him. "Let me get you a

taster." I turn and walk around, trying to act like I'm not dying inside.

I pour three small glasses before turning and placing them down in front of them.

"Can I get a soda water?" Charlie says to me, and I nod, shocked that he's not drinking with his parents.

"This is good," Quinn declares, taking another sip, "smooth."

Willow picks up her glass. "Oh, it doesn't even burn going down." She looks at her husband. "I love this." She throws back the rest of the shot. "Can I have another?"

"Relax there, sweetheart," Quinn says to her.

"I'm on vacation. Sitting with my son and my husband. I can't be safer." She looks at me. "I'll have another, please."

I smile at her. "You got it." I walk over and take a glass down and fill it halfway. I add a big cube of ice before making my way back and putting it down in front of her. "Happy vacation." I glance over at Quinn, who is looking at his wife with a glare, but you can see he doesn't mean it. "Are you guys going to try the food?" I ask, looking at Charlie. "I had the burger and it was so good."

"I'll take that," Charlie says, handing me the menu.

"I'll take that also," Willow agrees, as does Quinn, who also orders a glass of the new whiskey.

I walk into the kitchen, seeing the chef going back and forth. "How is it going?" I ask and he smiles.

"So good," he confirms. "I haven't stopped a second and I'm loving every single minute of it."

"Great," I say. "I'll take three cheeseburgers with fries."

"Coming up in about ten," he replies, dropping fries in the fryer. I walk out to see Brady seating two more people before walking to another table to take an order.

"It'll be ten minutes," I tell them, and Willow smiles at me.

"I'm so happy you're here," she says. I can see her cheeks are a bit pink, and I wonder if the whiskey is already working. "So tell us what you've been up to."

"Um," I start nervously, "not much, really. I was working for a bar up north." Charlie's eyebrows rise at that news. "Came home to help out. Not sure how long I'm going to be here."

"Maybe you'll change your mind and stay put," Quinn states. "Home is where the heart is."

"So they say." I smile at him. "I don't have any plans to leave for now." I avoid looking at Charlie but I can feel his stare.

Quinn looks around. "I forgot how nice it was in here," he says, picking up his glass. "What else have you done?"

"She's done so much," Brady breaks into the conversation. "She doesn't stop coming up with ideas."

"Excuse me," I say, turning and walking around the bar and heading toward the distillery part of the room. The darkened hallway is lit up by the small circle coming from the swinging door. I'm about to step through it to get my nerves under control, when I feel a hand around my wrist. I look over my shoulder as he turns me and

277

pushes me against the corner of the door. "Charlie." I barely have his name out of my mouth before his lips fall onto mine. His tongue slips in to play with mine. My eyes close as he kisses me, my head screaming at me that someone could see. My hands go to his sides, and instead of pushing him away, I squeeze him to stay where he is. He puts one hand over my head, while the other wraps around my waist and pulls me to him.

The kiss is soft yet intense, and when he lets go of my lips, I want to pull him back. "Hi," he says softly.

"Hi," I whisper.

"How is your day?" I blink, trying to get my bearings.

"Good. You?"

"Good," he replies, "my parents are in town." As if I didn't see him come in with them. "So I'll be coming to your house."

"Um, I don't think that's a good idea," I say, and all he does is grin before coming back down and kissing me.

"I'll see you out there." He gives me one more kiss before walking away from me. I hear the bell ring from the kitchen and walk back out, seeing that more people have arrived.

I grab the three plates of burgers before walking out and placing it down in front of Charlie and his family. "This looks so good," Willow notes, picking up the burger. "So tell me, Autumn, are you dating anyone?"

Twenty-Nine

CHARLIE

I PICK UP my burger to take a bite, my lips still tingling from kissing her, when my mother says, "So tell me, Autumn, are you dating anyone?" I swear I stop mid bite to look up at Autumn to see her face. And I don't think I am the only one who looks at her. I'm pretty sure my father does also, but all I can do is watch her face. "Does the silence mean you are or you aren't?"

She smiles. "Um…"

"Why don't we not put her on the spot?" my father suggests, taking a bite of his burger.

"Oh, I know who you could date." My mother takes a french fry and dips it in ketchup, and I really wish she would shut up right about now. I also really fucking hope she doesn't say me. "We should set her up with Emmett."

The minute my mother says that, I throw my burger back down on the plate. "No fucking way," I blurt a lot more tensely than I want to say.

"Why not?" My mother looks at me, waiting for me to come up with an answer, but the only answer I have is no.

"Yes, Charlie," my father chimes in, "why not?" I glare at both of them. My mother looks at me, waiting for an answer, but my father, he's got a look on him that is playful, almost as if he's enjoying this.

"She's gorgeous." Mom points at Autumn, and there is no denying that. "And he's good-looking."

"Willow," my father warns, and I look over at him.

"What's the matter, Dad?" I ask, and his look has changed from playful to almost lethal. "He's good-looking." It's funny that no matter how many years they've been married and even knowing how much my mother loves him, he still gets jealous when she talks about how good-looking another man is, even if it's in passing to my sister or even my aunts.

"I'm really not looking at dating anyone," Autumn interjects, and I look over at her. "I'm just focusing on the business."

"Now that's a sensible answer," my father says, "but all work and no play is not how to live a life."

"That's what I tell this one." My mother points at me with her thumb before picking up her burger. "It's fine he's doing his thing"—she waves her finger at me—"sowing the oats."

"Willow," my father snaps, turning to Autumn, whose face has now paled. "Can she have a water?"

"Quinn Barnes, don't you dare think you are going to take my drink away from me," she retorts. "These two are watching life just run away from them."

"Why don't we change the subject?" I pick my burger back up.

"Okay, fine," my mother gives in, "but I want you to be watching out for her." She looks at Autumn and then at me. "Make sure she's okay."

"Oh, I'll look after her, all right," I assure her, my eyes on Autumn as she turns her eyes to me. It's right then and there that I decide the only man who is going to fucking date her is me.

"What are we talking about?" Brady asks, coming to stand next to Autumn.

"Autumn and how she should date Emmett," my mother answers as my father puts his head back and looks up at the ceiling.

"She just had a date," Brady cuts in, and the burger in my mouth tastes horrible.

"With Emmett?" My mother gasps out and looks like she's about to clap her hands in glee.

"No." Brady shakes his head. "What was his name?" He snaps his fingers until he gets it. "Bryan."

"Can we stop talking about this?" Autumn urges while I put one hand on my hip, the other tapping the bar.

"So you are dating?" my mother asks her.

"It was one date," she mumbles, "and we decided that we were just going to be friends."

"Well, that's good. Have you been to the barn lately?" my father asks her, changing the subject.

"I have, actually. I went over there to ride Goldilocks," she replies and I wonder if she thought about lying to him, but then wonder if I told him she was there. Whatever the reason, I'm happy the conversation about her dating is fucking over.

"I met her today," my mother says. "She's so pretty."

"She is," Autumn agrees. "I have to check on the tables." She turns to walk away from us, leaving us with Brady as the talk turns to I don't know what because I'm only watching her work the room, smiling at people and conversing with them. It's different from when I came in here the first time and she would cower behind the bar.

She works the room, not noticing how the men look at her. She smiles politely, avoiding looking at them, as she goes back behind the bar but makes orders instead of talking to us.

We finish our burgers, and my father talks to Brady about buying some of the whiskey and taking it home. "Come and take a look in the back," Brady invites him and my mother, and they go with Brady, leaving me all alone.

I watch her make her way around the room until she comes back to me. "Where did they go?" she asks, picking up the plates, cleaning them up behind the counter before placing them into the dishwasher.

"Your brother is giving them a tour. My dad wants to take home a couple of cases of the new blend," I say. I want to ask more about the date she went on, but my mother comes back and the three of us talk about nothing in particular.

My father comes back after loading five cases into his truck, and they get up to leave. "I'll see you tomorrow," my mother tells Autumn, and Autumn just nods at her. I take one more look at her before walking out with my parents. My mother sits in the back as we drive back to my house.

"That was such a nice night," my mother says to me when we get home, and she steps outside. "We should do that again tomorrow."

"Yes," my father agrees as he holds her hand and walks up the steps to the front door, "just with less whiskey."

I chuckle when she slaps his arm. "Are you not coming in with us?" My mother looks at me because I'm standing by the truck.

"I'm going to go for a walk," I tell them.

"A walk where?" my mother asks, and my father stands beside her, with his lips held tight together.

"Around, I'll be back later."

"How much later?"

"Willow," my father cuts in, "how about we let him do what he needs to do."

"And what is that?" She glares at my father. "It's enough, don't you think?" My father puts his hands on her shoulders. "It's been eight years. It's time for him to come back to the land of the living and live."

"I'm living," I assure her as she sniffles back the tears running down her face. My father lifts his hand to wipe them away. "I promise, Mom, I'm fine." She turns to look at me. "I'm better than I think I ever was."

"I know," she responds softly. "I can see it. I can feel it." The smile on her face is soft as my father puts an arm around her neck and pulls her to him, kissing her on the top of her head. My mother didn't have the best childhood and was left for dead by her mother's husband, who was using her to steal people's identities. My mother is a computer wiz, so she sometimes works with my grandfather. She's the only one who can crack his firewall, and she's happy to do it each and every time. "We want you to be happy," she says. "The only thing a parent can wish for is that their child is healthy and happy."

"I'm getting there, Mom," I admit to her. "I might have been lost along the way, but I'm getting back." I'm not lying either, not like I used to do back then. Saying the words just to say them so she wouldn't worry. But she saw right through me, they all did. The only one I was fooling was myself.

"Okay." She wraps her arms around my father's waist. "We're here if you need us."

"Don't wait up," I say, pushing off and heading toward the forest. When I look over my shoulder at my house, I see they aren't there watching me. I make my way toward the cemetery, stopping at her grave site. "Hey," I say, getting down in a squat, "I know I haven't been here in a while." I don't know why, but I smile. "Not sure if you noticed or not. Or if you saw anything. I still miss you, but it's a different feeling now." My eyes are on her name like I expect her to say something to me, but the only thing in the night is the sound of crickets. I don't know how long I sit here; it could have been five minutes or it could have been an hour. But for the first time, leaving her is not with a feeling of dread. It's with a lightness as if the pressure on my chest has been taken off. "I'll come and visit again soon." I stand and put my hand on the cold gray marble. "I might even bring her with me." I smile and turn to walk toward her house.

I walk out of the clearing toward her house at the same time I see her walking out of the back door. She's out of her jeans and in another pair of shorts, but this time, they are tight and mold to her body. The tank top stops just under her tits, showing off some of her stomach, making my mouth water. She sits on the swing and pushes off, looking out, and I know when she sees me because her foot stops moving. "What are you doing here?" she asks as I take a step up.

"I told you I was coming here," I remind her as I walk up the steps and sit beside her on the swing, leaning sideways to kiss her neck. "Did you think I was lying?"

"Well..." she starts, unsure of what to say, "I thought that maybe with your parents here."

My hand finds hers on her leg as I pull her into me. Wrapping my arm around her waist, I pick her up. She gasps in shock as I place her on my lap to straddle me. My arms wrap around her waist, and I pull her to me. She's stiff for a couple of seconds before she melts into my chest and wraps her arms around my neck. Her head rests on my shoulder as her lips touch the side of my neck. "I missed you," I admit. "You don't have to say anything. I just wanted you to know." I feel her lips on my neck, softly kissing me, "especially after you left this morning."

"Charlie," she says, but her face never moves out of

my neck. "Just drop it."

"No," I say, tightening my hold on her. Was it the picture?" Her body goes stiff in my arms, "I moved Jennifer's picture." I tell her.

She moves away from me now, and I can feel her wanting to get off me. "Charlie."

"I put it in the living room instead of the bedroom." I inform her, "I didn't do it for you, I did it for me."

"No, you didn't," she snaps at me. "You are moving it back into your bedroom; that is where you want it."

"I want it where it's at, in the living room." My hands at her hips squeeze her. "I know you'll never tell me to move it. I know you'll never tell me to get rid of it, and that is all I need to know."

"I would never ever do that." She shakes her head.

"I know, baby"—I bend to kiss her lips—"but you're in my bed now, and I want you there more than I want the picture there." I see her look down at her hands on my chest. "She's where she needs to be." I don't want to drag out this conversation any more than I need to. "Should we go to bed?"

"Yeah," she mumbles. I get up as she wraps her legs around me and hangs on tight, as I walk to the back door and open it before stepping in and locking it behind me. She lets go of my neck, leaving one hand wrapped around my shoulder while the other one holds my face. She turns her head to the side as she presses her mouth to mine, and I forget everything from the outside and the only thing I have on my mind is her.

Thirty

THE SOUND OF soft bells fills my ears as the body under me moves to the side, making my eyes flutter open in time to see his naked back as he leans over the side of the bed and takes his phone out of his jeans. The sound of his belt buckle hitting the floor thumps right before the alarm is turned off. He places the phone on the bedside table before turning back to me and taking me into his arms. "Was that your alarm?" I turn my head to look over my shoulder and out the window to see the sun is coming up.

"It is," he mumbles, the sleep still in his voice as he buries his face in my neck.

"Shit," I hiss, and his head tilts back to look at me, "you were supposed to leave."

"Is that so?" he asks, his eyebrows pulled together. "Why is that?"

"Because your parents are at your house," I groan.

"Ugh, now they are going to know you didn't sleep at home." He buries his face again in my neck, but this time, pushes me on my back.

He kisses my neck, and my arms and legs wrap around him tightly. "I think I'm old enough for sleepovers."

He gets on his forearms to look at me. "They are going to ask all the questions." I put my head back deeper in the pillow.

"And I'm pretty sure I don't have to answer those questions." He bends his head to kiss my jaw as he moves back on his knees. My legs open for him, one leg going over his arm that is holding him up, as the other hand goes to his cock. I get up on my elbows to watch him fist it in his hand, rubbing it up and down my slit a couple of times before he looks up at me and slides the tip in. Both of us moan out at the same time. The hand that was holding his cock is beside my hip as he pushes more of it into me. He buries his dick all the way in me before his hand is between us as he plays with my clit at the same time as he fucks me. The sound of us heavily breathing now fills the room. He watches me watching his hand and his cock. "Every single time," he says, picking up speed, "feels like the first time." He moves a bit faster. "I want to spend the day fucking you." He moves the hand playing with my clit to my neck, squeezing me and pulling me down onto his cock to match his thrusts. "Make you come over and over again." I open my mouth to say something, but nothing comes out but a moan. My hand moves up to hold on to his wrist while he puts his forehead on mine. "Watch your pussy swallow my cock." We both look down. "Tighter and tighter." He pulls out to the tip before hammering back inside. I close my eyes, feeling the orgasm come closer when he snaps, "Watch us. Watch how you take me. Watch how your greedy pussy wants me. " His balls hit my ass while he slams into me. I want to open my eyes, but it feels so good until he pulls out of me. Then my eyes fly open. "I said watch me." His hips move back as he holds the base of his cock, moving it through my slit and to my clit, rubbing over it twice before sliding back into my pussy. "Greedy," he teases, smiling at me, "for my cock."

"Charlie," I hiss out his name as he slows his pace, leaving his cock planted in me halfway as his hand comes up and plays with my clit.

"Tell me what you want, baby." The way he calls me baby makes my stomach contract. "And watch me do it to you."

"Need you to fuck me, Charlie." I lick my lips, my hips moving up and down to get his cock more into me. "Need you to fuck me hard." His fingers move around and around on my clit. My whole body is tight. "Need you to fuck me so hard I feel you when I walk all day long." I look at his cock half in me, half out of me. "Can you fuck me that hard?" My eyes go from where we're joined to his eyes. "Can you fuck me that hard? That's what I want." He puts his hands by my hips, slamming into me. "Yes," I say breathlessly.

"Put your legs over my shoulders," he orders me through clenched teeth and slides so deep into me I feel him at my throat. I'm about to say how good it is, but

I can't because he's fucking me like he's never fucked me before. And he's fucked me hard before, but this, it's barbaric. Every single time he slams into me, the sound of our skin slapping together fills the room, but he picks up his pace over and over again. "Your pussy is so tight; it's sucking my cum right out of my balls." I don't have to say when I'm going to come because he tells me, "I feel you soaking my cock." My pussy clenches over and over on his cock. "Running down my balls." I can't help but cry out his name. "That's my girl," he praises, relentlessly pounding away at me. "Ask me for my cum," he urges. "Tell me you want my cum in you." I tilt my hips, hoping he goes even deeper. "Tell me you want me dripping out of your pussy all day long."

"Yes!" I shout.

"Say it," he growls, his teeth clenched together.

"I want your cum in me." I can't even focus because I feel another orgasm building. "I want to feel you all day long in me. I want your cum in me." My head goes side to side. "Fuck me harder."

"Any harder and I'll fucking break you." He can't even talk without panting.

"Then break me." I reach up and bite him right beside his nipple and that is his last straw. He doesn't stop, he thrusts into me harder and deeper until we are both going over the ledge. My hips thrust up to meet his until he plants his cock to the hilt, and I feel him coming in me. His mouth finds mine.

My hand leaves the sheet to cup the back of his head. My fingers play with his hair until I feel his twitching cock stop. He pulls his mouth off mine. "Fuck, just came harder than I ever have in my whole life." He looks down at his cock still buried in me. "And all I want is to fuck you more."

I giggle. "Is that a bad thing?"

"No, but I'm going to have to fuck you in the shower."

"Why is that?" I ask, confused since he's never taken a shower here.

"You want me to go home after staying out all night and smelling of sex?" he asks, and I roll my lips together.

"Good point." I move my hips, wanting him to fuck me more. "But aren't you still going to smell like sex if you fuck me in the shower?"

My legs fall off his shoulders, so he wraps one arm around my waist, pushing me onto his cock that is still hard in me, as he gets out of my bed. "One way to find out," he states, walking to the bathroom, "unless I fuck you and then you get out so I can wash."

He walks into my small bathroom, which is the size of his walk-in closet. "Or we could just shower."

My arms loosen from around his neck to hold his shoulders. "Or I fuck you on that counter"—he motions to the counter beside my sink—"and then shower." I don't answer him. I don't have to, my pussy answers for me. "Oh, you like that idea." He places me down on the edge of the counter, and I put my foot up on both sides. "Fuck, open for me." He pulls out his cock to the tip before he slides it back in. His hands go to the sides of my neck. "Last time was hard," he murmurs softly, "so this time I'm taking my time."

"Don't you have to get home?" I ask before his mouth finds mine.

"Don't care." That's the last thing he says, and the shower runs while he fucks me, taking his time. By the time he finishes, I've come five times and he's come twice. The water is ice cold by the time he finally pulls out of me and steps in the shower. "Fuck, it's like an ice bath."

"Shouldn't have taken your time fucking me." I laugh as he rushes to take a shower. He is almost finished getting dressed by the time I get out. My whole body is freezing, and I'm shivering. "Next time, we don't turn on the shower until we are getting in." I walk out of my bathroom.

"You have a robe?" he asks, and I shake my head. "Then put a long shirt on and come walk me to the door."

"You can go by yourself." I point toward the door. "You know the way."

"Yeah, but then I can't kiss you goodbye." I don't know why, but the words make my heart skip a beat. "I'm late as it is."

"You were the one who wanted to fuck me in the shower," I remind him as I drop my towel and grab my shorts and tank top, slipping them on. "You could have showered without me."

I walk to the end of the bed, where he waits for me. "What fun would that be?" He takes my hand in his, bringing it to his lips and kissing my fingers before walking to the back door.

I follow him out as he takes one step down and turns

to me. "I'll see you later." I don't know if he's asking me or if he's telling me. He puts his hands on my hips. "Have a good day." My hand comes up to brush his wet hair back before I kiss his lips.

"Have a good day, Charlie," I say softly as he turns and walks down the rest of the stairs. I lean against the post, watching him disappear into the forest, taking a second to take a deep breath in and out before walking back inside and getting dressed.

I pull up to the office earlier than normal because I decided to have coffee at my desk. My father's truck is already there, and when I walk in, I hear his boots as he walks out of the office. "Morning, sweetheart, I got you coffee." He smiles at me as I walk up to him and hug him, not thinking about the fact that he's gotten a bit skinnier since I've been here.

"You are my savior." I look up at him. "Always."

"Always will be," he mumbles before letting me go, and I walk into the office. "Have a couple of things to discuss with you," he says. "Sit down."

"This sounds official." I try to make it light, but his tone is anything but.

"It is," he states, "I'm not going to beat around the bush." He sits and puts his hands on his desk. "One, I found out that you took your own money to put into the company."

"Okay," I reply, and his eyebrows shoot up.

"I thought for sure you would try to make up a lie. Second, you are taking it all back today."

"I'm not." My tone is dead serious. "The company

needs it. I'll take it back when I can."

"And when do you think that will be?" he snaps at me. "I already have nothing to give you when I die. The last thing I want is for you to lose it all."

The minute he says those words, my chest gets tight. "The company is getting better." I try not to let my voice quiver.

"It is," he agrees, "but then what?"

"Then nothing," I retort, "this is what you are leaving me." I point out to the distillery. "This and your legacy. It's worth everything."

"Don't be silly." He shakes his head.

"I'm not." I slap the desk. "Now I know that it's been tough and I know we have a big hill in front of us, but we aren't going to get anywhere if we are just looking at it and not doing anything about it. So I'm going to do what I can and you two," I mention my brother, "are going to have to suck it up and let me." He glares at me. "The new blend that Brady made," I say. "We are going to have a private party to debut it and limit the invites to a hundred people for now. If people enjoy it, hopefully, it will attract more customers to the bar. Then we can host more events over the next few months, and if we are profitable, we can talk about adding tasting rooms and private rooms to hold the events. I've started working on a mailing list, and we're going to extend the invite to all of the people who've come in and ordered bottles of whiskey. We will charge them a fee to cover the cost of the food and some other things. We'll also include a tasting menu with different whiskeys, and fingers crossed, they'll like it and will order some of it."

"You think that will help?" he asks honestly.

"I have no idea, but I know we have to keep trying." I get up from my chair. "We've hidden for long enough." I swallow. "I've hidden for long enough. I did nothing wrong. I should have never let them run me out of town. But I'm back, and I'm not going anywhere. I'm going to walk with my head high." I close my eyes. "Okay, not like making direct eye contact, but I'm not going to be afraid of them anymore." He laughs. "But we are doing this party, and we are going to brace for the worst. But hope for the best."

He leans back in his chair. "After the party, you take back your money," he counters.

"After the party, we'll see how it goes, and I'll take back ten percent."

"You'll take it all back."

"Twenty percent," I counter, and he glares at me. "Also, that look doesn't scare me. I'm not a little girl anymore."

He tries not to laugh at me. "No, you aren't," he agrees. "I can see that being back home, you've got your backbone back." He nods. "Twenty percent, and if you don't take it, I'll fire you."

Now, it's my turn to laugh at him. "I think I own a third of the company."

He pushes back and gets up from his chair. "I had an idea about how to bottle the new blend," he tells me. "Take the bottle they used to use in the Prohibition era, and on the front, we do what they did back then, a doctor's note." He picks up a picture he must have found, and I see the front on the bottle.

"It looks like a script from a pharmacy." I see that the patient's name is on there with directions on how to take it. "This could be really cool. What if we did the theme from the twenties?" I start getting all the ideas. "You know who is going to love this?" I try not to laugh. "Brady."

"Oh, he's going to love this," my father agrees. "I'm going to go and bottle a few and see how it looks." He walks out and stops. "Love you, kiddo."

I smile at him. "Love you too, Dad." I watch him walk away from me with a vow that I'm going to do everything I can to make him proud of me.

Thirty-One

CHARLIE

I WALK INTO the bar just after seven, and see it's slower than usual, but it's also a Monday. I head to the bar, seeing Brady behind it. "Hey," I say, looking around to see if I spot her, but she isn't here.

The bell from the kitchen rings. "You can go get that and take it back to her," Brady suggests. "She's in the back going over the menu for the party."

"Okay." I walk over to the kitchen, finding the chef there smiling at me.

"Hello, Mr. Barnes." He nods at me. "You taking the food to Ms. Autumn?"

"I am." I pick up the plated burger. "Can I get one also?"

"Sure thing," he says and I walk out. It's been two weeks since my parents have been to town. It's also been two weeks that I've been at the bar every single night. I don't think it's a secret I'm there for Autumn, but I also haven't come in the bar and made out with her in front of everyone. Not that I would care, but I know she would. Even though we go to bed with each other every single night, and it's no secret when I leave her house and get home. I also don't give a shit if anyone knows, but I want to make sure she's ready for it. It's gotten to the point where I've even helped out in the bar on nights when they've been slammed. Which has surprised everyone, including them. It's like the black cloud of the Cartwrights has been lifted off them. But I also know it's because of all the hard work Autumn has been doing to bring in new business. In fact, every single weekend their tables are full, turning them over three times. They are even talking about hiring someone.

I walk into the back and find her with her head down as she writes things on a paper. "Knock, knock, knock," I say. She glances up at me and looks exhausted. "Brought you food." She's been working every single day for the past two weeks. Starting as early as I walk out of the house and finishing sometimes after midnight. Every single night we fall into bed with each other, and no matter what time I try to wake up before the alarm, I never do, and even when I do, she always wakes up when I get out of bed.

She smiles. "Thank you," she says as I walk around the desk and put the plate at the edge of the desk before leaning down and kissing her lips. "Hi," she murmurs softly when I let her go. "Is it busy out there?" She motions with her chin toward the door.

"Nah," I reply, "about six tables. I think he has it

covered. Eat." I point at the plate as she takes up a French fry and dips it in ketchup. "Are you almost done?"

"No." She shakes her head. "I never thought this party would be as big as it is," she admits, taking a bite of her burger and then offering it to me for me to take a bite of it. I shake my head, knowing that this is probably the only thing she's eaten today. "When I brought this up," she says, "I thought maybe thirty people."

"How many are you up to?" I ask. She looks at me, and I can see her eyes light up.

"Seventy-seven," she replies. "Do you know how many people that is?" I try not to laugh. "That's like a lot. The max is a hundred, so I'm happy it's almost there."

"Where are you going to put them all?" I ask and her whole face now lights up.

"We are going to close the bar for the day and do welcome cocktails in the bar. Then I'm going to have one side of the room cleared out and, on the other side, fit long tables down one wall to do a tasting menu. We are going to offer them chances to walk around. I want to get some of the pictures from back in the day set up all around with little facts about the company."

"You did this?" I ask, shocked about how creative she's been. "All these ideas?"

"Yes." She laughs as she takes another bite of her burger. "I've been going crazy trying to get all the things here, and everyone, of course, is like *cash only* since we're behind on some accounts, but we're catching up," she says, avoiding my eyes. "Thankfully, I have some money left, but it's all gone after this." She takes a deep breath. "The next step is probably selling the house." She trails off, and I get angry. "That's like the last thing I want to do. I don't think I'm going to have to do it. Business has picked up so much, but I can see the sky from under the water."

"Your father isn't going to let you sell your house," I say, trying not to sound angry or tense.

"My father isn't going to know." She shrugs. "I have to do what I have to do, Charlie. He's not getting better, and I can't have anything happen to him and have him, you know…" She can't say the words. "Worry that we're going to lose the business."

"Your father doesn't give a shit about that, and you know it." I sit up. "He cares that you are taken care of."

"I'll be fine," she states, not sounding as convincing as she wants to be. "It'll be fine."

"It will, baby," I assure her softly and then look over to see Brady standing there with a plate.

"You order this?" he asks of the plate in his hand.

"I did." I reach for the plate. "I'll pay when I come out front," I say, and he looks at the two of us.

"I think we owe you anyway," he replies, turning and walking out of the room.

"How do I get a ticket to this event?" I finally ask the question I've been dying to ask for the last two weeks since she started talking to me about it. Each day I would wait for her to ask me or wait to see if I saw anything on how to purchase tickets, but nothing.

"You want to come to the event?" She picks up her burger as I pick up mine. This is as close as we've gotten to having dinner together since that one night.

"Of course, I want to come to the event. I want to support you."

"Um…" She's not sure what to say. "The tickets are expensive, and you've already tried the new blend."

"Autumn," I say her name, "do you not want me there?" I try not to let it get to me, but I'm getting really pissed at the thought.

"I didn't say that," she says calmly.

"You also didn't not say it." I pick up my burger, trying not to let it get to me.

"Fine, I'll give you a ticket," she concedes softly, opening the drawer beside her and taking out something from her desk and handing it to me. "You get the first ticket."

She places the ticket in front of me, and I see that it's black and gold. "No, I'll buy a ticket," I say. "I'll pay Brady if you don't want to take my money."

"If I fight with you, will I win?" she asks.

"Baby," I call her the nickname I've been calling her more and more in private, "the only time you will win a fight is if we're fighting about which bed to sleep in." Her cheeks get pink as she looks at the door to make sure it's just the two of us. "Or what position you want me to fuck you in." She laughs. "Besides, I want two tickets."

"You're going to bring a date?" she asks. I can see the color drain out of her face, and I just stare at her.

"I don't know if Emmett will want to be called my date," I deadpan, without telling her there is no one I'm going to be fucking dating but her. "Is that okay?"

"Yes," she answers, the color coming back into her face as she closes her eyes. "I really need for this to work," she admits. "I'm exhausted."

"I'm going to take these plates to the front." I get up and pick up the plates. "Then I'll see if it's busy, and if not, I'm taking you home."

"Brady is just as tired," she states, trying to hide the yawn she's fighting.

"Brady comes in at noon some days," I remind her. "Brady isn't working eighteen hours a day." I walk out to the front and see only six people in tonight.

"Slow night?" I say as I clean the plates and put them in the dishwasher.

"We were slammed all afternoon with three fucking tours. I even had to cook a couple of burgers," Brady explains. "I'm about to do last call." He looks at his watch. "It's eight p.m. and it's a Monday."

I pull out two twenties and place them on the bar. "I'm going to take her out of here." I motion to the back, and he nods. He hasn't said anything to me about the two of us, but I know he's seen us a couple of times share a kiss in the back when we thought no one was there. "See you tomorrow."

"See you," he says, and I walk in the back and find her with her head on the desk.

I walk to the side of the chair and bend to kiss her cheek. Her eyes flutter open. "Come on, baby, let's go." She sits up, rubbing her eyes.

"Brady?" she mumbles as I pull her up from her chair and grab her purse.

"He's closing now," I inform her as we walk out the back door. I walk her to her side of the car, opening the door for her. "Get in." She looks up at me, and I can't help it. I bend my head and kiss her lips. "How does a bath sound?" I ask, and she moans in my arms. "I'll take that as a yes." I chuckle as she gets in the car, and I walk over to the driver's side, get in, and make my way over to my house. She puts her head on the window, and she's out like a light in two seconds.

"Where are we?" she asks when I stop the car, and she opens her eyes.

"My house." I get out and am about to carry her inside, but she gets out and meets me at the front door. I don't say anything to her as I walk in the house and head for my bathroom. I turn on the water and test it before walking over and grabbing one of the bath bombs I never use that are in a basket by the tub. She stands next to me as I sit at the corner of the tub.

"Are you coming in with me?" She steps between my legs as I look up at her, her fingers pushing back the hair at the side of my head.

"Do you want me to come in with you?" She nods as she crosses her arms in front of her and pulls off her T-shirt, throwing it to the side, followed by her jeans and then her bra and panties. She stands in front of me naked. My head bends forward to kiss her stomach. "Get in. I'll get undressed." My clothes join hers as she gets in and I quickly step in, sitting in front of her.

She comes over to me and straddles my lap. "Thank you for running me a bath," she says softly, my arms wrapping around her. Her mouth finds mine at the same time she reaches between us and sinks down on me. My hands grip her waist as she rides me, my mouth coming down to her nipple, neither of us saying a word. Even when we get out of the tub and head to bed, she slides in and meets me in the middle. Her head is on my chest, and in no time, I feel her heavy weight on me. It doesn't take me long to join her.

When the alarm rings, I'm on my stomach facing the bedside table. She's draped over my back, and I smile as she cuddles into me for a couple of seconds before rolling away from me and getting out of bed. She heads to the bathroom and comes back out fully dressed. Coming to my side of the bed, she bends to kiss my lips. "Have a good day," she says, rushing out of my house before I even have a chance to get up.

I toss the cover off myself and get out of bed, grabbing my jeans from last night and my T-shirt before sending Emmett a text.

Me: *I'll be there late.*

He answers with one word.

Emmett: *Okay.*

I walk out of the house and head toward the path that isn't worn out anymore. There is even some grass growing where it was just dirt. I walk into the black cast-iron fence area, heading straight to her. "Hey." I look down at her tombstone. "I guess you've been wondering where I've been." I smile as the tears escape my eyes. "Or maybe you haven't." I stare at her name engraved in the marble. "I'm in love with her." I expect the tightness in my chest to be so strong that it doesn't let me breathe, but it's not there. "I don't know when it happened, but it did." I wait for the guilt to come, but again, it's not there. "I don't even know if she feels the same way about me, but I'm going to say it tonight." I decide. "I don't even care if she loves me or not. I'll take her any way I can have her. She's the hardest-working person I know. She's kind. She's thoughtful. She's funny." I smile. "I don't have to tell you all this. You know how she is." I wipe the tears away from my face. "I want you to know that I will always love you." I take a deep inhale and exhale. "You'll always own a piece of my heart. But I've learned that just because I love you doesn't mean I can't love her. Because, fuck, I do. God, I love her so much." My heart feels like it's going to explode. "I fucking love her, and I'm not going to be sorry about that. I'm going to wake up every day thankful that I have her. Thankful I can look at myself in the mirror again. Thankful I don't have to hide how I felt about you to her. She knows, but it's time for her to have all of me. She probably won't take all of me, that's the kind of person she is. She'll leave a part of me for you." I touch the headstone. "I'll see you soon." I turn and head back to my house, knowing it's time to finally have that talk and knowing I'm free to have it.

Thirty-Two

AUTUMN

THE PHONE RINGS beside me, and I look over from all the papers on the desk and see it's Mildred FaceTiming me. I slide my finger across the green button and wait for the circle spinning in the center with her picture, telling me it's connecting. She comes into view, and I can't help but smile big and also get a little sad at not seeing her every day. "Well, well," she says, her hair piled on top of her head, and I see she is sitting in the office. The creak of the old wooden chair squeals out when she leans forward. "Look at who it is." I've been home about three months, and in all that time, I've called her twice, I think, maybe three times. I've been horrible at communicating with her and know I need to do better.

"I know." I put the phone in front of me. "I'm the worst. I should have called," I admit.

"Forget that." She waves her hand to the side. "How are you doing?"

"I'm holding on by a string," I admit and proceed to fill her in with everything that has been going on. "Which now leaves me with zero money in the bank and betting everything on the house."

"You'll never have zero in the bank," she assures me, "you know that. You should know after all this time that you are worth a million." I roll my eyes at her.

"Sometimes it helps having that million in the bank." We both laugh.

"You look different." She takes in my face. "Definitely look like you gained weight, thank God." I shake my head.

"I eat donuts for breakfast every single day." I joke back with her.

"It's not just that." She stares at me. "Your eyes don't look haunted like they used to." I don't know what to say to that. "You have a lightness about you that I've never seen before."

"Maybe it's the ghost from the past that has left my body." I shrug. "Maybe it's the lighting in the office." I look up and see the lights above me.

"It's none of that. So am I getting an invite to this big party?" I stare at her, my eyes big. "If you don't invite me, I can always call your father and take him up on that offer to go out with him." I blow up my cheeks, fake vomiting to the side. "Not like that." She laughs. "Besides, who gives it out on the first date? Send me the details, and I'll see if I can get someone to cover for me."

"Mildred," I say her name, "I think I'm going to have to give up the apartment. It's silly to just have it sitting there when you could be getting rent for it." She shakes her head. "I don't know when I'm going to be coming back."

"You aren't coming back." She says the words I haven't said to her because I was too afraid to admit I didn't have her as my safety net. "I'll have your stuff boxed for you and bring it when I come down."

"Mildred." I choke on my sob, knowing I really won't be going back. "What if things don't work out here?"

She laughs. "Silly girl. It's already working out." There is a knock on her door. "Now, I have to go but I want you to text me, yeah?" she urges, and I nod as the tears roll down my cheeks. "Don't be a stranger."

"Thank you," I croak out as she looks away from the screen as I see her blinking rapidly. "I'll see you soon."

"You betcha." I can see the tears in her eyes as she smiles. "See you soon." She blows me a kiss before she disconnects the phone. I put the phone down and close my eyes, counting to ten.

I open my email and send her the information for the night. I make sure there is no price anywhere and then check to see that Bryan has emailed me and told me he's gotten an order for forty cases, and I swear to God I about cry at that. He also has brought down his terms to twenty percent this time.

I get up from my desk, noticing it's a bit past five o'clock, so Brady will most likely be in the front. I walk out and see it's jam-packed. "Shit," I swear, walking behind the bar. "Why didn't you come and get me?" I ask as I look at the orders on the bar and start filling them. It takes twenty minutes to get through all the orders, and I look around to see more locals than strangers this time.

The bell rings in the back, and I serve the plates, only stopping when it's almost ten o'clock. We've been nonstop since five. I've only had time to take one sip of water. "You can go," I tell Brady. "I'll close up. You got last night."

"Where is your partner?" Brady asks, and I look at him. "He hasn't come in."

I know he's talking about Charlie. He's a topic like the elephant in the middle of the room. Neither of us talking about the fact that he's been a constant in the bar for the past two weeks. Or the fact he's caught me making out with him more times than I care to admit even though we were away from prying eyes. I know he's worried about the whole thing, but I also know he's not getting on my ass about it. I mean, I don't even want to think about what the fuck we are doing. "Guess not." I ignore the fact I'm worried about him, but I also know that it's not my place to worry about him. We are fuck buddies, or at least that is what I tell myself we are.

"You sure you'll be fine?" he asks, and I glare at him. "Fine." He holds up his hand. "I'll come in early."

"Okay," I agree, knowing full well that I'll also be in. "Have a good night," I say as he walks out toward the back. I serve the tables I have left and finally close up shop at close to eleven. By the time I clean up and walk out to my car, it's a little past midnight. I drive home, ignoring the way my chest tightens when I think about Charlie. The scenarios run through my head the whole time. Him at home sleeping. Him on a date. Him being anywhere but here and me wanting to know if he's okay.

Pulling up to my house, I see him sitting there on the second step, his arms on his knees, his hands in front of him. He looks up, and I see his face looks like he's exhausted. "Hey," I say, getting out of the car and slamming the door. He stands up by the time I make it to him, and he doesn't lean down to kiss me, like he always does, which makes my heart speed up even faster than when I saw him.

"Hey," he says softly. "We need to talk." His voice is tight, and I nod, walking past him toward the front door and letting myself in. We should have had this talk outside so I wouldn't have the images in my head. If he's ending whatever this is, I should not let him do it here in my house.

I put my purse on the table, trying to control my breathing. Trying to control the way my hands are shaking, trying to control myself. I turn to face him, and he stands in front of me. His hands go to my face, and he holds it in them. I look into his eyes, wishing I had left the lights on so I could see his eyes for one last time. He bends his head, and I inhale when his lips touch mine. My hands come up to grip his wrists as he kisses me. "I'm sorry I didn't come to see you," he apologizes when he lets go of my lips, his thumbs rubbing my cheeks.

"That's okay." I try to steady my voice so it doesn't shake with the way my heart is pounding.

"I was afraid that if I came to see you, I wouldn't be able to wait until we were here to have this conversation."

I swallow the lump as I step back, his hands falling away from my face. "And I wanted to do this privately."

"You don't really have to do all of this, Charlie." I try to let him off the hook. "It's—"

"This morning when you left me, I didn't go to work." His voice is soft, and I look at him confused. "I had something to do beforehand, so I went to do it."

"Okay." One of my hands grabs my index finger, twisting it nervously.

"I went to Jennifer's grave." I put my hand on my stomach to stop it from lurching. "I went to tell her I've fallen in love with you." The minute he says the words, I think the air is being sucked out of me. I have to put one hand on the table to stop myself from falling. "I told her she would always have a piece of my heart, but that it now belonged to you." The tears come so fast and so hard I can't even control wiping them, falling one after another on my hand that is at my stomach. "I told her it was time for you to have all of me."

"Charlie." I shake my head. "You don't have to do that. I know how much you love her."

He chuckles as he sniffles at the same time. "Exactly what I told her. I was thankful I wouldn't have to hide the fact that Jennifer meant something to me."

"I would never "—I shake my head—"ask you to do that."

"I know, which is another reason I love you like I do." I watch his Adam's apple rise and fall as he swallows. "You don't have to say anything. I just wanted you to know how I feel. I wanted you to know where I was."

"I thought you were ending things with me," I admit to him, and it's his turn to gasp. "I also was telling myself that it was okay. But it wasn't, I wasn't." My voice cracks, and I put my hand on my mouth. "This is more than anything I've ever felt before." My chest rises and falls. "I never thought in a million years, after the heartache I felt, that I would feel this fullness. That my heart that was shattered into a million pieces would feel like it's full again." I close my eyes. "The guilt of loving you and wanting you weighed down on me each and every day." He doesn't give me another second to myself as he comes to stand in front of me. "Not sure if I deserve it or not."

His thumbs catch the tears running down my face. "You deserve it," he assures me softly, "we deserve it." He rubs his nose with mine. "We deserve happy, baby."

"You think so?" I ask, my hands going to his hips, gripping his T-shirt in my hands.

"I don't think so"—he tilts his head to the side, his lips hovering over mine—"I know so, baby."

Thirty-Three

CHARLIE

"THE WATER IS ice," I complain, getting out of the shower and leaving her in there. "It's like ice pellets hitting my back."

"Stop being such a princess." She laughs as she puts her head back and lets the water rinse the shampoo out of her hair. "You swam in a creek before. It's not warm."

"I swam in a creek before when I was overheated, and it felt good." I grab the towel.

"Well, were you not overheated from banging me against this wall?" She hits the wall on the shower.

"It's not the same thing." I glare at her, and she laughs, and it literally warms my fucking soul.

"Then maybe you aren't doing it right," she teases me, and I turn my head and walk out of her bathroom.

"I'm doing it fine," I mumble as I pick up my boxers and slide them on before grabbing my jeans. "Do you want a coffee?" I shout to the bathroom, and she sticks her head out.

"You're staying for coffee?" she asks, and I put my hands on my hips.

"Did we not have a conversation last night?" I ask. All she can do is stare at me, but in a cute way, with her trying to hide a smile by biting the corner of her lip, and I can't help but walk to her. "What did I say last night?" She looks up at me, her hair wet and so are her eyelashes. I grab her face. "What did I tell you last night?" My voice is low as I turn my head to the side and kiss her lips. It's a short, wet kiss. "So?"

"You said you were in love with me." Her voice is higher than a whisper.

"So that means I stay for coffee," I inform her.

"Oh, okay." She tries not to smile but fails. "Then I'll have a coffee."

"I'll get right on that, baby." My hands drop from her freezing face. "Please get out of that fucking shower."

"I have to condition my hair still," she says. "It's fine. You get used to it."

"I also don't think that's how it works." I shake my head.

She pushes me away as she steps back in the shower, and I walk to her bedroom and then outside to the kitchen. I'm grabbing things to make coffee when I see movement coming from the front of the house through the window. I put the mugs down as the hair on the back of my neck sticks up. "What the fuck?" I move my head to the side and see him: the fucking reporter. He looks around to make sure no one is looking in his direction when he reaches out for the mailbox at the curb. I rush to get my boots on, head to the door, and open it before storming out there. There's a stack of letters in his hand. It takes me three strides to be in front of him, shocking him enough when I grab the front of his shirt. "What the fuck are you doing?"

His face pales, the letters falling from his hand. "Oof," he grunts, his hands going to my wrist.

"I asked you a fucking question," I hiss at him. "What the fuck are you doing here?"

"Get off me." He tries to fight me off him, but I'm holding on to him for dear life. The rage fills my whole body. "Get the fuck off me." He moves side to side to try to get my hands to get off him. "I'm fucking suing you for assault."

"Not assaulting you if you are on private property and I'm defending the person who lives here," I inform him, my teeth clenched together. "Now, I won't ask you again. The next person I'll call is the sheriff, who I think would be interested to know why you were touching someone's mail. I think that's a federal crime." There is literally no other color on his face. "Now, what's it going to be? You answer my questions, or I call the sheriff and you can answer his questions?" I ask, but I'm so far gone, the second the question comes out I expect him to answer me. "Tick, tock," I say, moving my hand to me and then back again, shaking him.

"Fine, fine," he concedes, and I loosen my fist and push him away from me.

"Talk." I fold my arms over my chest to stop from

punching him in the face. "What are you doing here?"

"I was hired by the Cartwrights," he says and everything in my body gets tight. "They are looking for anything that will prove she"—he points at the house—"was responsible for the accident in one way or another. That maybe the two of you were the reason he was drinking since you two are now, you know."

"You're shitting me right now."

"I'm not shitting you." He smooths down his shirt that is balled at the chest and wrinkled. "They feel like their son was done a disservice by Ms. Thatcher, so they would like anything that would make her look like she was a liar and an opportunist." I count to ten, or at least I know I should count to ten, but I don't.

"Get the fuck off her property, and if I find you even sniffing in her direction, you'll have to deal with me. And, buddy, word to the wise." I take a step forward. "I would not fuck with me."

He holds up his hands. "Yeah, yeah," he backpedals, "this town is shot to shit anyway." He turns and gets into his truck. I take out my phone and snap a picture of his license plate and send it straight to my grandfather.

The phone rings two seconds later. "We have a situation," I say, bending and picking up the mail as I fill him in.

He doesn't even tease me about being at Autumn's house at the ass crack of dawn. "This just shot up to the top of my to-do list," he states and then hangs up.

I look up to the sky before turning and walking back into the house at the same time she walks out of the bedroom, wearing the T-shirt I wore last night, a white towel wrapped up on top of her head. "Where were you?" she asks, looking at me standing here in my jeans and boots.

"Went to get your mail," I lie to her, holding it up.

Her eyeballs go big. "You went out to get my mail half naked?"

"I'm not naked." I put the mail on the kitchen table. "I'm wearing pants. If I went out in my boxers, then I would be half naked."

"Charlie," she hisses, "people could see you!" I raise my eyebrows.

"Are you embarrassed?" I tease her as she glares at me, and I snatch her around her waist. "I like seeing you in my T-shirt." I kiss her neck.

"Is my coffee ready?" she asks but wraps her arms around my neck, not letting me move away from her. "Say it," she urges, looking up at me. All night long if she woke up, she would whisper to me for me to say how I feel about her.

"I," I say, kissing her lips, "love"—another kiss— "you." This time, I slide my tongue into her mouth. I'm about to pick her up when my phone rings, and I know it's my grandfather. "I have to get that," I say, her arms let go of my neck.

"How about I make coffee, then?" She turns and walks into the kitchen as I put the phone to my ear.

"Not a good time," I mention, knowing I can't talk.

"Good, so you can listen," my grandfather says, and I watch her make us coffee. "I think it's a good idea you guys come visit us this weekend. Make sure this guy leaves town, and if not, there might be blowback. I don't want the two of you involved in whatever I have planned, since you are now involved with each other." He slides in that comment, and if this wasn't a tense moment, I would laugh.

"Got it," I confirm, knowing I probably don't got it. There is no way she is going to leave town so close to the event and knowing how busy the bar gets on the weekends.

"See you tomorrow," he replies and hangs up the phone.

"Everything okay?" she asks, and for the second time, I lie to her, and the guilt eats at my stomach.

"Yeah, I have to get to the barn," I say, and she nods, walks over, and grabs a travel mug.

"If you give me ten minutes, I can get dressed and drive you over there," she offers. I nod as she walks by me but stops to kiss my chest where her bite mark is before pulling my shirt over her head and leaving her naked in front of me.

"That's not going to get us out of here in ten minutes." I slap her ass as she walks away from me giggling. I prepare us both to-go coffees, and when she drops me off at the house fifteen minutes later, I make out with her like it's the last fucking time I'm going to kiss her. "See you later." I get out of the truck and walk up the steps to my front door. Walking in, I grab my truck keys before turning and heading right back out.

Hoping like fuck he's home, I pull up to his house,

which is farther away from town. The fixer-upper he bought a couple of years ago looks brand new compared to the one that is falling down beside him. Walking up the steps, I pull open the storm door and knock.

I hear him on the other side of the door before he pulls it open, wearing what I was wearing not too long ago. "Charlie," he says my name.

"I need a favor," I state and he moves away from the door and I step in to see that the front isn't the only thing that is new. The whole inside looks like it was redone. I also know he did all this shit by himself over the last eight years.

"What kind of favor?" he asks.

I explain to him everything that happened this morning, his face filling with fear and then anger. "What the fuck?" he hisses out. "Like can't they just leave her the fuck alone?"

"I need to get out of town and I need your sister to come with me."

"She won't go." He shakes his head, thinking exactly what I was thinking.

"I'm going to come in tonight, sit with you at the bar, and ask her to go with me," I say. "I'm going to need you to take my back on this. I'll hire a couple of people to help you at the bar. If she thinks you're okay with it, she might go with it."

"I'll take your back." He nods. "You sure about this?" I know the question isn't about the plan to take her away for the weekend. He's asking me if I'm sure about his sister.

"She's it for me," I confirm and his mouth drops. "Told her I love her yesterday. Only one other person I said that to. Not going to be another one. I'll be at the bar tonight and you take my back."

"Yeah," he agrees and I nod at him, turning and walking out of the house and heading to the barn. I walk in searching for Emmett, who is sitting on his desk.

"Why is it every single time I find you, you're sitting on this desk?" I joke with him.

"Why is it that every single time you are supposed to be here, you're not?" he jokes back with me.

"Need a favor." I look around to see if anyone is within earshot.

"Your card is all used up." He smirks. "Front and back."

"You know anyone who could serve in a bar for about a week?"

"Do I look like HR to you?" He laughs.

"Is that a yes?" I put my hands on my hips.

"I know a couple of the guys who are looking for extra money," he says, motioning to the young kid who we just hired. "I'm sure he can take drinks to a table."

"Good, bring him to the bar tonight," I say and turn to head to the house.

"Are you working today?" he asks, and I flip him the bird over my head.

That night, the three of us are walking into the almost full bar. "Time to see what you can do," I tell Bishop. I slap him on the shoulder as I walk to the bar. Autumn looks up at me as she slings her shaker over her shoulder.

"You're swamped."

"Yeah." She smiles. "Two tour groups came this afternoon and haven't left yet." I look to the side to see Brady stepping behind the bar, and we share a chin-up.

"I'll help, and so will my guy, Bishop," I volunteer, and Brady just looks at his sister. "He has experience," I lie to them. The kid just turned twenty-one and has yet to be in a fucking bar.

"Good," Brady says. "Come with me," he tells Bishop, who follows him as I walk around the bar.

The four of us work nonstop for two hours, while Emmett sits his ass down on his stool, surveying. Bishop comes back and is all excited about the extra tips he's earned, not bringing up the fact I'm also paying him double his salary at the bar for the weekend.

Emmett leaves with him, and Brady comes behind the bar. "You need to stop giving those tours." He glares at his sister, who shrugs. "When I do those tours, they leave. You do them and they all think they can be your best friend."

"It's not my fault." She laughs and then looks at me. "What's wrong with you?"

"I have to go home this weekend," I explain and her face suddenly changes. "Have to check out a couple of things." Lie three today.

"Oh." That's all she says, grabbing the rag and wiping down the bar.

"Come with me?" I ask and look at Brady, who shares a quick glance with me.

"I can't leave," she replies.

"Yes, you can, and she is going with you," Brady declares. "It'll be a holiday not having you here."

She glares at him. "Who is going to help you?"

"Bishop, kid is good and he's looking for extra work," Brady cuts in. "Can't do many weekdays since he works for this one." He points at me. "But he said he can do Friday and Saturday since he's off on the weekend."

I walk to her and put my hand around her waist and pull her to me. "Come home with me," I urge as she looks up at me. "I don't want to be without you."

She looks at me, then at Brady, who puts his hands together. "Please leave." He even closes his eyes, and if I would be able to give this guy an Oscar, I would.

"You're a dick," she tells Brady, then turns to me. "I have to be back by Sunday night. I have a meeting on Monday morning with vendors."

I nod. "We can do that." I will agree to anything to take her away and I was even okay with kidnapping her, but this is much better. "Let's get you home and packed."

Thirty-Four

AUTUMN

"I DON'T KNOW about this," I mutter from beside him, my feet up on the dash as I move them side to side, looking out the window at the trees zooming by. I've been like this for the past three hours of the drive, and we have an hour left. "Like, isn't it going to be weird?" I ask again for I think the hundredth time.

He reaches out his hand to put on my leg, the heat from his hand warming me. "It's only weird if we make it weird."

My head flies to look at him, shocked he would say it was weird. "But it's weird." I tuck my hair behind my ear. He's sitting there wearing a white T-shirt, his biceps making my mouth water. His hair is pushed back from the shower he took this morning before we left my house. After work, I went to his house while he packed his bag, and then we went to my house, where I packed. We left this morning when we woke up, stopping along the way for coffee and donuts.

"It's not weird," he corrects himself, "and if you feel weird, we can always leave."

I gasp, putting my hand on his and linking our fingers on my leg. "Not only am I going to be the weird one, then I'm going to have you leave, so now I'm a bitch."

"Baby," he soothes, bringing our hands to his lips and kissing my fingers. "Everything will be fine. It's not going to be weird. It's going to be fine, and it's going to be great." He looks at the road, and then his voice goes lower. "Baby," he calls me, and I look over at him, "I need to tell you something."

"I knew it," I say, making him laugh. "It's weird, right?"

"No." He shakes his head. "Not that." He tightens his fingers with mine. "I lied to you." My feet fall off the dash as I sit up straight. "Not really lied to you. That was the wrong word." My heart beats so fast I can't even say anything. "I don't have to go home for work." I wait, knowing there is more. "Yesterday morning, I caught that reporter guy sneaking around your place." My mouth opens in a gasp. "I went out to confront him. He's not a reporter."

"What is he?" I ask, my head spinning at this information.

"I think he's a private investigator, but he was hired by the Cartwrights." The minute he says that, I feel like I'm going to get sick. I pull my hand from his, putting both of my hands on my stomach. "He was trying to find information about you being involved with the accident."

I can't help but snort out at that part.

"How?" I shake my head. "Like, how would I be involved? I was sitting in the back, and he was literally crushed to the steering wheel. How did they think I could spin this?" I look at him, and he looks like he's hiding something else. "What else?"

"He might have alluded to us being an item back then, which is why Waylon was drinking."

"Oh my God," I snarl, looking up at the roof of the cab, "are they insane?" I go from feeling sick to my stomach to angry. "Forget I asked if they are insane, one hundred and fifty percent fucking insane to think that we were hooking up before. They are so delusional that they can't see the only one to blame was fucking Waylon, and obviously them for enabling his bratty fucking behavior." I shake my head. "How did you find all this out?"

"I may have threatened to beat the shit out of him and have him arrested for stealing your mail." I throw my hands up in the air. "I called my grandfather, and he said that we should maybe not be home this weekend."

"My brother and my father." My mouth suddenly goes dry.

"They're fine. Brady knows—" he starts to say and stops when I shriek.

"Brady knows?" My eyes glare at him. "Wow."

"I needed to get you out of town." He tries to plead his case.

"So instead of, I don't know, telling me the truth. You lied to me." I laugh and pfft out. "Great."

"It's not like that." He reaches for my hand.

335

"It's exactly like that." I let him slide his fingers through mine and bring them to his lap. "It's one thousand percent like that. You lied to me."

"I wanted you safe," he refutes, his voice tight, "and I'd do it again."

"What are we doing? I mean, we love each other, but what does that mean, exactly? Like, what are we doing with each other?" I ask. He just looks over, his eyebrows pinched as he pulls over to the side of the road and puts the truck in park before he turns to stare at me. "Because if we are together and doing whatever with each other, we can't be lying to each other."

In one move, he reaches over, unbuckles my seat belt, and reaches down with his other hand, putting the seat back before plucking me out of my seat and pulling me onto his lap. "That's the first time you said you love me." His voice is a whisper, making my heart soar.

"Did you not know?" I ask, my fingers playing with the collar of his shirt. "I thought you—"

"Autumn, I'm in love with you and only you. And I lied, but it wasn't technically a lie." I raise my eyebrows at him. "The point is, I'm telling you now."

"The point is, you should have told me this when it happened." I maneuver on his lap to straddle him. "I can't take lying."

"I know, baby, I'm sorry."

"This is the last time," I warn. "There won't be another time. I can't do the lying thing."

"Noted," he says, and I'm irritated.

"Don't 'noted' me, Charlie Barnes." I move to get off

him, and he grips my hips, pulling me back down on him. "What are you doing?"

"We just had our first fight," he mumbles, his hands moving up to take my shirt with him, and I smack his hands away.

"You do not think I'm going to have sex with you on the side of the road," I gasp, "in broad daylight." I get off his lap. "Maybe if it was nighttime, but definitely not now."

"So first course of action," he plans, putting his seat belt back on and getting his seat back into his place, "make-up sex."

I shake my head as I fasten my own seat belt, and he pulls onto the road. "So what did we learn from this?" I look over and ask.

"That in one hour, I'll be having make-up sex." He smirks my way, and my heart literally jumps in my chest at his smile. "And I'm never to keep anything from you."

"I mean not in that order, but..." I smile, looking outside and realizing if this would have happened three months ago, it would have probably broken me. It would have cut me off at the knees, but not today. I take it with a grain of salt. They've broken me once; I refuse for them to break me again. "Yes."

We pull up to his house in forty-five minutes, and the minute we do, he groans. "What are my parents doing here?" he whines. "It's time for make-up sex." His hand goes for the door handle as I slide my feet in my flip-flops.

"Charlie, don't you dare say anything to them," I

warn between clenched teeth when I see the front door open and Willow come out, followed by Quinn.

"What are you guys doing here?" Charlie asks as soon as he gets out of the truck, and I meet him in the front of it. The last time I saw his parents was two weeks ago after they visited Charlie for a couple of days. Each day, they would eat at the bar at night, and he would spend the night with me, no matter how many times I told him to go home.

"We brought over some food," Willow explains, looking at her son and then looking at me. Charlie comes to stand next to me and slides his hand into mine. Her eyes go big. "Oh my." She looks up at Quinn, who tries not to make eye contact. "You knew?"

"No," he lies. "I might have suspected this, but this is a shock to me also." He gasps. "You two are together?" He rolls his eyes. "Maybe if we laid off the special blend, we would have seen what was in front of *your* face." I turn my head to laugh against Charlie's shoulder as she glares at him.

"We're leaving." She shakes her head. "And you"— she points at Charlie—"we are going to have words later." She then looks at me, and her smile comes back. "It's good to see you, Autumn, I'm happy you're here." She then slides her eyes back to Charlie. "You, not so much." She walks to the truck, getting into the driver's side, and we all hear the sound of her locking the doors.

"Willow," Quinn says, walking to the pickup and trying not to laugh. He pulls to open the door and the handle drops back while she starts the truck. He knocks on the window. "This isn't funny," he says, and Willow just puts the music louder in the truck as she adjusts her seat.

"She's going to leave him here?" I say, shocked as she backs out slowly.

"Nah," Charlie says, "if she wanted to leave him here, she wouldn't have backed out so slow." He lets go of my hand, walking to the truck, and knocks on the window. "Mom, can you stay for lunch?"

She stops the truck at the same time Quinn walks over to stand next to me. "I hope you know that he's exactly like his mother." I put my hand in front of my mouth as Charlie talks his mother into staying for lunch.

"I'll get the bags," Quinn offers, walking to the back of the truck and stopping when Willow comes to stand beside him. "You almost ran over my foot," he accuses, and she ignores him but doesn't walk away from him. "Our son is home. Give me a kiss and let's have lunch." She looks up at him, the look of love written all over her face.

I'm so engrossed in them I don't feel Charlie put his arm around me, looking up at him. "See, it's not weird." He bends his head and kisses my lips softly before whispering in my ear, "Don't think I'll forget about make-up sex." I laugh at him as he turns, and we head into his house.

"Are you done with this?" I get up from my chair and walk over to Charlie's side of the table to grab his plate. His hand comes out as he rubs the back of my leg. I look down at him as he looks up at me. The smile on his face makes his eyes light.

"Yeah, baby," he replies softly, and I know I shouldn't care that he's calling me baby in front of his parents, but I do a bit. But not that much because I lean down and kiss his lips, because I want to. Because it feels right. But more importantly, because I can.

I grab his plate and see Willow watching us, her hand going to her own plate as she gets up and grabs Quinn's plate. The two of them made up by the time they walked in. "You don't have to clean up," I say. "Charlie can help."

"He has to get the bags," Willow says, and I look over to see the bags at the door, but I just walk back into the kitchen with the plates in my hands. "I'll go get the rest," she tells me but doesn't move. "So you and Charlie," she starts, and I put the plate down, trying not to be nervous but failing.

"I know it's a shock," I start, my voice quivering, "and trust me, we weren't expecting it to happen." The tightness in my chest gets even tighter. "It's not just for fun. I know I'm rambling, but I can't help it. I ramble when I'm nervous." I lift my hands and drop them into the sink.

"There is no reason for you to be nervous." She smiles at me as she blinks away tears. "We owe you more than words can say right now."

"What?" I question her, confused as she grabs one of my hands.

"I just had lunch with my boy, and he sat there, and he smiled—not a fake smile but a real fucking smile that went all the way to his eyes." I try not to laugh at her saying the F-word, especially since she whispered it. "I sat there, and he laughed like I haven't heard before. Like I've been praying for for the last eight years. He sat there, and I could tell he was happy. He wasn't faking it. He wasn't saying it to say it. He was actually happy, and he's thriving, and you are part of that reason." I start to say something, but she holds up her hand. "You brought me back my boy. I didn't think I would ever see him again." She wipes the tears away. "You brought my boy home." She smiles at me. "Now, we've been in your hair long enough." She turns. "So I'm going to let my husband," she shouts toward the men, "take me home and make up for the fact that he lied to me."

"I didn't lie to anyone. Did you ask me?" Quinn defends himself from the table in the other room. "No, you didn't."

She winks at me. "So now I have to ask you things, and you not tell me?" She puts her hands on her hips and walks into the room. "What else are you keeping from me?"

He groans, and I hear the chair creak across the floor before I see him bend. The next thing you know, she's over his shoulder. "What are you doing?"

"You are begging to fight with me." He smacks her ass. "I'm going to give you something to fight with me about." He walks out the door and slams it after him. I look over at the dining room when I hear the sound of the other chair scraping the floor.

Charlie now comes to my side as he bends down and

picks me up over his shoulder, and I laugh. He slaps my ass. "You owe me make-up sex." He walks over to one side of the house. "Plus interest."

Thirty-Five

I'M SLIDING ON my suit jacket when I hear a knock on the door. I walk out and head toward it; I can see figures through the glass window. I'm almost there when there is another knock on the door. "I'm coming," I say, pulling it open and staring at my sister, Grace, in shock. "What the hell are you doing here?" Her husband, Caine, stands behind her, wearing a suit very much like mine. My parents pull up behind them, and then a couple of my aunts follow. Everyone is dressed to the nines. The last time I saw them was when we went home to escape the man lurking around. It took my grandfather two days to find out who he was and to deliver him a message that he was messing with the wrong people. Which isn't surprising since my grandfather runs the biggest security firm in the country. It took him less than an hour to cut ties with the Cartwrights, and we found this out through an email he sent to them quitting. Since then, we haven't seen him around town, and from what my grandfather told me this morning, he's in New York.

"Is that any way to talk to your favorite sister?" She steps in, kissing my cheek.

"You're my only sister," I remind her, turning and seeing Caine hold out his hand to me and shake it.

"I told them it wasn't a good idea, but I'm usually never listened to." Caine walks in with Grace toward the living room.

"Usually?" I watch him grab her hand.

"Ever," Caine corrects himself. "It's like I talk for nothing since no one listens to me."

"Oh, don't you look nice," my mother says, coming to me and getting on her tippy-toes to kiss my cheek, then flattening down the front of my jacket.

"What is everyone doing here?" I ask, shaking hands and kissing cheeks.

"It's your girl's big debut. You didn't think we'd miss it," my father explains.

"Does she know you're coming?" I ask the question, though I know full well she has no idea, or else she'd be double stressed. Considering for the past four days she's slept maybe two hours each night, waking up, gasping for air with nightmares that she forgot to do something, which wasn't the case.

"She has no clue," Caine replies. "I also said it was not a good idea to ambush her at her job." He looks over at Grace.

"I'm not ambushing anyone. I got an email and bought tickets to the event"—Grace avoids looking at him and instead looks at her nails—"in your name."

"You're welcome." He nods at me.

"Okay, this is fun, but I don't want to be late." I look at the room as they all get up and head toward the door.

"How are we going to plan this?" Grace asks, stepping out of the door.

"You planned all of this," Caine reminds her, his hand doing a circle of everyone in my driveway, "but you didn't plan how to execute this?" He shakes his head and laughs.

"I don't think I invited you," she hisses.

"You didn't have to invite me." Caine smiles at her. "Because I bought a ticket."

"Okay, you two. I get the whole he said, she said. Let's get mad at each other, but you aren't really mad at each other. But Autumn has killed herself for the past month putting this together, and we will not ruin it." I look at everyone. "We are on our best behavior."

"Wow," Grace interjects, "you really do love her." She smiles. "I'll be on my best behavior."

I get into my parents' car, and I'm out of it before he puts the car in park. The parking lot is filled, every single parking spot has been taken, so people are now parking along the street. We walk to the doors of the bar, met by two pillars of balloons at the front with a big chalkboard that says private event.

Pulling open the door, I step in and see how she transformed it. It looks like we are back in the twenties. The room is dimly lit, and black tablecloths cover all the tables. Wooden barrels are all over the place with pictures on them and little pieces of information beside them, along with a bottle of whatever whiskey goes with the picture. I look around the crowded room, spotting Brady standing with his father beside him, both of them in suits as they talk to a group of people in front of them.

My eyes scan the room, and I finally spot her on the side, talking to a man who looks like he's my grandfather's age. Her face is smiling, but she looks nervous as fuck. I can tell by the way her chest is rising and falling in the black satin dress she is wearing. It goes all the way up to her neck, the sleeves stop just after her elbow, as it goes tight at the waist and then hugs her hips until her mid-thigh. It's the first time I've seen her this dressed up in a while, and my cock pays attention right away. "Finally." I look over to see my grandfather standing there with a glass in his hand. "What took you guys so long?"

"Pops," I say, shocked. "What are you doing here?" I go to hug him, and he slaps my back.

"Bought tickets," he deadpans, and I shake my head. "I had a friend of mine who I thought would like this event."

"A friend of yours?" I ask, confused, as he brings the glass to his lips and takes a sip.

"Yes," he confirms and then motions with his head toward Autumn, "that's my friend." I watch as Autumn talks. "He owns Southern Tea. He is the largest wine and spirits distributor." He takes another sip. "I might have given him a bottle of the new blend."

I stare at him as he smirks at me. "I guess right time, right place," I say, and then see my family walking around the room, taking in all the pictures. I look over at Autumn and see that she's shaking the man's hand, and the handshake lasts one second longer than it should or than I want it to last.

"Relax there," my grandfather advises, "his wife is right there." He motions with his chin to the woman in the corner talking to Brady now.

"Excuse me," I say, walking away as he chuckles. Her eyes find mine, and I can see some tears in them, and my pulse races.

"Hi," I say when I get close enough to her, wrapping an arm around her waist to bend down. Usually, I kiss her cheek, but not now, not tonight, actually, no fucking more. I kiss her on the lips, and she even gasps before my lips touch hers. I can hear whispers from some of the local people here but have zero fucks to give.

"Hi," she replies, trying not to act like I didn't just throw her off her game, but seeing the look in her eyes, I know I did. "Charlie," she says my name, "meet Montgomery Johnson." She smiles at the man. "This is Charlie Barnes."

"We've met." He shocks me. "When you were a little kid chasing the horses." He laughs and sticks out his hand to shake mine.

"That sounds like me." I take my hand off her waist and shake his hand, but then slide my hand into hers. She squeezes my hand tightly as we make small talk. Brady comes over and asks if he can give him a tour of the distillery. The two of them take off, and I look down at her. "Are you okay?"

"No." She shakes her head. "Can you come with me?" she asks, and I nod as she turns. I stop after one step when I see the back of her dress or, better yet, the lack of the back of her dress. Her whole back is bare, with a sash bow that ties at the base of her back, right above her ass. I blink twice before I follow her closely, blocking her from people's view behind us. She pushes open the door to the distillery, and I see most of my family with her dad as he shows them the process of the machines. She opens her office door, the curtain down on the big window that looks out. I follow her in and close the door. She turns to face me and bends over with her hands over her mouth and nose.

"Baby?" I ask softly, and she stands up.

"Do you know what just happened?" she says, her voice shaking and now one lone tear comes down her face.

"I have no idea, but I really fucking hope it's good." I walk to her, my thumb coming out to catch the lone tear.

"He distributes to forty states and wants to add us to his catalog," she tells me. "He says he's going to personally make sure that everyone tastes our whiskey." I smile at her. "Do you know what that means?" I wrap my arms around her waist, pulling her flush with my chest. "Charlie, this is massive." She puts her hands on my biceps. "This is—"

"You did it," I say softly. "You worked your ass off, and look at everything you did." I kiss her lips. "And it paid off." I slide my tongue with hers as we make out in her office. "We should get out there," I say once I let go of her lips.

"Um, yeah," she agrees, stepping out of my arms. "You kissed me"—I tilt my head to the side—"in front of everyone."

"Okay."

"Are we doing that now?" she asks, and I put my hands in my pockets. "Like, we kiss in private." She wrings her hands together. "But we've never, you know, in front of everyone."

"Do you not want to kiss me in front of everyone?" I ask, getting pissed.

"That's not exactly what I said," she retorts, and I raise my eyebrows. "It's just that everyone is going to see and, well, then you know how gossip is..."

"Are you ashamed of me?" I chuckle nervously.

"Charlie," she says, "don't be ridiculous. I'm doing it to protect you."

"Noted," I say. "But I don't give a shit if people gossip. I don't care if people take pictures and post it on flyers in the middle of the town square." I shake my head. "So now that we've concluded this portion of our talk, how about we get out there so we can celebrate?"

"Okay," she agrees, walking to me and taking one of my hands in both of hers, "that sounds like a plan." I pull open the door and walk out with her. "Also, we are going to discuss the dress."

She looks down at her dress. "What's wrong with my dress?"

"You're missing a whole piece in the back," I explain, pushing the door to the bar open as she laughs at me. I spend the night by her side, her hand in mine most of the time or my arm around her shoulders. There is no mistake at the end of the night that we are together. We get a couple of raised eyebrows and a couple of finger-pointings, and each time I make sure to lean down and kiss her lips. "Give them something to talk about," I mumble to her each time.

We spend the night at my house, her dress in a heap at the front door, the rest of her clothes beside the bed. Her body curved into mine. Everything else is not even a blip on our radar.

The next morning, I bring her coffee in bed. "Will you come with me?" I ask as she looks up at me. "I want to take you somewhere."

"I'll go anywhere with you," she agrees, getting up and sliding into her dress again. We go to her house, and she changes before I take her to the cemetery. She looks out the window as I drive up. "You okay with this?" I ask when I put the truck in park, and she nods, getting out of the truck.

I slide my hand in hers as we walk over to the grave. "I haven't been here in eight years," she admits to me softly. "I couldn't." My thumb rubs hers as we stop in front of Jennifer's tombstone. "I miss her," she says. "There isn't one day that goes by I don't think of her at least once." She wipes the tears away from her face, looking up at me. "She loved you so much."

I nod. "The feeling was mutual."

"She must be pissed at me now that I'm with her man." She laughs through her tears, and I look down at her.

"I don't think she cares," I say honestly.

"Then you don't know anything." She lets go of my hand and wraps it around my waist. "I would be pissed if you got with my best friend." I wrap my arm around her shoulders and pull her closer to me, kissing her head. "But then Jennifer was nicer than me."

"She might have done this," I suggest. "She knew the both of us were hurting and needed each other."

She looks up at me and then looks back down at the tombstone, squatting down in front of it. "I miss you so much," she now whispers to her, "there is so much that has happened." She laughs now as she wipes away a tear. "I bet you know already." I smile as I listen to her talk to her. "I promise that I'll take good care of him." I close my eyes, blinking my own tears away. "We both love you so much and we'll never forget you." She presses two fingers to her lips before putting them on Jennifer's name.

She stands up beside me as my hand moves to grab hers, sliding it with her fingers and feeling her. Making me settle just by her touch, she looks up at me. The streaks of tears down her face as she smiles, inhaling deeply before saying three words that I don't think I've ever wanted to hear more in my life, "I love you."

Here, in the middle of the cemetery where my dreams were shattered, I feel whole again. I feel like whatever path I was on and then did a detour led me to this moment right here. To this woman right here. To the fact I love her with every single fiber in my soul. I love her to the point that I never, ever want to be without her. I love her to the point where I don't think I could breathe without her. She has cured me, and she had no idea she was doing it. I had no idea she was doing it until it was right there in front of me. "I love you."

Epilogue One

AUTUMN

Six Months Later

"HEY," BRADY SAYS, coming into the office with two plates in his hand, and my eyes light up.

"One of those better be for me," I reply as he sets one plate with a burger and fries in front of me and then places his own in front of him as he sits down in his chair.

"Last time I came in here with food only for myself, you stole it from me." He picks up his burger and takes a bite. "Didn't even offer me anything."

I pick up a french fry and dip it in the mountain of ketchup the chef put on there for me. "It was delicious."

"What are you doing?" he asks, looking at all the paperwork in front of me.

"Preparing my speech for the State of the Union." I scrunch my nose up at him.

He ignores my joke. "We need to hire another server," Brady suggests. "One isn't enough on a Saturday. Even you have to agree."

"I do," I agree with him. "We need at least another two." I take a bite of my burger as my eyes go to the papers that were in front of me not long ago. Invoices that are all current with the way the bar has taken off. It's like we are back and even better than ever. "I had to soak my feet in an ice bath when I got home."

"Well, I'll put the notice up on the door like I did the last time," he says, "and we also need another bartender." I look at him. "You can't be doing the office and then the bar every night."

"You sound like Charlie," I point out to him. "I'm fine. I'm more than fine now that nothing is threatening me and my family," I admit to him. The Cartwrights have slunk into whatever hole they are in now. Now that Harmony left Winston, they are trying to do damage control to show everyone how amazing they still are. Apparently, according to the gossip going around, she left him six months ago. Why anyone is surprised is beyond me since he makes it no secret that he cheats on her. The number of times I've seen him out with different women is crazy, and if I were her, I would light all of his shit on fire.

"You are, but we are doing pretty well now," he declares, and I chuckle. "Very well, considering all of our debts are paid off, and we have regular runs with orders that are backed up. Plus, the tours are still going stronger than ever. We sell more cases than we've ever sold."

"Why don't we wait a couple of months and see?" I try to meet him in the middle.

"You said that last month," he points out, "and we've already passed the quota for this month." He then points at the whiteboard I hung in the office with a goal that we need for the month. "The private tasting events are booked solid for a whole year, Autumn." His voice starts to go up. "What else is new?" I try to change the subject.

"Not much," he says, "I think the house next to mine got rented out."

"The one that is run down?" I ask.

He nods. "Saw someone over there this morning trying to calm down the overgrown weeds."

"Every single time I come and visit you, I have a feeling it's going to fall like a stack of Jengas."

"Hire the fucking bartender." He puts his hands on his hips. "Or you know what, I'll do it myself."

"Fine, fine." I hold up my hands. "I'll do it. Jeez." I inhale. "I was just trying to spend time with you."

"You want to spend time with me?" he retorts. "Invite me over for a meal. Now I have to go out for a bit." He doesn't wait for me to answer him. Instead, he just walks out of the office when my phone rings, and I see it's my father.

"Hello." I put the phone to my ear.

"Did your brother talk to you?" he mumbles, and I laugh. It's been a rough six months; he's getting weaker as the days go by. Even he had to admit that he needed part-time care, so we have a nurse who comes in and helps during the day for a couple of hours. I usually bring him breakfast and then Brady heads out to take him lunch and the nurse is there to help him warm up his dinner.

"Hello to you too, Father." I ignore his question.

"Well, did he?" He also ignores me. "You either hire someone, or I'll come and do it myself. Walker and all."

I chuckle. "Simmer down there, Pops," I joke with him. "I am literally putting the notices in the paper as we speak."

"Don't toy with me," he barks, and I just laugh.

"Dad, I swear I'm going to put it in the paper," I assure him softly. "Now, if you let me go, I can do it."

"You better," he snaps. "I love you." His tone changes. "More than you will ever know."

"I love you more," I say, hanging up the phone and feeling the little pang I usually feel when I hang up the phone with him. Wondering if it will be the last time, knowing that even though we have prepared for it to happen sooner rather than later, I'm still not ready. I don't think anyone is ever ready.

I place the ads in the paper, finish doing all the checks for the month, and I'm getting up to head to the front when the back door opens and Brady comes back in. "Have you been gone all this time?" I ask, looking to see it's almost five o'clock.

"Yup," he confirms, and it looks like he just stepped out of the shower. "Why are you still here?" he asks. "Isn't tonight your night off?"

"I was just leaving." I pick up my purse and sling it

over my shoulder. "See you tomorrow."

"Yeah," he says, walking straight to the front of the bar. I get into my car and make my way over to my house, enjoying the sounds of the birds chirping all along the way. Spring is in the air for sure.

I call Charlie the minute I park my car, and it goes straight to voicemail. I'm walking into the house as I'm about to leave a message when I stop dead in my tracks. My whole house is empty. There is literally nothing in my house. The table is gone, and the couch is gone. I walk into the house and head to the bedroom and see that it's also been stripped. I turn to head to my closet, every single piece of clothing I own is gone. Not one fucking hanger swings in place. I turn to walk back out of my room when I hear the front door open and then shut.

Walking out, I see Charlie coming into the house, and his eyes don't even scan the room. As if my house has always looked like this. "My stuff is gone." I blink twice. "Like, every single piece of everything is gone." I turn around, wondering if I should call the police. I put my hand to my head. "How did they take all of the stuff and not leave anything?" I look at him, and he doesn't even look fazed that someone broke into my house. "All of my things are gone."

"They aren't gone," he reassures me, his voice not rising like mine. "I moved it out." He walks into the room, standing in front of me. "We moved it out, started this morning when you left. Just finished not long ago."

"Who is we and where did you move it to?" I ask and he just looks at me. His beautiful face tries to fight smiling at me, but he just smirks and then grins. The face I look for every single night I'm behind the bar. The face I look at right before I fall asleep. The face I wake up to each and every single day and have for the last eight months. The face I want to stare at for the rest of my days.

"Me and a couple of guys from the barn. Your brother came and helped."

"Brady came here?" I say, pointing at the wooden floor. "To help you move my things out?"

"Yup." He puts his hands in his back pockets, the T-shirt pulling against his chest.

"Where are my things?" I ask again.

"Took them to my house, our house now."

I put my hands on my hips. "You took all of my things over to your house?"

"Our house," he corrects me. "It's been over six months. I'm done with this back-and-forth bullshit. Half here, half there. Playing heads or tails to decide where we sleep at night."

"So you thought 'hey, let's just take all her stuff to my house' instead of talking to me about it?"

"Yup." He nods. "Another thing, besides you moving in with me." He takes one hand out of his back pocket, tucks it in his front pocket, and takes something out before getting down on one knee. The phone drops from my hand, clattering onto the floor. "We're getting married." My hands go to my face. "I want you to move in with me, and I want to marry you. I'm not waiting forever either. Meaning, if I could convince you, I would do it tomorrow." He holds out the ring. "I'm not wasting more time with you not being my wife," he says softly. "I want to have my ring on your finger. I want your ring on my finger. I want to have babies with you. I want to fight with you for fun." I laugh since we never, ever fight. It's a strange thing; maybe it's because we've been friends for so long, but there are no fights. "I want it all, and I want it with you."

"Charlie." That's the only thing I can say.

"That isn't how you say yes," he jokes. Taking my hand, he places the ring on my finger, and I gasp when I look down. "I don't want to hear anything either. I went with my mother."

"This is massive," I declare, looking down at the huge ring on my finger.

"You can hand it down to our daughter or our son, whichever you want."

"I want my father to walk me down the aisle," I say. "I don't know how much time we have."

"Does that mean you'll marry me?" He smiles, and I grab his face in my hands.

"That means I'll marry you. Tonight, tomorrow, this weekend." I kiss his lips. "In this lifetime and the next, I will marry you each and every single time." He gets up from his knees, swinging me around. "You are everything I've ever dreamed of but thought I would never get."

"Dreams come true, baby, we're proof of it."

Five days later, in the middle of his backyard, with all our family and friends, wearing a wedding dress I didn't even think would be possible to get on such short notice, my father walks me down the aisle to the man who made me see that I am worthy. Who showed me what unconditional love is. Who showed me what real love feels like. I became Mrs. Charlie Barnes.

Epilogue Two

CHARLIE

Five years Later

THE SOFT BELLS ring and my eyes flutter open, taking in the almost dark room. The sunlight tries to come through the side of the shades. I turn to my side to stop the alarm from ringing, shutting it down before I turn the other way, reaching for Autumn. "Morning," I mumble as my hand touches the empty space where she is supposed to be sleeping. I get up on one elbow, looking over at the baby monitor by her side of the bed, and see Landon, our three-year-old son, still in his bed, "Baby," I say softly, looking back at the door to the bathroom and seeing it open but no noise coming from there. I flip the covers off of me, getting out of the bed, and looking down at the phone that is right next to the picture of the three of us, taken last summer when we went to my parents' house. Autumn is tucked to my side, her arms around my waist, while I hold her shoulder with one arm and Landon with the other. The three of us posing for the camera. It is such a beautiful picture I also had one made for my office.

Grabbing a pair of shorts before I walk out to the kitchen and see it's empty also, I look around. "Autumn," I say her name louder, looking around the room and spotting pictures of us all over the place.

The table in the corner of the living room still has Jennifer in the middle, with pictures of us all around it. I'm about to take out my phone when I look out to the back patio and see her sitting in the swing. I let out a breath I didn't even know I was holding, as I make my way to her. Pushing open the back door and then the screened storm door, her head turns to look at me. "What the fuck." My voice is tight, and her eyebrows shoot up.

She has one leg tucked under her as she pushes the swing with her other foot. It's the same swing she had at her house; we just moved it over to ours. " Good morning to you, grumpy pants." She is wearing a loose, long-sleeved gray, off-the-shoulder shirt with matching shorts. That is exactly what she wore to bed last night before I peeled it off of her. She holds the white coffee mug in her hands. " Did someone get up on the wrong side of the bed?"

"No." I sit down next to her, wrapping my arm around her waist and pulling her to me. She holds the coffee cup above her head, laughing as I tug her over my lap and she straddles me. I bury my face in her neck as I wrap both arms around her waist. I close my eyes and my heart starts beating normally now that she is in my arms. "How am I supposed to make you breakfast in bed for our anniversary if you leave the bed?"

She leans the side of her face on my head. "Happy anniversary," she responds softly. "I think you gave me my gift this morning, at like three, when I got up to use the bathroom and came back to bed, and you mauled me."

"I didn't maul you." I smile. "You were just wearing too many clothes." She laughs. "What time did you wake up?"

I finally let her go. She sits back on my lap, brings the cup to her lips, takes a sip, and then offers it to me. "This is cold," I retort when I take my own sip. "How long were you out here?"

"A little while," she replies softly and avoids looking at me, instead she turns her face to the side. "Was just sitting here thinking."

"Yeah," I ask, knowing something is up with her, "and what were you thinking about?"

She shakes her head and puts her hands on my chest, right where my heart is beating. "I was just…" she trails off. When she looks up at me, I see tears in her eyes, and everything inside me freezes. "I was thanking Jennifer." I lean over to the side, putting the coffee mug on the table before giving her all my attention.

"Autumn." My voice comes out in a whisper.

"I know, I know," she starts, wiping her tears off of her face, "but I was just, I don't know, thanking her without trying not to feel guilty about having you."

I hold her face in my hands. "I believe in my heart this

is where we would always be." My thumbs catch her two tears. "That regardless, this right here with you and our son is where I would have been."

"You can't say that." Her bottom lip quivers. "You don't know."

"You're right. I don't, but what I do know is that my life with you, with Landon, it's not something I would trade, for anyone, ever." I kiss her lips, our foreheads connected

"I'm pregnant," she reveals softly. My eyes fly to hers, and my heartbeat speeds up, listening to the words, blinking a couple of times, wondering if I'm hearing things or not. But the smile on her face, the way her eyes light up, I know. "I'm three days late. I woke up this morning and took the test."

I bring her face to mine, sliding my tongue out and into her mouth, her hands roam up my chest to around my neck. Pressing her into me, I'm about to carry her to bed when the door opens, and Landon comes out with tears running down his face. "Mama," he cries out, coming to us, wearing his tractor pj's, "I thought you left me." He uses his palm to wipe the tears from his face as Autumn turns and holds out her hands for him.

"I would never leave you." She moves back on my lap, turning him and sitting him down between us. "Never, never." She kisses his head, my arm holding them to me.

"*We* would never leave you." I look at my wife. "Do you know what today is?" I ask him and he rests his head on Autumn's chest. "It's the day Mommy and Daddy got married." He looks up at me. He looks exactly like me, minus his eyes, which are just like his mother's. The mirror to his heart, like hers.

"Do you love her?" Landon looks at me and then his mother, then back at me with a smile, and I give him the same smile back. "He loves you," he tells Autumn, who just laughs at him.

'Yeah." She nods her head. It's something that started when he was two-years-old and I walked into the house one day and said, *"Landon, you know what? I love her."* *Then I kissed her lips, making him laugh. So ever since then he asks me every single time I get home, "Daddy, do you love her?"* She kisses the top of his head before looking at me. "I love him too. How about we go and get breakfast going?" she asks him and he jumps off of me and runs toward the door, and we watch him run into the house.

"Thank you, baby," I tell her, and she turns to look back at me, tilting her head to the side. One hand goes to wrap around the side of her neck, and the other goes to her stomach. "Thank you for taking my shattered dreams and making them real, mending them so they are so bright they're hard to look at."

"No," she refutes, getting off of my lap and holding out her hand for me, "thank you for mending all of my broken pieces and putting me back, not like I was, but better than I've ever been." She turns. "Now come and feed your wife and children." I get up, slipping my hand in hers.

I watch her walk into the house before turning and taking a look at the blue sky and silently saying, *Thank you, Jennifer, for giving her to me.*

9 781990 376986